A PITCH

By Harold Kasselman

IN LOVING MEMORY OF RUTH AND AL KASSELMAN

ACKNOWLEDGEMENT

Special thanks to Sean Conley Esq. whose patience and expertise with technology issues allowed me to format this novel into an e-book. I also want to thank my daughter Jaime Brooke Kasselman and so many friends who read the novel and gave me encouragement. Some of you are mentioned as characters in this novel.

Disclaimer

This story is a work of fiction. Any names used herein are entirely fictional and do not represent any real person, except when used for historical context.

TABLE OF CONTENTS

INTRODUCTION

My name is John Cowan, a baseball writer, but during one season I had to reinvent myself as a half-assed lawyer to do my job. I spent more time attending press conferences and interviewing attorneys than I did analyzing baseball box scores. It was not something I ever imagined would happen, but then who could have foreseen the cascading events that unfolded that year. I got to know some of the participants in a drama that began on a baseball diamond and ended in a legal debate. As I write the story that I hope you will read, maybe you will find the answers that still evade me.

I was doing a story about the stellar crop of rookie prospects that year and I found myself in Philadelphia to watch a young pitcher for the Phillies by the name of Tim Charles. It was the last game of a three game series on a Sunday night with the Mets, and I was there to evaluate first hand for my readers whether the kid was a legit future star, or just another overly paid, one-year wonder.

I never did get to write the story about the other rookies because what happened that night made me abandon my efforts, and redirect them to the story I am about to tell you. Rather than use the first person style of narrative, I would rather you learn what happened without me as an intermediary. I'll simply give you the facts as they played out on and off the field. I had the benefit of sitting down and conversing with many of the people you will meet in a short while. It is their eyewitness accounts, including court testimony, which provided me with the ability to share the events of those days with you.

The real enigma, as I reflect upon that baseball season, is how the sport lasted so long, apart from labor-management disputes, free from judicial intervention. My hope is that I never live to cover a story like it again.

There is one final warning. To grasp the heart of this story I have to provide baseball background that may be alien to some. I ask your forbearance, but I have no doubt, as lawyers are fond to say, you need to know the facts to understand the issues.

Chapter 1
June 21

There was an undercurrent of excitement amongst the sold-out crowd at Citizens Bank Park. The home team's young rookie pitcher was to start against their traditional arch rival the New York Mets. There was yet another emotion that many in the stands and players on the field shared. It was a sense of dread that something ugly might happen between the two ball clubs in front of a national television audience. Some spoke openly of that fear as fans watched the players warm up before the game.

The Phillies had not contended for several years. Still, hope filled the air that summer because the young man warming up on the pitcher's mound for the home team was ten million dollar bonus baby Timothy Charles.

He was just twenty, but he was everything scouts had envisioned when the team drafted him two years earlier. At 6' 6" he had grown two more inches since the draft, but still retained that wiry 215-pound frame that effortlessly propelled the baseball. His fastball was clocked in excess of 100 mph on occasion, and he perfected a motion that hid the ball from the batter's eye until a moment before it crossed the plate.

The fastball was not the only weapon in his arsenal. He had a curve ball that buckled the knees of even the most aggressive hitters. Many compared it to the stuff of Sandy Koufax, Nolan Ryan, or Clayton Kershaw. Charles got the job done with those two pitches, but he also had a decent slider and was working on a change up with pitching coach Terri Rowlands.

On this Sunday, Charles would pitch the last game of a three game series. To say that there was no love lost between the teams would be an understatement of epic proportions. The rivalry traced back to the 2007 campaign when then Phillies' shortstop Jimmy Rollins announced at the end of spring training that his team was the team to beat in the NL East. The heavily talented Mets team took great offense but they blew a commanding lead in September and the Phillies claimed the divisional title on the last day of the season. Rollins won the Most Valuable Player award to further the Mets' humiliation.

That animosity grew more intense the next year when Carlos Beltran took the lead in 2008 by boldly announcing to the baseball world that the Mets were the team to beat that year. Ironically the Mets imploded again in the latter part of September and helplessly watched as the Phillies went on to win their first World Series since 1980. In 2010 the Phillies won their fourth consecutive divisional title Late in the season Chase Utley slid late into second base on a hard take-out slide on the Mets' second baseman much to the ire of several of the Mets' players who hinted at future retaliation.

Then two seasons later the irrepressible Mets outfielder Mike Zahn proclaimed that the Phillies were on life support. The Phillies were an aging team and critics felt that their place in history was a distant one. Many of the players from those days still carried their dislike for one another, and even younger players adopted the institutionalized animus.

The Friday night opener renewed the smoldering feud when the Mets' closer threw a pitch that struck Phillies' star second baseman Elliot Butterworth which resulted in a broken finger. That injury forced him onto the 15-day disabled list. Notably, the pitch that struck Butterworth came immediately after a three-run homer that put the game comfortably out of reach for the home team.

Everyone in the stands and in the dugouts believed it was *a purpose pitch*. In other words, it was intended to send a message to the Phillies not to dig in their heels at the plate. As a result, the home plate umpire issued warnings to both managers that any further retaliation would result in ejection for the offending pitcher and manager.

The loss of Butterworth would be a blow for the team, and it was fervently felt by his teammates and the new manager. Buck Sawyer only had a one year contract. He was old school both in discipline and in the strategy of the game. He believed that pitchers had to employ intimidation as part of their repertoire. As a corollary, he believed that, if his players were the targets of dirty slides or *purpose pitches*, his staff was to retaliate in kind. Buck made no secret of his style of play, and he expressed it more than a few times to his players both informally and at team meetings. He was the polar opposite of the Phillies' beloved former manager Charlie Manuel. Manuel was a father figure who gave his players the freedom to play the game without an omnipresent manager. Sawyer was in your face daily

It was a style and philosophy not uniformly embraced by his pitching coach or members of the team. Many players had loyalty to their team, but they also had to think of themselves as individuals competing in a marketplace.

If a player were to get hurt in his free agency year, he could lose out on an opportunity to make the equivalent of a healthy state lottery payout. Equally clear was the reality that retaliation sometimes led to a cycle of violence between the two teams. If you were the recipient of *a brush back pitch*, that was one thing, but a fastball in the ribs or elbow could lead to an extended loss of playing time.

So on the Friday night opener, the benches poured onto the field after Butterworth was hit, but the teams merely practiced the unwritten ritual of baseball fights. They mingled, pulled, and gestured, but no punches were thrown and players held tempers in check. Even Buck Sawyer seemed calm, but that was merely a façade. Inside he was coldly calculating, and he vowed to himself that a Mets' player would pay a price for the injury to his all-star second baseman. Retribution would be had by Sawyer through one of his pitchers. The rest of the league - as well as the New York Mets would know what to expect if anyone tried to hurt one of his own.

After the game, Buck called next day's starting pitcher Doug Adams into his office. The guy had George Clooney-like looks but with a dusty brown colored hue in his hair He had graduated from Wharton with a master's degree in business after several years of off-season study. Adams was so knowledgeable about the finances of the game that he negotiated his own contracts. Accordingly, he saved the substantial fee that would have gone to an agent. He may not have been the most popular guy in the clubhouse, but he had the respect of his teammates. Perhaps because of his business acumen, he was voted the team's representative for the players' union.

Buck was looking at video of the game and was still fuming when a freshly showered Adams sat down in his manager's office.

"You know that prick hit Butterworth deliberately, don't you, Doug? We're gonna pay them back in spades! I expect you to take care of business tomorrow night. I intend to equal the playing field. I'll let you decide who to take out, but do it early in the ball game. I want them sonsa bitches to know it was payback. I look at it as an eye for an eye."

Adams wasn't shocked, but he was uncomfortable with the notion that he was to be the avenger for his manager's face-saving "honor" play. He detested Buck Sawyer. It was as if they were from two different cultures. Buck toiled in the minor leagues his entire career and had just made it to the majors this year. He took long bus rides and slept in cheap motels for chump money to stay in the game for thirty years as a player, coach, and manager. He worked his way up the Phillies' organization because he was loyal, didn't buck the chain of command, and had a penchant for recognizing great talent in young players.

In fact his most notable contribution to the franchise was scouting Tim Charles. Buck had coached the Phillies minor league team, the Clearwater Threshers, in Florida, when he was asked to scout a high school sophomore pitcher in nearby Sarasota. He took the hour ride on several occasions to see the youngster pitch. By his senior year Charles became a "can't miss prospect."

It was in large measure due to the efforts of Sawyer that the Phillies selected Charles number one in the amateur draft. It was soon apparent that the organization would repay Buck with a managerial spot at Reading the AA team. With Charles' success at Reading under Buck's guidance, Sawyer was tapped to manage the major league team when the prior manager was fired.

Adams gazed at the spittle on Buck's chin from the tobacco juice that failed to find its way into the empty Sam Adams bottle that served as a spittoon and ashtray. The college grad cursed his misfortune. He felt comfortable on the team, but the lure of old school baseball did nothing to ignite his energy. He was driven by personal goals.

He cared about winning and the good of the team, but he was not the cheerleader type. He saw himself as a professional man with skills to be sold to the highest bidder. Sure, he'd rather be on a winning team - that brought more opportunity for publicity and endorsements. He was a commodity in a business that long ago ceased to be just a game. He was like a mercenary who refused to get too close to his teammates because they could be traded or sign elsewhere and become opponents at any point.

Rather than start a confrontation with his beefy red-veined faced manager, Adams chose not to respond directly. The presence of four other bottles of beer convinced Adams that there would be no backing down by Sawyer.

"I've been around this game a long time. I'll do my job."

"Good. That's what I expect from you. Your team needs you to step up and be a leader."

Adams didn't wait around for Buck to clarify things. He was already late to meet his catcher for a few drinks at a center city bar in the Rittenhouse Square section. He wanted to go over the scouting reports of a few of the newer Mets. He looked forward to a more festive atmosphere with the homegrown veteran Bobby Carson who was the starting catcher.

Shortly before 11:00 PM, Adams met Carson at a prominent Philly spot and devoured two glasses of pinot noir at $14.00 a pop, but that was of no concern to him. What was on his mind was Sawyer's directive. He was a player rep and a fellow union member. He would not intentionally put another union member in the ER; it simply wasn't him. After the two discussed pitching strategy, Adams approached the subject of retaliation that gnawed at his skin.

"I've got myself a little predicament, and I want your take on it. Buck wants me to take out one of the Mets because of Butterworth, and he wants it done tomorrow night."

Carson wasn't surprised He too felt that something had to be done. He opined out loud about which player on the opposing team would take the hit.

"I think the Mets depend on Leyton. Without him, they'd fall apart".

Kenny Leyton was their speedy second baseman. As the lead-off batter, he was considered the spark plug of the team. His loss would at least equal that suffered by the Phillies.

Adams countered with Luther Wynne, who played shortstop and irritated the Phillies with hot dog antics by showboating around the bases and giggling in the dugout.

"I'll tell you straight. I won't intentionally throw at his head, but I'll make him dance at the plate. Buck may not be satisfied, but I draw the line when it comes to putting someone's career in jeopardy. And let me remind you that Wynne may charge the mound, so get your ass out in front of him before he takes a shot at me. Can I count on that?"

Bobby looked a bit hurt by the question. It was an unwritten custom in baseball that a catcher always protected his pitcher if he was charged by an enraged batter.

"Hey, I'd love to tackle that dipshit. I don't even need your sorry ass as an excuse."

"Fine. Look for the pitch to come at Wynne in his second at bat. I don't want to make it too obvious. The thing that pisses me off is that I'll get tossed from the game, and I need the work. But we have to do something. Here, let me have the bill. You go home and get some sleep so your reflexes are sharp to cover my back".

"Wow! The conservative MBA is loosening his money belt. This is a night to remember".

Chapter 2

Citizens Bank Park was sold out for the 22nd consecutive home game of the season. The resurgence of the team in the division standings was one reason. Second, the young flamethrower Tim Charles was leading the league in strikeouts, and was second in earned run average among starting pitchers. He, along with the ageless Nolan Albright, Scott Jeffries, Doug Adams, and Jeff "Tiny" Rommer rounded out a very formidable pitching staff. Veteran Ron "The Barber" Barkowsky, a Camden City native, was an occasional spot starter and reliever.

The Phillies had a totally different line-up from their pennant winning years. They had homegrown talent in Butterworth, and a prodigious RBI producer in their first baseman. Sophomore year man Colby Green was at second. Julio Herrera, whose glove work was magical, won the job at third. His plays were invariably in the top ten gems shown nightly on ESPN.

In the outfield, other than big Miguel Morales, the Phillies depended on speed and defense rather than raw power. The bench had a good on-base percentage, even if it lacked walk-off homerun power. This was a well-balanced team. Of course the Braves and the equally dangerous Washington Nationals were also favored by some, and it was clear that the race would go down to the wire.

In the clubhouse some of the Phillies players played cards in the afternoon, while others chose to listen to music to relax before the game. Others spoke openly and with some degree of hostility about the loss of Butterworth.

Julio Herrera was one who bitterly complained that the Mets' hurler had deliberately gone after Butterworth. He was especially pissed that the umpiring crew had not ejected the pitcher.

"We have to protect our players or we'll be standing out there with a target on our heads. The umpires won't stop it, so we gotta do it ourselves. Ain't that right?" asked Julio.

His message reverberated. Several of the guys looked toward Adams and the relief pitchers to see whether they were listening. Adams continued to read Forbes magazine but a couple of the relievers nodded in agreement. Veteran pinch-hitter Tom Klingler, quipped "Baseball is as much about intimidation as it is about talent."

"That's no lie" yelled an excited Herrera, "and today's a good day to prove we're no candy-asses. My main-man Bobby Carson, whatchu say"? Julio asked.

Carson had a leadership role on the team by virtue of his catching position as well as the way he played the game. He was the prototype of a team player and played the game hard. He ran out slow ground balls and hustled on every play regardless of the score. He was a manager's dream.

"Julio, I hear you man."

Carson didn't feel it was necessary or helpful to be explicit, but he left the clear impression that he would have their backs.

Later, as the players streamed onto the field, the air seemed to be filled with the acrid aroma of testosterone mixed with adrenalin. Neither team had fraternized with the other club's players during batting practice as was often the case. Adams finished his warm up pitches on the sidelines and debated within himself the merits of what he was about to do. He hated getting ejected from any game. He felt like he was better than any long reliever on the club, and he didn't want the bullpen depleted for the Sunday night televised "game of the week." Additionally, he needed to get another one in the win column.

The first inning was uneventful and there was no score in the top of the second when Luther Wynne came up to bat. Herrera could barely contain the smirk that appeared on his face. He figured that Wynne would be the one selected to pay for the injury to his teammate. In the dugout Sawyer also waited and wondered who Adams had chosen for retaliation.

Adam's first pitch was a fastball on the outside corner, but a bit high for ball one. Wynne, batting right-handed against the lefty Adams, leaned over the plate in a relaxed style that would, even under ordinary circumstances, prompt a brush back. And so the lefty threw a high heater around the chin of Wynne that produced a howl from the crowd as if they had been the recipient themselves. Mets' fans booed the gall of Adams. The count was 2-0 when Adams decided it was time to pay his obligation.

His next pitch was a curve ball that broke hard on a downward plane and struck Wynne rather harmlessly on the top of his left foot. The pitch was so benign that the plate umpire awarded first base to the batter, but failed to eject Adams or even issue a warning. At third base Herrera was stunned and confused by the half-hearted effort of Adams. He glared at his pitcher and hoped that this was just a set up for the real drilling.

But Adams got the next batter to hit into a ground ball double play, and. the cleanup hitter flew out to left to retire the side.

Herrera ran to the dugout and waited there for Adams to take his slow walk from the mound. When Adams reached the first step, Julio literally confronted him.

"You pussy! Is that what you call protecting your players? You're a joke man! You threw that pitch like a little leaguer. Who the hell's gonna respect us now? You hear me man? Look at me when I'm talking to you"!

Herrera's agitation went from words to physically pushing and taunting Adams. "Can you fight you little girl? You got no *cohones*!" But Adams kept his distance and went to the water cooler.

All of this was in clear view of the Mets' dugout, and their broadcast team showed the internal squabble twice after commercial break. Carson and two of the coaches pulled Julio away and kept the men separated. Sawyer went over to Herrera and told him that he supported the point that he was making, and that someone would deliver the message for the team.

"Nice job out there, Adams," mocked Sawyer. "You have them crappin' in their pants. What the hell was that pitch? Ya think that evens things? You're nuts if you do."

Sawyer was worked up, but his bench coach reminded him that the cameras were locked on him, and that he needed to take it to the runway if he wanted to dress down Adams.

In the home team's broadcast booth, the color analyst and the play-by-play announcer could not ignore the episode when they were back on the air. The long time analyst knew instinctively the cause of the bench confrontation.

"Herrera was expressing the time-honored unwritten code amongst ball players that 'if you hit one of my teammates, we will retaliate in kind.' Apparently that curve ball that Adams threw didn't satisfy Herrera, and he let Adams know it in no uncertain terms."

"That's not a good omen for things to come between these two teams because tensions will rise and expectations for further reprisals will increase for both sides," said the Phillies' announcer.

"That's true, and it's especially bad news for the Phillies because there will be dissension in their clubhouse. Sawyer wants to avoid a schism on this team. Now, there are examples of teams who could still win in a tense clubhouse, even teams that had fistfights among themselves, like the Oakland A's and Yankees of the 70's, but they are the exceptions."

"I'm wondering whether Buck may have to suspend Herrera for that outburst" said the play-by-play announcer.

"That's doubtful, but Buck will have to bring these two guys together in a three-way meeting." said the analyst.

Adams returned unperturbed to the mound and continued to pitch effectively, and at the end of the eighth inning the home team led 3-1.

In the ninth, Sawyer replaced Adams - who had thrown 105 pitches - with his closer. The Mets countered with back-to-back singles to start the inning. The next batter struck out for the first out and that brought up Mike Zahn, their power-hitting right-fielder. The left-handed Zahn took the first offering from the Phillies closer and launched a one-hop grounder up the middle towards second. The second baseman quickly whirled towards second and threw a perfect toss to shortstop Colby Green, who pivoted across second and began his throw to first to complete the double play. The speedy

Leyton was motoring to second as fast as he could to break up the double play.

Leyton bore down on Green and slid with his cleats high in the air. He made contact with Green just as the ball left the shortstop's hand and plowed into his upper thigh. Green tumbled hard onto Leyton.

In the meantime, the first base umpire had already made the out sign to end the game, but that did not end the field activity. Leyton tried to push Green off of him but Colby Green took exception by putting Leyton in a wrestling hold. Mets' players poured onto the field to back their team leader. That prompted the Phillies to scamper on as well. Even the bullpen pitchers surrounded second base.

"This could get ugly real fast," warned the Phillies' analyst. "These guys simply don't like each other. Let's hope no one gets hurt." Most of the players merely mingled around. The proper protocol, as practiced for generations in the unwritten baseball code, is to make a perfunctory showing of solidarity for your teammates by gesturing rather than actual fighting.

This code was not to Buck's liking tonight, and he charged over the mound towards the rugby-like scrum of men at second base. He was met there by Zahn who had changed direction from first and headed to second. Sawyer tried to tackle the larger Zahn, but two other Mets' players interceded and sent Sawyer flailing to the ground. His pride and rump a bit damaged, he was privately grateful that two of his coaches held him back from further pain or humiliation. He couldn't believe how winded he was from the little action he had taken. He felt older than his 58 years but the smoking and drinking had caught up to him. Well, he thought, he showed his players he meant business- even if he fell short of his goal.

Other players continued to push and menace at each other, but because the game had ended, police broke up the opposing sides and order was restored with little damage.

Gregg Martin, a former ballplayer for the Phillies, was down on the field for a post-game interview. He was unable to get anyone from the winning team to talk except Herrera, who was still mingling around looking for some renewed action.

"Julio, nice job out there. This is a good win against those Mets again tonight, but what is this brawl going to mean for your club's morale?"

"It will definitely bring us together man. We have to go out there and execute our game every day, and not be intimidated. This will give us an extra incentive to want to sweep those guys."

" Does this brawl end the retaliation by both clubs?"

Julio wasn't willing to commit because in his mind his team had now suffered twice at the hands of the Mets, and the score was not yet settled.

"Let's see what tomorrow brings, but we need to protect our players" said the young third baseman.

"It looks like things are still brewing down here. Back to you in the booth," said Gregg.

In the radio booth, color commentator Joe Forte, also a former Phillies' player, made it clear to his listeners that peace was not at hand.

"That slide by Leyton was downright dirty if you ask me. Nobody takes exception to a clean take out slide, but that was cleats-flying-high and it went too far. It was deliberate. If

I'm out there on the mound the next time that Leyton bats, he'll see some chin music."

"Yes Joe, but do you do it the next game, the next series, or just at some point during the season"? asked his partner in the booth. " Retaliation will mean automatic ejections and possible suspensions."

"No question about it, but the team comes first and you need to show your players that you're willing to sacrifice a suspension for them. If not, you lose their respect, and they won't have your back when you need them."

"Well, that's a wrap from Citizens Bank Park tonight, where the fighting Phillies took the second game of a three game series from the Mets and the fireworks were out prematurely here in June" said Martin.

In the clubhouse, Colby Green was getting treatment for cuts and bruises he suffered on the slide from Leyton. Sawyer called for a closed meeting so the press was excluded. Buck was on his fourth cigarette since the game ended, and his face continued to reflect the beet pallor that was present when he was incensed; an emotion often seen by his players.

"Men," he began," I'm old school, and I'm proud of it. There are certain basic rules that still remain a part of baseball. One of them is that you gotta protect your own if they're thrown at, or when somebody takes out one of us on a dirty play. We have to play hardball, and that means playing the game the way it's supposed to be played. We need to respect each other enough so that we do what's necessary to protect our baseball family.

We lost our All-Star second baseman for several weeks because of a *purpose pitch,* and today we pissed away an opportunity to respond in kind with Wynne at the plate. The Mets have to learn that we won't turn the other cheek. Joe Garagiola said,

'Baseball is a game played by human beings and governed by unwritten laws of survival and self-preservation.'

"That was true 60 years ago and it remains true today. This is a game of the survival of the fittest. You have to be skilled, conditioned, and be willing to defend yourself to survive in this game so that you can claim a title after 162 games. The game of baseball is really no different today than it was when Cobb played, or when Mays, Mantle, and Aaron did in the Golden Era. Think about what pitchers like Drysdale, Gibson, or Randy Johnson would do. Pride and respect is the engine that drives the great teams to win the World Series. We got there in the past, and I want to take us there again. Are you with me?"

The players rarely saw Buck so emotional and many were actually moved by his words. They responded with loud cheers and applause. For young Tim Charles it was moving yet very unsettling. He heard the jab that Buck threw at Adams, without naming him, and he felt the words by his manager were now directed towards him.

"Now boys, I'm going to say this just once more, and I expect that my words will be taken seriously. I want Leyton to pay for what he did to Colby. I don't give a flying fuck if he's run over at second base, stepped on, hit in the head by a throw when he runs toward a base on a force play, or frankly beaned in the head. In fact I hope one of you sticks it in his ear! I want it done with a fastball and not some change up or breaking pitch. We need to put him on the disabled list."

"One other thing before I let you go. I can't stress enough, especially now, what I have posted here in the clubhouse. As you walk past it, pay attention to it and live by it. Get some rest and I'll see you here tomorrow at 2 PM."

As Sawyer left, Adams shook his head and said "asshole" loud enough for others to hear. It was met by silence save for Herrera. He couldn't hide his emotions and responded to no one in particular that "Buck knew how the game was meant to be played."

As Tim Charles, the following night's starting pitcher left, he paused at the framed quote that was on the wall. It read:

"What you see here, what you say here, what you hear, when you leave here, let it stay here."

Charles felt sick to his stomach as he pondered the words of his manager. Did it really fall on him to keep the unwritten law of retribution? Was he up to it? Why had he been scheduled to make the next start?

Chapter 3

Timothy Matthew Charles was born and raised in Sarasota, Florida, adjacent to the Gulf of Mexico. For the middle-class Charles family, it was an ideal place to raise a family. It was a modest house that was home to his father Jeff, mother Lois, and siblings Walt and Joyce. Jeff Charles was a schoolteacher in nearby Bradenton and coached the high school team. Lois needed to supplement his income and worked as a legal secretary for a local firm. Still, with gorgeous beaches nearby, and beautiful sunny weather all year, the Charles family felt blessed.

Tim inherited a passion for baseball from his dad, who played Minor League ball in the Florida State League. He would play catch with his son from a very early age. Tim would later credit his dad with developing his skills and his knowledge of the traditions of the game. Tim was a fierce competitor despite his reticent personality off the field. He never wanted a manager to take him out of a game.

The bond between father and son was cemented when Jeff took his son to his first baseball game at the age of seven. It was only a spring training game, but to Tim it was almost a spiritual event. Tim lived within walking distance of Ed Smith Stadium, at that time, the spring training facility for the Cincinnati Reds.

Sarasota was a great location for a baseball freak like Tim. The month of March, when spring training began, was even better than Christmas break. On the weekends, Jeff and his son would take in games in Sarasota, or in Clearwater where Tim would see his future team the Phillies play ball.

They were a close-knit family, and shared a strong faith in their Lord, which regularly took them to church on Sunday. They had relied on their faith when the family considered whether to let Tim enter the baseball draft after his senior year at Cardinal Mooney High School or go to college. The family could not afford to send Tim without scholarship money, but that was no concern after Tim was named to the All-American team. When Buck Sawyer went to their home and talked to the family about the Phillies organization, he brought a few former major league players from the Phillies organization.

Buck summed it up simply: "Tim, you have been blessed by our Creator with great talent, and He has a plan for you in this game. Why put your career at risk by playing four years in college? You don't want to put your arm in jeopardy before you sign a big league contract. Think of your future son."

That logic and the prospect of a ten million dollar, three -year contract - convinced the family to sign with the team after he was drafted. He got one million up front as a bonus.

In his first full season in pro ball, Charles lived up to his potential. During that summer his parents drove to the Clearwater Stadium to see him pitch. He needed their presence because Tim was not the most outgoing young man on the team, and he missed his home a great deal.

Now home would be in a new location. He bought his parents a house in nearby Lakewood Ranch. It was a stunning sum of money for him, a $350,000 four-bedroom house on a lake, with its own pool. He was grateful to do it, and it would be his off-season home as well, until he was ready to live on his own. As a reflection of his gratitude to the church, he donated $25,000 to his local parish. His present to himself was a convertible Mustang.

By August of his first season, Tim had progressed well beyond anyone's expectations, and the young sensation was brought up to the parent club on September first when the rosters were expanded. Charles pitched well in his three starting appearances. He had more strikeouts than innings pitched, and had pinpoint control. If there was one criticism management had for the kid, it was his apparent unwillingness to move batters off of the plate when they dug in against him. As a result, Charles gave up three home runs in his short stint with the team. They chalked it up to his youth and lack of experience.

When the regular season ended, Buck Sawyer had a talk with his young apprentice and told him that he would be given a full opportunity to make the major league roster when he went to spring training the following February. In the off-season, Tim worked extremely hard at his training program. He was wiry and nimble and never seemed to have a dead arm. Most of his power came from his legs. That gave him the ability to propel the ball and lessen any strain on his shoulder or elbow.

When he returned the following year, he was touted as one of the top ten rookie prospects by the famed and respected Sporting News. Yet the timid and shy youngster remained humble, and celebrity didn't swell Tim's head. Unlike some in the league, he avoided the glare of the media as much as possible. He did what the club asked of him, but the media and fans couldn't get enough of his boyish good looks. When he smiled his dimples and that closely trimmed blonde hair made him look even younger than his chronological age.

Tim was more than happy to give back. He signed autographs at every venue both before and after a game. He would get ribbing from some of the veterans, but deep down they envied his innocence and respected his patience and gentleness with the fans.

His play on the field did nothing to disavow the baseball pundits. He was simply terrific. He had a sixteen inning scoreless streak before he gave up a two-run homerun to Dave Romm of the Reds. By the end of spring training there was no doubt in anyone's mind that he had made the team. He was two months shy of his 20th birthday.

Just three months into the season, Charles faced his first critical test in the majors. It wasn't a bases-loaded jam with Bryce Harper or Andrew McCutchen up at the plate. It was a choice he had to make about his own code of conduct. How would he deal with morality on the playing field when his team demanded something that he felt was out of character?

He couldn't sleep after the Saturday night game. He was about to pitch before a packed stadium the next night in view of a few million fans on Sunday Night Baseball. If that weren't enough, he was in the middle of a virtual baseball war between his team and the divisional rival Mets.

He stayed up late in his center city apartment with his roommate Bradley Schofield, a speedy outfielder. Brad had been in the league only a few years himself, but at 27 was savvier than Charles. The topic of conversation was naturally Buck's speech and the animosity that was keenly felt in the two prior games.

"Hell no, man, there is no way that this is over. It's just a question of when and how the next one comes. Hey roomie, you're not going to be the first guy to nail a batter in retaliation. It's not that big a deal. It goes with the territory.

The Mets expect   it sooner or later. But if it you don't have the gonads you can let one of the bullpen guys do it for you."

"But I don't want to let the team down. I dreamed about playing in the majors for as long as I can remember. If I punk out, what will people think?"

"Dude, you know what some of the guys will say. They'll call you a pussy. They'll say you're gutless - maybe that you got no respect for the game."

"Oh, thanks man, you're all heart."

"Look roomie, Adams is still getting paid, and he wimped out. What's the big deal?"

"The big deal is guys are pissed at him."

"So, you still have me and Doug as friends."

"But everyone else will think I don't have their backs."

Tim could not forget Sawyer's words about sticking it in someone's ear. It unnerved him to think of it, but he felt a deep obligation to the man who had been his benefactor. He realized he would be suspended, but that was the price the team and Buck felt was necessary. As he gazed vacuously at the ceiling, he recalled a painful episode he had experienced in his junior year of high school.

The baseball team captain and head honcho Clark Draper called a team meeting in mid-season. Draper's manipulative and egocentric personality spawned adulators and sycophants alike. The players listened intently as Draper relayed a conversation he had earlier with Coach Braddock. Draper explained that the coach planned to promote a kid from junior varsity as an extra infielder. The problem was, as

Draper saw it, the new kid wouldn't fit in because he was gay. Rather than make the whole team uncomfortable, Draper argued for an alternative solution. He ordered his teammates to ostracize and shun the kid until he broke and quit.

It would have worked except for the reserved yet bold act of courage displayed by Tim. On the second day of practice, while everyone else ignored the neophyte, Tim pulled a stunt vaguely reminiscent of Hall of Famer Pee Wee Reese in 1947. Reese had simply draped his arm around the shoulder of Jackie Robinson during a road game in a show of support when opponents, fans, and even some Dodger players wanted no part of a black man in baseball. In the same spirit, Tim put his arm around the shoulder of the dispirited youngster on the dugout steps and assured him that his love for the game would overcome any obstacles.

Given Draper's exalted status, the results were not unexpected. The new kid stuck it out and performed solidly, but Tim bore the consequences of scurrilous rumor for the rest of the season. Those moments were not lost on Tim now as he faced another challenge just a few years removed from his high school lesson. As Yogi Berra once said, "it was déjà vu all over again."

He wanted spiritual guidance, but he knew there was nothing in the Bible to justify deliberately hurting another competitor. So he didn't pray for an answer. He finally fell asleep at 5:00 AM. When he awoke he was no closer to an answer.

Chapter 4

"Welcome to ESPN Sunday Night Baseball on a beautiful summer evening at Citizens Bank Park, the home of the Philadelphia Phillies," said television anchor Joe Ludwig. He summarized the prior games of the series for his listeners.

"For those who aren't aware, Elliot Butterworth was hit in the hand by the Mets' reliever Friday night and Doug Adams hit Luther Wynne Saturday night. That led to a high slide by Leyton into Colby Green on the last play of the game.-an amazing finish to a hard fought game. By now most of you are probably aware of the melee that occurred as the game ended .The last play and the ensuing brawl have been shown repeatedly and dissected on the airwaves.

"The umpiring crew chief was required to submit a written report of the incident and background to Major League Baseball within twelve hours of the brawl. That office studied the video of the game, the report from the crew chief, and expedited their decision. The commissioner's Vice President for Discipline, has already issued a five-game suspension for Buck Sawyer and Mike Zahn. Mets' second baseman Kenny Leyton was suspended three games and fined for his flagrant take-out slide. No action was taken against any others.

"But all of them will be at the ball park tonight because all filed an appeal on the length of their suspensions. That means they are available to play while the grievance process occurs," said Ludwig.

"On the mound for the Phillies tonight is youngster Tim Charles, a flame-throwing twenty year-old right hander. He'll be opposed by the Mets' veteran Juan Rojas. What do you see from this youngster, only one year removed from the minors, asked Ludwig of his color analyst"?

"He's the real deal. He's been clocked at 100 mph on the radar guns and he can keep up that velocity late into the game. He can throw like that because he gets tremendous torque from his legs as Nolan Ryan and Tom Seaver once did.

"He's got great movement on the ball. He's baseball smart beyond his years, and he pitches, not just throws. He changes eye level on the batters too. He moves the ball up and down in the zone so they don't know what to expect from his location. Add in a devastating curve ball, and you have the makings of a potential Cy Young Award winner."

Down on the field, Charles was finishing up on the sidelines when the bullpen coach handed him the ball and reminded him to do what he had to do out there. "Buck's depending on you", added the coach.

Charles took the long walk out to the mound where he was met by the equally direct Julio Herrera.

Herrera asked "Are you ready to take care of business"?

Charles replied that he felt strong during the warm up.

"I don't mean that kind of business. I mean the pay back."

Charles just shook his head and looked down at the pitching rubber. He was so consumed by his predicament that he barfed in the clubhouse amidst the derisive chants of his teammates who good-naturedly scoffed at the rookie butterflies. They didn't understand that the underlying bout of nausea was more about the manner that the game would be played rather than his performance In the dugout, Adams approached the troubled youngster and took him aside.

"Kid, Buck is a short-timer. He's in a one year contract, and it's unlikely he'll be back. You'll be here for a long time. There's a middle ground. You don't have to do what Buck asked, but you can still shake up their hitters. A little chin music will take them out of their stride. Throw it close enough to the head that they play scared. Then maybe you won't get ejected."

It was hard for Adams to discern whether he had had an impact on the kid. Charles merely nodded in acknowledgement but didn't convey what he was thinking. He just sat in a corner of the dugout and waited for the top of the next inning.

Before long, it was the sixth inning of a nail biter. The Phillies led 2-0. Charles put his decision behind him and concentrated on winning, but time was running out; Leyton would bat second this inning. A momentary lapse in concentration caused him to groove a fastball down the middle that resulted in the first Met to reach second base on an extra base hit. As Leyton made his way from the on-deck circle to the plate, Gregg Martin told the local affiliate audience "If I'm out there on the field, I 'm waiting for my pitcher to take aim at somebody."

"I don't know if you want to put the winning run at the plate with no outs by plunking Leyton, but we'll see," added his partner Joe Forte in the booth.

"Leyton takes his time as he gets into the batter's box. He looks toward the third base coach for the sign. Would he be bunting with two runs down"? asked Forte. Then he called the next pitch.

"*Leyton squares as if to bunt. Charles in the stretch, checks the runner at first, he lets loose with a high inside fastball. Oh no! He's hit! The ball hit him square on the head near the ear portion of his helmet. Leyton is grimacing in obvious pain. His face is contorted almost beyond recognition as he holds his head. He's wobbling around home plate trying to maintain his balance. Now his knees crumble and Leyton falls sprawled out on the ground! The capacity crowd is as silent as mourners at a funeral. They sit transfixed by the horrifying image on the field. His helmet came off as soon as he was hit. This looks bad, and you have to hope that he hasn't suffered a serious injury. The ball sounded like a firecracker when it hit Leyton. I see some movement from Leyton so that's a good sign. Both teams are standing at the edge of their dugouts intently watching."*

"That's right, but you have to feel for the young pitcher too" said Martin. "He went down on his knees and put his glove over his head as if to shield himself from the scene in front of home plate. I'll tell you, it didn't seem like Leyton saw the pitch coming. He stood there like the he was paralyzed. He made no effort to get out of the way. You wonder what went through his mind."

In the ESPN booth, Ludwig told his listeners "The ball gets on you so quickly you barely have time to react. The ball Charles threw was clocked at 95.There is so much to report here fans as the trainer for the Mets and their manager tend to Leyton Umpire Mike Kastle has ejected both Tim Charles and manager Buck Sawyer, but they are still milling around on the field. Charles said something to Kastle after he was tossed. Let's look at the replay and see if we can figure out what he said. As the crew and the rest of the television audience watched the replay, Ludwig called it from the booth.

"It looks to me that Charles said he didn't mean to hit Leyton."

"I agree that's what he said, but I think Charles threw that pitch deliberately," replied the color analyst. He may look horrified, but it's more from the realization that he's in trouble with the commissioner's office. In the context of this series, I have to believe it was intentional. This is going to cost him several days in suspension time. Kastle is warning both benches now that any other *purpose-pitch* will result in further ejections."

Ludwig then brought it back to the playing field. "Juan Rojas is jawing at Tim Charles, and Mike Zahn is being held back by Bobby Carson. Players are pouring onto the field and it looks like another melee may break out. But now there's a burst of applause in the stadium."

"It looks like Leyton is conscious. He's trying to get up, and trainer Mitchell Schwefel is restraining him. He's talking to Leyton and apparently testing his eyes or vision. Now he's slowly helping the second baseman to his feet, and the crowd and both teams give him a standing ovation. Schwefel continues to talk to him and perform some physical tests but it looks like he may be okay. I doubt that he'll remain in the game. Mets' manager Aurelio Ruiz has signaled for a pinch runner as Schwefel helps Leyton to the dugout.

"The Phillies' new pitcher middle relief man Skip Wilder will get all the time he needs to warm up because of the ejection to Charles. Both teams are returning to their respective dugouts. Let's take a commercial break and digest what we just saw fans."

In the Mets' clubhouse, Schwefel told a reluctant Leyton that he would be accompanying him to the hospital to do further tests. By this time, Leyton's wife Theresa, who was at the game, joined her husband in the trainer's room. She encouraged Ken to go for tests, and he was glad to have her with him. He hated hospitals and was relieved to have her by his side.

"Gee honey, I don't even remember getting hit, but I'm okay."

"Is there anything hurting babe? Please be honest with me."

"Other than seeing some stars and ringing in my ear, I feel pretty good. I could probably play Tuesday."

"You must be out of your mind. Don't you read about players with concussions coming back too early? Do you want to be demented when you're fifty? Why don't we listen to the doctors before you decide what to do, okay"?

It was a short ride to Center City and Jefferson Hospital where they took Leyton. It was now only twenty-five minutes after the beaning. In the ER, they were met by Drs. Howard and Lynn Sheldon. The latter was an ER doctor while her husband was a specialist in traumatic brain injury. They had Leyton sit upright on an examination table. Mitch Schwefel provided background to the physicians about the injury. He also told them that Leyton's pupils were dilated upon initial examination on the field.

Howard Sheldon wanted to know if the patient had ever lost consciousness, and Schwefel told him that it was unlikely for two reasons. First, he had gotten to him very quickly, and second, Leyton seemed to recognize him. The doctor, however, found significance in the fact that Leyton had partial amnesia of the event. Now, however, he was aware of his surroundings and knew his name.

Lynn Sheldon tested the cranial nerve again to see if Leyton's pupils reacted normally to light. That checked out. She found no abnormality with his tendon reflexes, such as the knee-jerk reaction. Likewise, there was appropriate sensory function, as evidenced by Leyton's wince to a pinprick. Yet Leyton admitted that the ringing, although more subdued, continued to exist, as did his perception that he was seeing stars.

"It looks, upon examination, that you have what we call a 'grade two concussion,' Mr. Leyton, she said. I'll order a blood test to look for unique proteins that show up in the blood after a head injury, and that will help to confirm the presence of a concussion."

"Is it serious?" asked Theresa.

"Well," interjected Howard, "every concussion should be taken seriously. This is a mid-range concussion. The good news so far is that I feel or see no evidence of bruising or fracture. We need a CT scan to look inside your head. The procedure will take about forty-five minutes, but it is imperative to look for any signs of bleeding or fracture."

"When can I play ball again"? Kenny wanted to know.

"Let's wait to see what the CT shows us but I'd say conservatively you shouldn't play for two weeks. Don't even exercise for a week. Now why don't you go with my wife so we can both evaluate your CT scan, okay?"

"Sure thing Dr." said a dejected Leyton. "I'll be fine Theresa. You stay here and we'll go home soon."

"I hope so , but don't get upset if Dr.Sheldon wants you to stay the night for observation."

"Hey babe, listen to the rest of the game will you, and let me know how we did."

"Okay, maybe it will take my mind off of you. I hope they suspend that pitcher for the season. He hit you in the head. He could have killed you."

"It'll be alright, honey. He just did what was expected of him. He just let it fly a bit too close to my noggin'. I'm just glad everything is still in place in my head."

Lynn Sheldon wheeled him away and Theresa found the lounge to watch the game. She could barely record the images in her brain, but she was happy to see that the Mets had taken a commanding lead off the Phillies' relievers, scoring four times in the two innings after Ken was hit. The game ended with the Mets on top 6-2. At least she would have some good news for her husband when he returned.

An hour later Lynn Sheldon returned with Leyton.

"Well, I still have a brain, honey! Isn't that great? Tell her it's true, Doc!"

"So, I can confirm the presence of a brain, Mrs. Leyton. I can also tell you I see no evidence of hemorrhaging or fracture, so that much is good. Your husband tells me that the ringing and stars have subsided entirely. All of that is promising, but I am a bit concerned about the initial amnesia, and I do think it wise to stay the night while we keep you under observation. The blood test also shows the presence of unique proteins that are indicative of a concussion, so I am fairly certain you have sustained one. I'll get you a bed once you provide us with your insurance and other details.

"Doc, I'm feeling normal now. If it's all the same to you, I would just as soon go home to my family. We have the day off tomorrow anyway, so I promise to stay in and rest."

"Ken Leyton, you are impossible! You're lucky you aren't in a coma, and I want to be sure you're okay. I'd feel much safer if you would just stay. I can sleep on a chair."

"I quite agree with your wife, Mr. Leyton. You would be doing yourself a disservice to leave. Concussions are not always predictable, and complications can occur."

"I appreciate that, Doc, but if I start to feel badly again, I'll go straight to the hospital near us. I just can't stand being in a hospital, and unless I'm unconscious, I'm not going to be talked into staying."

"Well, it's against my medical judgment, Mr. Leyton, but I can't prevent you from leaving. In any event, Mrs. Leyton, please watch him closely for any changes like headache, nausea, or irritability. If he complains that he feels like he is in a fog, get him to a hospital ASAP."

"I sure will, and he will stay there if I have to handcuff him to a bed. Thanks for trying, but you can see that he has a hard head, Doctor."

In the ER, team trainer Mitch Schwefel paced nervously until a smile crossed his face when he saw the Leytons approaching the exit. He too urged Leyton to reconsider, but was assuaged by the promise to seek medical help if any symptoms set in. He wished them a good evening and told them he would report the news immediately to manager Ruiz.

By the time they drove home to Voorhees it was almost midnight and Ken was exhausted. They were met at home by Theresa's parents, Donald and Elizabeth Cox, who were overjoyed that their son-in-law was back home safely. They had spent the evening with their grandson James trying to keep him occupied with toys while they waited for word from their daughter.

Ken was exhausted and after grabbing some Oreo cookies and milk, he excused himself and went upstairs with Theresa to see their son before bed. Ken felt lucky to have such a wonderful family and to be able to play a kid's game for a living. He was grateful that as he laid down that he was off Monday as the Mets traveled back to New York. He wouldn't admit it, but he couldn't imagine having to play the next day. He was dead tired.

Chapter 5

On Monday, sports radio and television concentrated on the beaning of Ken Leyton. The majority of the listener calls merely chalked up the incident as a necessary component of the game. Even the commentators justified it as an understandable corollary to the spiking in the ninth inning of the second game of the series. True, feelings in New York were running very high, but their more knowledgeable baseball fans understood what had taken place. They may have believed they had gotten the worst in the feud, but they were sophisticated enough not to be self-righteous about it.

The Philadelphia Bulletin led the morning edition with the line "Second Casualty of Baseball War." The New York Tribune banner headline was "Open Warfare Declared." Both assumed that the pitch was intentional. Both recounted stories and quotes from yesteryear concerning the use of the bean ball in the history of the game.

But in the late afternoon, one show in particular raised a controversial argument ESPN's "Today in Sports" debated the issue of whether the act by Tim Charles went beyond what is deemed acceptable and tolerable by the rules and customs of baseball.

Mike Greenblatt asked his counter-part Alex Turner an intriguing question. "Does what Charles did last night amount to a crime? I don't know what it's called in the law, but does that intentional beaning rise to the level of criminality"?

"That's interesting. I hadn't really considered that, but it's worth talking about," said Turner.

"I'm just putting it out there. I haven't really come to a conclusion myself", said Greenblatt. "But if Leyton suffers some kind of serious injury, and if he is out for an indefinite time, maybe somebody ought to think about what the consequences should be."

"Your point is well taken, although I do feel some sympathy for the kid who threw the pitch. From all accounts he is a youngster with good character. And I'll lay odds someone on the managerial side told him to take that action to retaliate for the injury to Butterworth and Green. But it raises the whole issue of whether the unwritten code of conduct in sports can trump the laws that you and I have to abide by."

"Hopefully the injury to Leyton isn't serious, and that there is no reason for anyone in or outside of the game to have to answer that question," said Greenblatt.

On the MLB network many commentators questioned whether Charles intended to hit Leyton or whether the pitch was supposed to be chin music and got away. Al Lester, a former pitcher for the Mets, pointed out that Leyton was the first batter Charles had hit in the majors. He felt the pitch had merely gotten away from the kid.

"Look at how the kid reacts when the ball hits Leyton. He falls to his knees and puts his glove over his head in what seems to me to be genuine remorse. Then you can see him talking to umpire Mike Kastle. If I'm reading his lips correctly, it looks like he is saying he wasn't trying to hit him."

But Manny Reynolds, a former Seattle Mariner second baseman, pointed out that Charles had the second fewest walks per innings pitched in the eastern division and that his control was very accurate. In his mind there was little open for dispute.

"I think it's obvious what we're looking at here. This was a payback pitch and not just a brush back. That's scary when you're throwing in the upper 90s. I hope Major League Baseball comes down hard on him. Hey, it's easy to say that you didn't mean to hit him. Anybody can say it; it doesn't mean it's true."

"It's unfortunate," said former pitcher Gary Udell, "but let's face it, bean balls have always been a part of the game. It's a risk you have to assume if you're a batter. Baseball is a game of physical contact too; it just isn't thought of in the same light as hockey or football. All the same, it's a lot more physical than people think. You don't play hardball baseball thinking it's a game of chess. You know when you step in the box that the pitcher will jealously guard that plate. He may let you have a small part, but if you lean too much or relax out there, that pitcher has just as much a right to the plate as the batter. That's where intimidation and bean balls play a role."

Jay Parker, the baseball historian, put the debate into proper perspective.

"Look, this isn't something new. A player expects his pitcher to get even. It's the law of retaliation. Barry Bonds was furious at his teammates in 2002 because he was getting hit so much that he openly complained in public about the lack of protection from his own pitchers. They hadn't retaliated. Former Arizona Diamondback's GM Kevin Towers publicly chastised his pitchers for failing to protect his hitters in 2013.

Billy Martin's credo was also based on the art of intimidation. He had no problem ordering his pitchers to hit opposing batters to get an edge. It is, as your other guest just said, an inherent risk of the game that has become acceptable by long-term custom.

I'm not sure of when and where you draw the line, but I do know that it will take something significant to change that cultural phenomenon in baseball," concluded Parker.

No one that evening could have anticipated that the event that took place on Sunday night would be the catalyst for a series of consequences that would shake the very foundations of baseball in the ensuing days.

Initially, what seemed no more than a concussion that would keep Leyton out of the lineup for a few weeks, rapidly changed in the ensuing hours after he left the hospital.

Chapter 6

Theresa couldn't sleep. She was lying on her side with her eyes open and watched as Ken breathed deeply and rapidly throughout the night. She silently prayed that he would be himself in the morning. She was out of bed early to greet young James, or "Jimbo," as they called him. It was 6:30 when she came downstairs to make him breakfast. She would let Ken sleep for as long as he wanted. There was no reason to rush. She would insist that Ken go on the disabled list or at least stay away from the park for several days.

Nevertheless by 10 AM she began to worry. She went upstairs and gently shook her husband. He asked her to let him sleep longer. When he assured her that he was fine, she left him to finish his much needed rest. When James walked into the room at noon, his father got up in bed and hugged his son.

"Did you do good in the game, Dad? "

"I didn't play long, Jimbo. The ball hit me in my head and I had to go home."

"Does it hurt?"

"Not too bad, son. I can still go swimming after lunch if you want."

"Yeaaah for us!"

But Ken was pushing himself to look normal. His head hurt and he felt seasick. He'd take some Tylenol with lunch and that would do the trick - at least he hoped so. For now he'd shower, dress, and spend some time with his in-laws. Maybe he would even stay over again rather than drive back to their home in Morristown, New Jersey. He would be more comfortable at home, but he just didn't feel up to the two-hour drive today.

Ken assured Theresa that he was merely tired from the excitement and that there was no reason for alarm. He ate a ham sandwich as he fought the temptation to keep it all down. After lunch he kept his promise and got in the pool with James. He caught James as he jumped in the pool more times than he could count, and winced as James hollered with excitement. The shouting seemed to pierce through his head. Maybe, he thought, it was just the headache getting to him. In any event, he wouldn't disappoint his son until James told him that he had enough.

Damn, he was so tired. He knew he needed more rest, so he told Theresa that he was going to lie down again for a nap. Theresa still did not suspect that anything was wrong. Wouldn't anyone need rest after a concussion? She had not been made privy to the headache or the other symptoms, so she decided there was no reason for panic. She reasoned it was just part of the body's way of healing itself.

At almost 5 :00 PM, she decided to wake him. When he got up he had trouble seeing his wife. There were two women in front of him and he felt confused.

"What time is it?" he managed to say.

As soon as she heard his words, Theresa knew something was very wrong. He spoke as if he were in slow motion. He told her he was seeing double.

"I'm taking you to the hospital. Don't even try to argue with me. Please get dressed. James can stay with my parents. I'll be right back. I'm letting them know we're leaving."

"I guess you're right, honey" said her resigned, and increasingly frightened, husband.

When she returned to the bedroom, her husband was sprawled on the carpet. She ran to him and yelled for him to tell her what happened, but he was unresponsive. She could hear him breathing but each breath sounded like it was sapping all of his strength. She ran for the landline and called 911.

"911, what is your emergency please?"

"It's my husband. He's unconscious. Please send an ambulance!! Please, before it's too late!"

"Is he breathing?"

"Yes he is, but it looks like he might be in a coma. Please just send someone out now!"

"Just one more question, try to remain calm. I am sending someone out now as we speak. Did something happen? Did you have a fight? Did he have an injury?"

"No! We didn't have a fight. He is Kenny Leyton. He is a baseball player and he got hit in the head last night during a game, but he was fine. I don't know what could have happened."

"Okay Mrs. Leyton, please don't move him. The paramedics will be there in a couple of minutes."

Theresa frantically called for her dad to stay with James while she went to the hospital with her husband. She vaulted down the stairs and waited until she heard the sirens outside and ushered the two paramedics up to the guest bedroom where Kenny still lay. She jumped in the ambulance with them and they headed for Virtua Hospital in their Voorhees town, just a short ride from her family's home. They were at the hospital by 5:13 PM. Theresa was told to remain in the waiting room. She could barely breathe, but she did as she was told.

Leyton was rushed to the ER while paramedics briefed doctors on the medical history they learned from Theresa. Doctors again ordered a CT scan and MRI while a nurse hooked Leyton up to a respirator to ensure that enough oxygen was getting to the brain from the flow of blood. The staff knew from a feel of the neck and the skull that swelling had taken place. Intravenous fluids were introduced to prevent his blood pressure from falling too low and also to enable blood and oxygen flow to the brain. He was stabilized for the moment.

A review of the second brain scan validated the initial impressions of the ER staff. Leyton was suffering from a cerebral edema. His brain had filled with water and was cutting off his body's blood supply to the spinal cord. He was rushed to a surgical room where doctors initiated a ventriculostomy. The procedure produces a small hole in the skull and a plastic drain tube is inserted. The purpose is to drain cerebrospinal fluid from the inside of the brain to relieve pressure on the brain. Leyton remained in a coma with no change in his vital signs.

Dr. Paul Skyversky sat down with Theresa and told her that his condition had not improved. He laid out one further option for her to consider. She listened as if in a stupor. The words carried no meaning. Everything had happened so fast that she was unable to process it. She was jolted to alertness when Skyversky told her he planned to open her husband's skull and take out a piece of the skull to relieve the intracranial pressure.

"How can this be happening? How much time do I have to decide?"

"I am afraid we are up against the clock, Mrs. Leyton. He's in a coma, and unless we do something, I am not very optimistic. Frankly, his chances are not good either way."

"Oh my God, this can't be real. What should I do? I'm not prepared to make this decision."

Nevertheless, she reluctantly agreed to try the last horrifying option. Theresa went to the hospital chapel to wait and pray. She tried but couldn't stem the fear that she already knew how it would end. In the same instant she felt anger rising within her towards the man who had done this to her beloved husband.

Chapter 7

Ken Leyton was pronounced dead at 7:23 PM. The massive swelling of the brain had made recovery a virtual impossibility. Dr. Skyversky broke the news to Theresa in the corridor where she stood with her father. She was filled with bewilderment, confusion, and pain. The anger would return later.

"How," she asked, "could this happen when we were told that there was no fracture or bleeding in the brain"?

"Unfortunately, a CT scan doesn't always pick up swelling, or even a small subdural hemorrhage. Even if it isn't there initially, the fluid can increase over the next twelve to twenty-four or even forty-eight hours. A cerebral edema is sometimes missed on a CT scan. I don't want to give you a medical lesson now while you are in shock, but I assure you it happens."

"Please, explain it to me Doctor. I need to understand why my husband died."

"In any trauma to the body, such as a blunt force to the knee, there will be swelling of the tissues surrounding the location of the wound. It is no different with a head injury. Your husband was hit by a tremendous force that produced a traumatic brain injury. The brain is in a closed space and it was jostled back against the skull from the power of the pitched ball. That brain injury caused it to swell. Because the brain is in a closed space in the skull, it can only expand so much until there is nowhere else it can go. The brain then puts downward pressure on the spinal cord. This cuts off the blood supply to the spinal cord that controls all bodily functions. Soon respiration is halted and the patient dies.

"We tried everything we could to alleviate the swelling and fluid, but your husband could not survive the surgery. If he had, there is every reason to believe he would have had permanent brain damage that would have left him in a vegetative state.

"I truly am sorry, Mrs. Leyton, for your loss. I wish we'd seen him sooner."

"I saw no signs of anything wrong. He was tired, but I thought it best for him to rest. Should I have seen there was something wrong?"

"Mrs. Leyton, you can't be expected to be a mind reader. If your husband was having symptoms and didn't share them with you, there was really nothing you could have done."

"I didn't even have a chance to say I loved him. The last thing I said to him was telling him that he was going to the hospital. I can't believe this. How will I tell his son? He idolizes his father."

"I can help get a grief counselor here to help you and your son. Call me anytime and I'll set it up."

"I have so much to do and I can't even grasp this."

"Come on home Theresa, your mother and I will help you with everything that needs to be done. We'll get through this together, as impossible as it seems now", said Donald Cox.

Theresa and her father left for home, where they forced themselves to speak of the funeral arrangements. It was like an out-of-body experience for the widow, who barely had time to internalize the loss and the sorrow that would accompany her for the next several years. She allowed herself to nestle in the arms of her mother and feel the security that only her parents could now give her. She would wait until morning to break the news to James. That night Theresa cried softly in her bed until she fell asleep.

When she awoke, she thought of Ken, and then she thought of the man who had murdered her husband. For the first time, she saw clearly what had to be done. She vowed to herself and to her husband that his killer would be held responsible. She owed it to Ken and to their son to see that justice was done.

Chapter 8

The shocking death of Leyton sent reverberations well beyond the realm of the baseball world. After the headlines on Tuesday concerning the tragic death of Leyton, there were editorials in both Philadelphia and New York papers. They questioned the use of the brush back tactic for any purpose, especially when aimed near the head. But today the print and broadcast media broadened the inquiry. They took up the lead of the question raised by ESPN a day earlier. Should an independent investigatory body look into the tragic episode to see if criminal charges should be brought against the pitcher who threw the deadly pitch? Or, they opined, is this best left to the office of the baseball commissioner and those in the profession to sort out?

The unique and tragic story prompted several national journalists to contact the Philadelphia District Attorney's Office on Broad Street early Tuesday. Erica Benson, the executive assistant to District Attorney Nancy Artis, had never been so inundated with emails and phone. Rarely had requests for information gotten so chaotic that she couldn't keep track of them. Exasperated, she got up and knocked on the DA's door.

"Nancy, I don't know how to handle all these calls. I need to give them something. Everybody's calling about the death of that ball player. It's all over the news and they want to know if you're going to do something about it. What do they want from us? This happened at the ballpark during the game didn't it? What's it got to do with the DA's office?"

"Well, it's an unnatural death and I suspect that's where we come in. Technically it's a homicide Okay, set up a press conference for 11:00 this morning. I should be briefed enough to handle the press by then, and ask Steve Burkett to get here on the double". Burkett was the First Assistant to the Chief DA and he had over two decades in the office.

He strode into her office at 9:30 with a smirk on his face. "Good morning boss! Looks like an uneventful start of the day, wouldn't you agree?"

"Dammit! I've been getting messages on my Blackberry since 4 AM, and I can't count the number of phone calls and emails. I told Erica to set up a press conference for 11:00 today, but I don't know what the hell to tell them."

"Tell them very little. Don't accept questions. Give them a brief statement to hold them off until we can get the management team together to discuss a game plan. We don't want to get out ahead of ourselves and commit to some action that we may later regret."

"Fine, but what do I say in the statement other than our deepest sympathy for, what's his name?"

"Kenny Leyton."

"Right, I never heard of him. It's a tragedy, but I don't know how else to characterize it yet."

"That's my point! They want to know if we're prepared to issue an arrest warrant for the pitcher Tim Charles. Simply say that we have not, at this time, sought an arrest warrant. Tell them that pending further review we will issue periodic updates. Tell them you wish you had more, but that's all you can say for now."

"Okay, that sounds good, but we have to provide some details or they'll hover over us like locusts until we offer up something concrete. In the interim please have the press assistant, the chief of homicide, and the chief of major crimes ready for a working lunch."

"You got it. Good luck out there. I hope they don't devour you. I'm just starting to get to like you."

"Don't be so cocky, or I'll have you go out there to handle the conference."

At 11:00 A.M., the Widener Building at Three South Penn Square was mobbed by television cameras and reporters all anxiously waiting for Nancy Artis to tell them what the next step would be. The question had been posed by the editorial staffs of the print media and the baseball pundits. Now they wanted to tell the public whether their elected officials would actively engage in the controversy. In this tumult Artis stood at her podium and read from a prepared statement.

"My staff and I extend our heartfelt sympathy to the Leyton family. This is a shock to all sports fans throughout the nation. This is a time for somber reflection for the family of Ken Leyton and Mets' fans who grieve the passing of their beloved fallen leader.

"In that spirit, my office will soberly look at the video of the game as well as the two prior games. We shall patiently gather information to initially determine whether any criminal investigation is warranted. I have not at this time authorized the issuance of an arrest warrant for any individual. I will issue updates as we make progress. I know you want more specifics, but I am simply not in a position to do that now. I will not take any questions at this time. Thank you."

As she gathered her things, a reporter from a New York paper yelled out "Will you order an autopsy?" Another from the Philadelphia Bulletin asked if she had spoken to Mrs. Leyton. Artis ignored the questions and strode from the podium to shouts of disapproval from the fourth estate.

Turning to the cameras, a reporter from New York's SportsNet cable network asked rhetorically "What can't the Philly DA see that a couple of million fans saw all on their television sets Sunday night"?

Back at her office, Artis was not surprised to hear that the phones were still ringing incessantly. Members of the Chamber of Commerce wanted to talk to her, brass from the Phillies wanted a meeting with her, and the mayor wanted her to call. They all wanted to stress the adverse impact that a prosecution would have on the City and the Phillies. The team brought in plenty of revenue. The loss of the young star would dramatically hurt the team and the substantial businesses that made their money from enthusiastic packed stadiums. Everything from hotels, restaurants, transportation, food suppliers, souvenir vendors, city taxis, and good will toward the city would be impacted negatively by a prosecution.

She took a call from the Phillies' chief executive officer. He expressed the view that this was a matter for the baseball commissioner and not the criminal court system.

"Ms. Artis, I realize I have a substantial interest in the outcome of your decision, but I respectfully suggest to you that the commissioner has the necessary tools to do what is necessary in this instance. He can impose enough sanctions to satisfy the call for swift punitive action.

"And I want to point out that the call for a prosecution is not all pervasive. There are many who agree this should not be criminalized. This is a tragedy for both young men. Charles is just 20 and he will never get that out of his mind. For all we know, he may be finished as a professional in this game as a result of this tragedy. He may not be able to focus again. Let the duly elected commissioner make the call. I just hope that you won't let the press coerce you into making the wrong decision. I am confident you have what it takes to do what is right rather than to bow to pressure."

Nancy thanked him for his viewpoint and cautiously told him that she was not looking to make this a "cause célèbre." "But I can't make any promises to you until my staff and I have reviewed the facts," she said. "I understand your position and I will give you the courtesy of a call when we have made a decision on whether to prosecute."

She looked down at the pastrami sandwich with deli mustard on her desk and buzzed Erica to tell her that her stomach was lobbying for chicken soup. She had enough acid in her stomach to fill a car battery.

Nancy Artis was no shrinking violet. She spent several of her early years in the DA's office and handled high profile trials. She went into the private practice of law and was successful defending physicians in malpractice cases. She made enough money so that at 50, she was able to accept the Republican Party's offer to run for District Attorney against the incumbent democratic DA. It was almost against all odds in the overwhelmingly Democratic City of Philadelphia, but somehow in she pulled off the upset of a century in winning the election.

Still, she was a realist and knew that one big mistake in her first term could lead to defeat. At the age of 54 she didn't want to return to the long and grueling hours of private practice.

Now, as she waited for her staff to join her, she wished she had an escape valve from the potential bombshell that the baseball death had brought to her door.

At noon, with staff seated, she began with a summary of the events of the previous days. She could be frank with her upper management team. They were not naïve about political ramifications to this job.

"So, the way I see it, we have a no-win situation on our hands. If we decline to prosecute, the cynics will criticize me for protecting a hometown hero. And no doubt Mrs. Leyton will vilify me. If we do prosecute, everyone from the mayor down to the hot dog vendors at the ballpark will hang me in effigy. I won't be able to go anywhere without an armed security force. People will protest at my home. Do I sound in panic mode? That's how I feel right now.

"I have to stand for election again in two-and-a-half years. That's not long enough away for the public forget. We may not even be into the trial stage for another year if we prosecute. That means it will still be relatively fresh in the public mind. I can see the primary challengers lining up already to unseat me. No doubt it will all be framed in terms of the ambitious DA who had visions of herself in the governor's chair or on the Supreme Court. Who knows what outrageous lies they will fabricate. I don't for one minute think that I 'm overstating the consequences. I'll probably have a favorability rating below 25% by primary season.

"On the other hand, we have an unnatural death that was witnessed live by more than 43,000 people and on television by perhaps a couple million more. It may have occurred in a unique arena by consenting adults, but if Charles killed Leyton, there is no other name to call it but homicide. You can argue over the degree of homicide, but I don't see any way this can be called excusable or justifiable homicide. Now that I have framed the issues, does anyone have some ideas on how we approach it? I'm all ears."

Barbara Harrison, the media officer, wondered aloud if we could stall to see what the baseball commissioner intended to do. "If the sanction is severe enough, maybe the widow and the public will cool off on any criminal prosecution."

"I don't think that's a reasonable expectation. We can expect an uptake in the drum roll for a criminal investigation if it looks like we're just playing for time," said Burkett.

"I have an idea that may sound like a Hail Mary but it's legally sound. I don't know if it's wishful thinking, but..."

"Okay, enough with the qualifiers, let's hear the idea and then we can decide if it's from the tooth fairy or not," said the DA to her homicide chief, Ira Slavin.

"Well, this may be a hair brained idea."

"Ira, get on with it, will you please?!"

"I was just thinking that the best way to pass the buck would be to have another jurisdiction take the case."

"And how would that be accomplished?" asked Burkett.

"This is the scenario. The victim actually died in New Jersey, right? Okay, that means that either the Philly DA, or the county prosecutor where the person died can prosecute the case."

Nancy was stunned and confused. "I don't get it. The guy was beaned in Philly. That's where the homicidal act occurred. Where does New Jersey come into play?"

"He's right. The criminal code confers jurisdiction to New Jersey if either the criminal act or the resulting consequences of the act occurred in New Jersey," replied Steven Burkett.

Slavin explained that the act was in Philly, but if the coroner or medical examiner determined that death was as a result of the thrown pitch, the result of the pitch was consequently a subsequent death in New Jersey.

"We had cases in the past where there is a mob- or gang-killing and the body is dumped in Delaware. Delaware authorities could legally prosecute, but we do because we could prove the shooting happened in our City. We had the witnesses and the evidence of the crime here so we were able to prosecute," said Slavin.

"So what you're telling me is that the authorities in New Jersey could assert their jurisdiction and handle the case, am I right? " asked the intrigued DA.

Burkett wanted to know where the victim died, and learned from Harrison that he died at Virtua Hospital in Voorhees.

"That's in Camden County "said the homicide chief.

"Well that's a very interesting scenario people, but I see one flaw," said Artis. "How in the world do I get the Camden County Prosecutor to play ball? No pun intended."

"Well, I know her fairly well," said Burkett. "We went to law school at Rutgers and I run into her every year at alumni events or at District Attorneys conventions. I could call her."

"Excellent! Now see if you can get her on the phone and ask if we can pay her a visit to discuss the matter."

At that moment, Erica buzzed Artis with news that Theresa Leyton was in the waiting room asking to see the District Attorney.

"Oh Steve, make that call to the prosecutor now! I think the screws are about to tighten."

Chapter 9

Theresa Leyton was clearly a youthful looking twenty-nine. At 5' 6" and 125 pounds with a lithe body and brunette hair often in a pony-tail, she was still asked for identification at liquor stores. Now a widow, and the mother of a four-year-old son, she allowed herself one night to grieve the sudden loss of her beloved husband of seven years. She had met Kenny in her freshman year at the University of North Carolina at Chapel Hill. Ken was two years older and the talk of the campus because of his baseball prowess.

They shared many interests, including a love of sports, and a fierce competitive style of play. While Ken was laid back off the playing field, Theresa was best described as a Type A Personality. She didn't take well to coming in second either in sports or scholastics. Perhaps because she was an only child, her parents yielded to her every whim. As an adult she came to expect the same attention from others. If she were disappointed, her wrath could be fierce and uncompromising

So Ken was content to play the submissive role in the marriage. To him their mutual backgrounds and physical attractions far exceeded Theresa's petulance. It helped too that both grew up in southern New Jersey, and that they shared a cultural bond because of their roots and Protestant faith.

. Theresa was not a stay at home wife, and she had visions of a career which included her own business sometime down the road. So it was consistent with her personality that she could compartmentalize her personal tragedy and concentrate on seeking redress from the Philadelphia District Attorney the day after her husband was killed.

She left her son with her parents, who still lived in the house where she grew up in Voorhees, New Jersey. It borders its larger neighbor, Cherry Hill Township, where Kenny attended school, and it's close to the ballpark in Philadelphia. It seemed like homecoming for Theresa and Ken whenever the Mets traveled to Philadelphia to play. They usually stayed at the home of Theresa's parents for the series so they could combine family and business.

Theresa had witnessed the horror of Sunday night at the game while her parents babysat. The painful progression from exuberance, when it looked like Ken would recover, to the shock and disbelief when doctors told her that Ken had not survived, would have immobilized most spouses. Yet Theresa was only steeled that much more to see to it that people were held accountable for her loss.

Erica led Theresa into the DA's office, quickly sized up Leyton's demeanor, and headed straight for the door. Nancy Artis rose to greet Theresa and said sincerely "Mrs. Leyton, on behalf of my office, please accept our sincerest sympathies to you and your entire family for the tragic death of your husband. I cannot imagine what you must be feeling and going through. It must seem like a nightmare from which you cannot awake. The entire city mourns the loss of your husband. What can I do for you this afternoon"?

"That is very kind of you to say. I guess it all hasn't fully hit me yet so I must be running on instinct. But since you offered, there is something you can do for me. I heard the statement you made to the press on the radio, and I'm perplexed. Why it is that the pitcher hasn't been arrested and in jail? What else would you need to prove that he killed my husband"?

"Well, I realize that it may seem so plain to you, but there are certain fundamentals that my office will have to examine before we allege that a crime was committed. After all, some may view this as a tragic accident. The pitch may have been thrown while he was off balance, or the ball may have slipped from his hand as he was in the process of throwing. There are a lot of things that could have happened short of a crime. Now I can appreciate that you want something done-"

"I want justice for my husband, Ms. Artis. He was just thirty-one years old, and he didn't die from any accident," corrected Theresa. Everyone saw what happened, and the fans know the bitterness between those two teams. It doesn't take a genius to figure out what happened."

"Ultimately you may be right Mrs. Leyton, but I'm a public prosecutor and I must make my determinations based on proof. I only ask that you be a bit more patient. The criminal justice system sometimes moves laboriously. You need to concentrate for the next few days on your family. The system will sort through this in due course."

"Frankly, I am perfectly able to multitask if necessary. I may be unfamiliar with the justice system, but I don't want my husband's death chalked up to some cliché about the unfortunate necessities of the game."

"I can assure you that I will give this a priority, but I'm afraid that I'm not in a position to authorize an arrest warrant at this time. I don't expect to give you a definitive answer for the next several days. Please be patient."

"This is not what I was expecting to hear Ms. Artis. I won't be one of those women who bury their spouse and move on with their life. I'm doing this because it's right and because justice demands a prosecution for this crime. I won't sit on my hands for long. Here is my telephone number at my parents' home. I will be in South Jersey for quite some time. I expect you will keep me advised as the case progresses."

"I certainly will keep you fully apprised of things as they occur, Mrs. Leyton. Let me show you out."

As Theresa left the office, Nancy slumped down in her chair and said a silent prayer that Burkett would have success with the Camden County Prosecutor. "What a cluster bomb this is going to be," she said out loud to an empty office. She wondered whether there really was a chance to pass this hot potato to another agency. She hoped Burkett had some good news for her. Otherwise, it was going to be a long and prickly next few days.

Downstairs, a television reporter, who was hanging around the offices of the city's top law enforcement official, recognized Mrs. Leyton from her pictures in the newspaper. He yelled for his cameraman to get over to him before she left. He caught up to her and asked her why she was there.

"I'm here because I don't want my husband's death to be labeled an unfortunate accident. I want the Philadelphia DA's office to do their job and to arrest Timothy Charles. He killed my husband in front of millions of people, and he is still a free man."

"Can you tell me what the DA told you, Mrs. Leyton"?

"What she told me makes me doubt that I will get justice in this City. They want patience, and I'm not willing to give it. If I have to get every wife on the Mets' team down here to protest, I will. I want him behind bars by the time my husband is buried. That's all I have to say right now, excuse me."

"Let's get this back to the studio in time for the 5:00 news. We'll use this for the lead. What a lucky grab from out of nowhere"! said the reporter to his crew.

Back in the DA's office, Nancy Artis had a brief conversation with her first assistant about his call to the Camden prosecutor. She was pleased with the result. The Prosecutor had agreed to a 9:00 meeting at the Camden City office the next morning. Burkett asked that it be limited to the Prosecutor and her first assistant prosecutor and she had agreed.

That evening Artis saw the local news interview with Theresa Leyton. She winced at the prospect that the story would get legs and be picked up nationally. It didn't take long before she got her answer.

Chapter 10

The controversy was highlighted on national news. Legal experts were questioned by network anchors about the merits of the widow's position. Noted legal scholar Lee Soliman warned against "a rush to judgment", but acknowledged that a criminal case could be initiated if, after balancing the competing interests at stake, it was apparent that anything other than a criminal prosecution would trivialize the incident and make it more likely for similar incidents to occur.

Most agreed that a prosecution could be brought, but were uncertain about the slippery slope such a course of action could set. Lawyer and agent Bruce Butler questioned the impact of such a prosecution on the game of baseball. What, he opined, would it do to the balance of power between the batter and the pitcher if the brush back or bean ball could be criminalized?

Baseball legends offered their insights. Will Campbell, a Hall-of-Famer and legend in the game said that he was hit almost 200 times in his career. He noted it was all a part of the game, like an unwritten rule that was just accepted by everyone. He emphasized that he had never even charged the mound for the pitcher.

Historians pointed out that early 20th century players considered the bean ball an art. It altered the way a batter would feel at the plate and change his confidence level. It was part of the strategy of the game. Why, they asked, should Charles be made a scapegoat for what the game had long ago accepted? The grieving widow was just knee-jerk reacting against the young kid and hadn't thought it through. They argued that with time she would come to see that even her husband wouldn't have wanted a criminal prosecution.

Unfortunately for Nancy Artis, some on the Mets, who were willing to go on the record, rebutted that argument. Mike Zahn, Leyton's closest friend on the team, was convinced that the pitch was both willful and deliberate. He felt that baseball had to make an example of Charles for the sake of all players and for the memory of his friend. He said he would join a protest if the City did not prosecute. Fellow outfielder Scooter Barnett echoed the same sentiment.

As a result, when she finished her nightly glass of red zinfandel, Nancy knew she would have to be at her best when she advocated the next morning in Camden.

Chapter 11

Grace Moore was a first in many respects. She was the first career prosecutor to have risen from the ranks of the office in her county to be nominated by the governor for the top job as Prosecutor. The custom had been for the job to go to a respected lawyer who had worked for and paid their dues to the political party with which they were affiliated. Nor had it been necessary for the lawyer to have been experienced in criminal law. What mattered was that they had worked pro bono for the party in various legal causes. The job was considered a prime political plum for patronage purposes.

So it was truly a first for Moore to get the nomination. She was also the first African-American lawyer, and the very first woman to ever hold that coveted position. At 46, she too had twenty years of experience in the field. What she had that Artis lacked was job security.

Moore, as all county prosecutors, was appointed to her job by the governor for a five-year term. She could be reappointed to another five-year term if the governor's party won reelection. She, however, did not have to run for office at any point. She could not lose her job as a practical matter absent some misconduct in office. The nature of her appointment allotted Moore more job freedom regardless of public opinion polls or even, for the most part, political implications. She did not have the same level of pressure from the general public as that of an elected official, and it made her job much less stressful.

At 9:00 AM, Moore's counterpart from across the Delaware River was greeted in front of the modest building at 25 North Fifth Street in Camden City that housed the majority of the various units and squads that made up the Office. The number of lawyers stood at sixty-six, compared with over three hundred at the DA's office.

The building itself was finished in 1994 and was obsolete in terms of space the day it opened. Like most governmental offices, the design and furniture would not appear on the cover of any style magazine. In fact it would be a suitable candidate for a makeover by the HGTV network. The rugs had stains throughout that almost looked as if they were a patterned style. The chairs had cushions that looked and felt like they had been used for teenaged sleepover parties. Most employees sat at cubicles with little space or privacy. Windows were at a premium. Those who were lucky enough to have one usually had a depressing view of a parking lot or a building that looked like it was days from being demolished.

Artis raised an eyebrow at Burkett when they walked in the doors to the small reception area. They were quickly scooted up to the third floor, which housed the office of Prosecutor Moore. The office was unremarkable with modest space. It was just enough to allow for a wooden table that could seat six to eight people for conferences. A flag of New Jersey flanked the Red, White, and Blue in the corner, and photographs of the Governor and Attorney General adorned the wall.

Moore got up from her desk to greet her colleagues and then she introduced them to her First Assistant, Jaime Brooks, who knew even less than Moore about the purpose of the visit. After the formalities, all agreed to be on a first name basis.

"How can this office be of assistance to you, Nancy?" asked Moore.

"I'll be frank. I'm not going to try and snow you. I'll lay out my cards for everyone to see. I know that what I'm about to suggest is a bit unorthodox, but I'm in a political bind. I'm in an overwhelming minority party in my city as you know, and I have to face an electorate in the not-too-distant future. Are you familiar with the tragedy at the baseball stadium? "

"Yes, I've been following the story and caught the interview with the widow. I don't envy your task, Nancy."

"I was actually hoping that you would envy my task."

"What do you mean?"

"I am here because I am going to urge you to undertake what would normally be my turf and my responsibility to fulfill. I want you to accept the job of investigating, and potentially prosecuting the pitcher who killed Ken Leyton."

"Why would my office want to prosecute an act that happened in Pennsylvania? I realize he died in New Jersey, but you have all of the witnesses in the City and it was the site of the alleged crime. If I took the case, it would look like some kind of power grab."

"No, no, we would hold a joint press conference and announce that we mutually agreed to have the prosecution in New Jersey. We would simply say that we are doing this to avoid any appearance of a conflict of interest. Leyton's wife has already said publicly that she couldn't get a fair shot from the City. By taking this action, we tell the public that we are doing everything we can to ensure that we eradicate any potential bias that the City government could have in favor of the team and the Charles kid in particular.

"You don't have to worry about opinion polls and elections, and you can use your discretion to prosecute or not without worrying about the political fallout. I won't stand a chance in the next election or even the primary if I prosecute that kid. I'll have to practice law in the Pocono Mountains region. Even that may not be far enough away."

"I appreciate your frankness Nancy, but do you really think the talking heads will buy it? I mean, don't you think they'll see the underlying political motive for the move? You may look even worse if you do bow out."

"I'm willing to take that chance. I've given it a lot of thought, despite the short time span, and I feel comfortable with the choice."

"I'd like a little time to discuss it with Jaime before I can give you an answer, but I do agree that there would be nothing legally inappropriate for my office to prosecute the case."

"Yes of course, and I don't want to add any added pressure, but someone will have to do an autopsy and it would be much less costly and less hurtful to the family if it were done before, rather than after, the burial."

With that understanding, the DA and her top assistant made their way back to their office leaving Grace and Jaime to ponder the ramifications of the proposal.

"Can you believe the moxie of that woman"? asked Grace.

"This is the first time I can remember being asked to do something as a political favor. I'm astounded. She wasn't even subtle. On the other hand, that may be a point in her favor.

"She's right. We have to move quickly, and if we accept, it will be a tremendous siphon on our resources at a time when we're barely able to stay above water. A case like this will be expensive, and it will be a full time job for whomever you decide to assign to it."

"Oh, I've already decided that. You're the first assistant for a reason. I trust your judgment and legal skills, so there really isn't much point to debate - unless you don't want to do it."

"You know, I have mixed emotions. My adrenalin is already in overdrive just thinking about it. This would be the case of a lifetime because it's unique and has such ramifications for the game of baseball. To be frank, I've been a Phillies fan my whole life, and I'd hate to be the one responsible for putting their star pitcher behind bars."

"That wouldn't be the case. It was his conduct on the field that brings us here, and it will be for a jury to decide whether he is guilty of a crime. Then it's up to a judge to decide if he belongs in prison."

"Okay, I'll do it if you want to take this on, but under one condition. You do the press thing. I don't want to have to spend my time talking to the press and answering the usual loaded questions. You can talk to Matt Lauer or Chris Matthews."

"Hey, I'm only human, I don't mind being on national television. My children would get a kick out of that. All kidding aside, that is a consideration in my judgment. With all of the press and visitors to Camden City, that will bring in quite a bit of money for our local merchants. Maybe some will stay over at hotels in the surrounding towns. In any event, it will bring in some needed cash for the county. That can't help but make the freeholder board look kindly upon our requests for funding when the next budget comes along."

"That's why you're the Prosecutor. You see the big picture."

"Then are we on the same page, Jaime?"

"It looks like we're all in."

"Okay, I'll contact Artis and make her happy, and I'll leave the job of calling Leyton's wife to you. I'll get her number from the DA."

"Wonderful! —that's so generous."

Chapter 12

The first thing on Jaime's mind was to call Theresa Leyton before the press conference. They would get off to a poor start if she heard it from the media before he had a chance to advise her of the new plan. Dealing with a victim of a crime was one of the most difficult aspects of his job. That was even more compelling in a homicide case. Most victims understandably thought with their hearts rather than their brains. They were suspicious of the motives of the prosecutor. It wasn't unusual for a victim to claim that the prosecutor was in bed with the defense lawyer. The allegations imagined that the sell out to the defendant was because the prosecutor was too busy or too afraid to take the case all the way to trial.

Jaime understood that and tried not to take it personally, especially in a homicide. It was unique in every way. The victim's family had to live every day with the pain that comes from losing a family member. Some never recovered. That's what made it so hard for them to accept legal explanations from prosecutors concerning shortcomings in the state's case. For them, it was too often a matter of an open and shut case. To Jaime, as well as his fellow prosecutors, such cases rarely, if ever, existed.

So he worried about how the conversation would go and decided that he would try to spell things out more when he saw her in person rather than on the phone. He phoned and spoke to her politely but briefly about the upcoming joint statement. She wanted to ask more about the process and his opinion of the case, but he assured her that if she came by his office tomorrow that he would be better able to inform her in more detail. It went better than expected, and he got the impression that she was relieved just to have the matter out of the hands of the Philly DA's office. He had until 2:00 PM the next day to do some digging so he could fill her in on what she could expect.

With that temporarily out of the way, he called Gary Slater, an assistant in the homicide unit to come to his office for a chat. Gary was a bit high strung and Jaime gave him the impression that it was to be a dressing down. Jaime got a kick out of busting his chops, but he had total faith in Gary's work ethic and enjoyed working with him when the occasion arose.

Gary came in with a look like he was going to upchuck at any second. It made Jaime laugh out loud.

"Thanks for the laugh, and I'm sorry if I had you going. Actually, I have something interesting, and I'd like your help ."

"Wow, I was holding my cheeks together so I wouldn't leak. I thought for sure I screwed up, but I couldn't figure out how. What can I do for you, boss?"

Jaime brought him up to speed but left out the political aspects of Artis' meeting with Grace.

"I'd like you to do some research for me as background for a potential prosecution. If we go ahead, I'll be asking you to assist along the way. That okay with you?"

"Sounds great!-What kind of research?"

"I need to know whether there has ever been a prosecution stemming from a death during a baseball game. Obviously I'm looking at a beaning, but I'll take any manner of homicide. If so, what was the charge, the legal issues, the defense, and the outcome? I believe there was somebody who died during a game, but I can't remember his name. It was a long time ago. See what you can find out there too. And, unfortunately, I need it by the end of today. Can you drop what you're doing and spend some time on this now?"

"No problem. I'll get right on it."

In the interim, Grace Moore and Nancy Artis decided to hold a joint press conference at 4:00 PM that afternoon. Both agreed to stay to the basics and to avoid a question-and-answer format. Less is more was the mantra for the day. In that spirit, Nancy began by reiterating that she promised to keep them abreast of any new developments in the case. When she got to the substance of the conference, the startling revelation brought a string of unfiltered exclamations from the reporters assembled there. "Does this mean Philadelphia is incapable of handling this case, Ms. Artis?" "Aren't you abdicating your duties as a DA?" asked another.

Artis stayed the course recommended by her advisors. She maintained that the perception of fair play was the basis for the decision. Her office was doing this to avoid any appearance of a conflict of interest. She had full confidence that the Camden County Prosecutor would impartially investigate the case, but that the DA's office would assist in many practical ways.

For her part, Moore explained that the DA would help in enforcing New Jersey subpoenas on Pennsylvania residents that would normally have no legal validity. With the DA's help, that Office would get Pennsylvania courts to enforce the subpoenas issued by Camden County and thus make any witness liable for contempt should they refuse to appear.

"That will be a huge weapon in our arsenal should we take the matter to a grand jury and then to trial," said Moore.

With questions still forthcoming, both women decided they had done their duty to the fourth estate and ended their conference. All in all it could have been worse. Artis offered to buy Moore a martini at the Palm Restaurant on Broad Street, but Moore wanted to get out as soon as she could. She did, however, assure Nancy that she would take her up on the offer in the future and it wouldn't just be a martini.

At the end of the afternoon, Jaime listened as Gary ran through what he had found during his legal research of the homicide issue.

"Boss, this will be a first. There is no precedent for it that I have found at the Major League level. We'll be making new ground in a homicide case.

There are a few aggravated assaults that have been prosecuted, but not injuries that led to a death."

"That's what worries me. We could end up looking like zealots by the media if we push ahead with this. I can see the headlines: 'Ambitious prosecutor seeks to make a name in baseball death'! But to me this is a classic case of manslaughter. It fits the definition of a death from reckless conduct almost perfectly."

"I agree and I wouldn't be embarrassed to argue that in front of a jury."

"Okay, but we aren't going to hang this kid either. I'm not going to issue an arrest warrant yet. I think what we do is gather as much information as we can through a grand jury investigation. We fairly present the evidence and the law on manslaughter to them and we let them decide if it was a crime. If they indict, then we seek an arrest warrant."

"Have you been able to figure out who the guy was that got killed before in baseball"? asked Jaime.

"Yes, it was Ray Chapman, but I could only find a book about it, not any court decisions. I have nothing to do tonight, and the book called *The Pitch That Killed* by Mike Sowell isn't too long. I can find the relevant portions tonight and see if it gives us any more insight."

"That would be helpful, and frankly if I get the chance I'd love to read it too. Please brief me in the morning. Have a good night and give my best to Angelique. Tell her that I apologize for taking you away from your evening together."

"When are you going to find someone? All work and no play, well, you know."

"Yeah, and when I least expect it, I'll find the right one - isn't that how it goes? Don't let the door hit you in the ass on your way out, Gary."

Chapter 13

The next morning, Jaime listened intently as Gary summarized what he had read the previous night.

"It was the only time in Major League Baseball history that a player was killed during a game. It happened on August 16th, 1920. Carl Mays was pitching for the New York Yankees. Mays threw an underhanded motion so low to the ground that he almost scrapped his knuckles when he pitched. He had a reputation for deliberately hitting batters. He was despised by opponents and even by many on the Yanks.

"Ray Chapman was an extremely popular shortstop for the Cleveland Indians. He was the first batter in the fifth inning. On the very first pitch the righty Mays threw a pitch that struck Chapman in the left temple area. Remember they didn't wear helmets in those days. The ball hit him so hard that it came back to the mound and Mays thought it had struck the bat. Chappie, as he was called, slumped to the ground but was later able to walk off the field with help from players.

"Long story short, he died about 4:00 AM the next morning from fractures of the skull after an unsuccessful operation to stop the bleeding. Now the initial reaction of his teammates was that it was not an intentional bean pitch. It wasn't until several days later that they started to say that it was done deliberately. Many wanted Mays banned from baseball and some teams threatened to boycott any game in which Mays pitched, but that never happened."

"What happened in terms of the police?" asked Jaime.

"Well, Mays immediately claimed to the home plate umpire that the ball was scuffed up and that's why it got away from him. The umpire unfortunately threw the ball out of the game so it was never available for inspection by the authorities. The next day, a police captain from the Manhattan DA's office came to his residence and asked him to accompany him to the precinct. He went with a lawyer provided by the Yankees. He was encouraged to give a statement and he did. Mays claimed that he threw a fastball and Chapman couldn't get out of the way. Mays also expressed great remorse, but argued that the act was an accident.

"The homicide DA took his statement and decided to close the book on the incident. He felt it was a tragic accident that was unavoidable in a game that had elements of danger in it. He had no precedent at that time and saw no evidence for a prosecution."

"You mean that was the only investigation done?"

"Yes, and other than an editorial call from one Cleveland newspaper, there was no real effort to charge Mays with a crime. In fact, Mays started for the Yankees just five days after the death of Chapman. The American League president took no action against him."

"That's amazing, but I'll tell you something. At the very minimum we're going to thoroughly examine every aspect of Charles' pitch before we close any book on Leyton's death. He deserves at least that much from us. In any event, it's the Attorney General's policy to send any potential homicide to a grand jury for their review to see if it was justifiable, excusable, or a form of murder. We'll use the subpoena power of the grand jury to bring in witnesses to testify so that we can present a full picture of the circumstances of this case. This will be a first for the criminal law and for baseball. I just hope we can do justice in whatever direction it takes us."

Chapter 14

The next step for Jaime Brooks was to contact the medical examiner's office. If he were going to make this a criminal case, he would have to prove the cause of death. He would need an autopsy to prove the death was a result of the pitch and not any other cause, such as sudden stroke or heart attack. He wanted to start the preparations immediately so that the body would be ready for the funeral home when the burial was to take place. He alerted the medical examiner of the location of Leyton's body and asked that the body be taken to the morgue. He requested that the autopsy be held up until he spoke with Theresa Leyton at the 2:00 PM meeting.

Jaime also had an investigator personally deliver a subpoena to Virtua Hospital for the medical records librarian to prepare and produce all of the records pertaining to the treatment of Leyton. Those records were to be returnable to a grand jury sitting on the 22nd of June. Jaime would share that information with the medical examiner for his final report on the cause of death.

The day was flying by and before he knew it, his long-serving secretary Bea Kaelin advised him that Theresa Leyton was waiting. The time was 1:35 PM. He decided to call the Office's Victim/Witness Coordinator to join the meeting. Linda Margarita was a veteran and knew how to treat victims. It was a difficult job, and Jaime knew he would need help with Leyton. He would introduce Margarita early in the case so that she could be his liaison with Leyton. That would free him from the need to personally explain every detail of the process to her. If something major developed, he could intercede, but he had to construct a division of labor so he could spend his time on the case itself.

After the introductions and the renewed offers of sympathy, Jaime told Theresa of his intention to have the body autopsied.

"Why is that necessary, Mr. Brooks? Everyone saw what happened. Why must my husband's body be violated even more than it has already?"

Jaime patiently explained why it was necessary. "Mrs. Leyton, if we pursue a homicide case, we are required by law to have an autopsy. I know that is what you want. In fact, with due respect, your consent is not necessary for us to perform one, but I would like your permission."

"But my family still wants a viewing, and I wouldn't want him to be so disfigured that it would have to be a closed casket."

Jaime tried to assure her that an open casket would still be possible. He also advised her that her funeral home could contact the medical examiner so that the body could be released to them after autopsy. Theresa reluctantly agreed and then raised the topic of arresting Charles.

"There will be plenty of time for that. I'll convene a grand jury to investigate the matter and provide them with witnesses and the law. When appropriate, they can decide what the proper charge, if any, is to be brought. If a homicide charge is returned, we will issue a warrant for his arrest."

"So you are saying in the meantime he gets to play ball and live his life as a free man? I thought you were representing me!"

At that point, Margarita interjected. "Actually Theresa, the prosecutor does not represent you. He represents the public at large. It's his job to see that justice is done, and not merely to convict someone. Ethically, he has to be fair to both sides. A lawyer for the defendant has his sole duty to that client, but a prosecutor represents the state itself. It's the state that brings the charge in the name of the people."

"Now that doesn't mean we are at odds, Theresa. In fact, at some point, if there is a formal charge by the grand jury, I will advocate on behalf of the state for the charge that is brought," added Jaime.

"The point is that the death of your husband would be a crime against the state. Of course you and your loved ones are the victims, but the prosecution is in the name of the state. I hope that make sense."

"Well I still think he belongs in jail sooner, rather than later. When will you start this grand jury?"

"In about a week, but the process may take several days, or even weeks, so you need to be patient. I can't discuss with you what witnesses say in the grand jury, but Margarita can help you with general questions. Any testimony at the grand jury must be kept secret unless an indictment is returned. At that point, I can discuss strategy based on what witnesses we will use."

"This will be a murder case, right Jaime?"

"It will be whatever the grand jury decides, but I would not get my hopes up for a murder indictment. Cases like this are usually charged as manslaughter. That is a homicide, but it is one that is less serious than murder because it's based on reckless conduct that led to death, rather than deliberate conduct. I don't want to get technical, but we're ahead of ourselves here. There has never even been a prosecution for homicide in this country based on our facts. Let's just proceed and see where it goes.

"In any event, we have a long road ahead. First things first, and that is the autopsy. It will take a week or so after the autopsy for the report to be completed. The autopsy will be done tomorrow morning and will last a couple of hours. At that point, you can have the funeral home call that office to release your husband's body. Is there anything else?"

"I'm sure I'll have plenty of questions, but I'm just glad that the law is starting to take action. I want justice done. Promise me that."

" I promise you that I will use all my resources to see that the state and you get a fair and thorough investigation, and prosecution if the grand jury indicts. I can't make guarantees other than that."

Mollified for the moment, the widow shook Jaime's hand and followed Linda Margarita from the office. Jaime would soon learn the cease fire was temporary.

Chapter 15

The Mets were to open a series at home with the Marlins that evening, but Leyton's teammates informally petitioned for the game to be cancelled. Mets' ownership took the lead in getting approval from the Marlins to postpone the game for one day in observance of the sudden and tragic events of the two prior days. The commissioner's office made no efforts to block the overture.

On Wednesday, the Mets' organization prepared a fifteen minute tribute to Leyton in the form of a scoreboard video that highlighted his productive career. Representatives from various police districts appeared in kilts and played bagpipes; celebrities sang "Amazing Grace" in tribute. The uniform of Leyton hung in the dugout and would remain there for the remainder of the season. All Mets' players wore Leyton's number 26 in the form of a patch sewn on the shoulder of their uniforms. The crowd stood in silence as religious leaders from the city said prayers for the baseball icon.

Perhaps to emphasize the extent of the tragedy, MLB Commissioner George F. Wilson issued a disciplinary decision in a directive that was released at 8:00 PM that same evening. Wilson was in his first year. He had been elected by the owners because of his love for the game of baseball, his experience on committees dealing with policy, and the gravitas that his name lent to the office. Those factors outweighed the votes of those owners who disapproved of his conservative-purism philosophy towards the game. In a prepared statement, Wilson said:

"The game of baseball has suffered one of the greatest losses in its long existence. Not since 1920 has a major league player given his life on the playing field. All who love the game will mourn the tragic loss of Ken Leyton. He played the game with passion, and gave his all to each at bat and every play on the field. He epitomized the kind of man who would have gladly played the game for the boyish thrills that it gave him, rather than the financial rewards that it afforded him. His baseball family extends their love and compassion to all of the Leytons in their time of mourning.

"In his memory, Major League Baseball will henceforth rename the coveted Most Valuable Player award as the Kenneth Leyton Award. It is my hope that this gesture will ensure that all future generations who play this game will always recognize his name and the ultimate sacrifice that he made to the game."

In a separate statement, Wilson handed down a 15-day suspension for Phillies' manager Buck Sawyer, and in a startling move, he suspended Tim Charles for thirty games pending a fuller investigation of the motives of the actors involved in the fatality. He hinted that the suspension could even include a potential lifetime ban. In addition, Wilson announced that he was forming a committee to study the potentiality of outlawing the use of the bean ball pitch from the game and what penalties would flow if someone were to violate the ban.

The composition had not yet been determined, but Wilson pledged a diverse range of opinions would be sought. He said he would include opinions from not only inside the game, but from journalists, historians, and physicians. The committee was to report its findings at the completion of the World Series.

The consensus of the baseball media was that an indefinite suspension was not only unusual but also a foreshadowing of something bigger to come, especially if

Charles were to be charged criminally. The next day, some in the media raised the issue again of how safe current helmets were for a hitter.

Bill Landsburg, a staff writer for ESPN, reported that Leyton had refused to wear the newest advancement in helmet wear. The Rawlings Company had introduced a new model S100 Pro helmet a few years ago which was tested to withstand a fastball pitch of as much as 100 mph. It was made with a new aerospace-grade carbon that had a lower volume of material but provided the same protection as the former S100 model. The helmets used by players through the 2012 season could only withstand impacts of 70 mph.

The 2012 MLB/players five year contract had mandated the use of the Rawlings S100 pro helmet for the 2013 season and for the duration of the contract. Despite the improvements in the newer model, some players objected to the reduced comfort level of the helmet and demanded a return of the older style. As a result, an agreement was reached to amend the contract to allow players the option of wearing the older model, which only withstood impacts of 70 mph, if they had over five years of major league experience.

Leyton was on record as dismissing the new helmet. Ironically, it was not because he found it uncomfortable. Rather it was strictly baseball superstition. Leyton had 200 hits with the older helmet but fell to 175 hits with the newer helmet. He blamed it on the helmet and nothing could dissuade him. Landsburg raised the question of whether Leyton could have survived if he had chosen to use the mandated helmet, since the pitch was clocked at 95 mph. He also questioned whether the helmet worn by Leyton fit him properly because it came off the moment of impact.

Presciently, he questioned whether that would be an issue if there were to be a trial.

April Gardner of the MLB Network questioned the need for the committee's very existence. She pointed out that the official rules of baseball had already made it unlawful to "intentionally pitch at the batter." She opined that the commissioner was aiming more specifically at banning pitches to the neck and head region. She, for one, could not believe such a rule would be workable. Why not make the use of the new helmet mandatory with no exemptions? It had taken a decade or more when helmets were first introduced before they were made mandatory.

"The death of one man should be proof enough for anyone that any advancement in the safety of equipment should be implemented - regardless of the objections of the players," argued Gardner.

The news of the suspensions shook the Phillies' brass hard. How long could they be competitive without their ace starter? How long would he be shelved due to the suspension? Those questions, as well as the legal troubles that were brewing, permeated the front office and the clubhouse.

Terri Rowlands was named acting manager effective the next day. Because there is no appeal process for managers, Sawyer had no option but to accept his punishment. Tim Charles was in the clubhouse when Terri called him in his office after the Wednesday night game. Sitting with Rowlands was the general manager of the team, Leon Rayford Roberts, who spoke for the team.

"Tim, I regret that you won't be able to suit up with the team until the suspension is lifted. That means you aren't even allowed in the clubhouse. You can sit in the stands, but officially you have no roster spot. I know this is tough for you son, but I have no choice in the matter. You can, of course, socialize with the team after the games. You can also file an appeal with the players union to see if an arbitrator will reduce it. Have you considered getting a lawyer, Tim?"

"Gosh no sir, all of this has happened so fast. I didn't even think I needed a lawyer. I wouldn't know where to turn for help. I don't know anybody here except my teammates. I called my parents, and they're coming up as soon as they can, but they aren't familiar with Philly either."

"Okay Tim, take this card. It's the name of a lawyer in a respected Philly firm. He's done legal work for us in the past. The team president has offered to pay legal fees for you, but you may want to get your own lawyer. We'll absorb the first $100,000 in fees that are generated. After that, we'll have to take another look at things. If I were you, I would contact him tomorrow and get some legal counsel, because it looks like New Jersey is considering a prosecution."

"I'm much obliged to the organization, sir. I just can't believe this is happening, but I appreciate your advice. I don't know what I'll do for money while I'm suspended. I spent a lot of my bonus money already."

"We're all in your corner, Tim. The organization thinks that prosecuting you is over the top and we feel ultimately that there will be no case, but for now, all we can do is uphold the commissioner's decision. Get yourself representation."

Tim left the office and made his farewells to the team. Adams told him to call anytime if he was feeling down or if he wanted to appeal through the union. Adams told him that Sawyer was responsible for everything. and that he would make that clear if he ever had to testify. Players embraced him and offered support. His roommate asked if he was going to attend Leyton's funeral.

"I want to go, Brad, I really do, but I don't know how people would react. They may not want me there. I don't know if I should reach out to the family or just send flowers, but I would like to go to the church. Maybe my mom and dad would drive up there with me."

"Why not ask your lawyer what he thinks before you decide to go."

"I will, but I have to call him and set up an appointment. Tell the other guys I'll miss them, and I hope I'm back before too long."

The Phillies' management also hoped Tim would be back, but they had to consider their options. They couldn't, of course, go with a four-man rotation in this day and age. The staff would likely break down late in the season if that happened. They didn't want to look desperate for a trade because they would get taken by rival clubs that would want inflated value in return for a starting pitcher. The farm system had a few prospects, but they worried about bringing up someone who was not yet ready for prime time. In the end, they opted for the farm system and brought up twenty-two year old Scott Hill from AAA Lehigh Valley. He was a mature right-hander with good stuff and control, but his fastball topped out in the 91-92 mph range so he wouldn't approach the dominance of Charles.

Management would make another move the next afternoon that rocked the City and the team. The ownership and GM were taking a lot of heat from the press. Speculation was rampant that the fatal pitch had been ordered by Buck Sawyer. Many were calling for his resignation from the team.

Sawyer had only been in the job for a short time, but stories of his hard drinking and boorish behavior were already well known to upper management. They were second-guessing their pick when Doug Adams met with Roberts in the morning. Adams told the GM of the order he had gotten from Sawyer to retaliate against a Mets' player. He went even further and detailed the manager's speech after Saturday night's game that made it clear that Sawyer wanted to hurt someone enough so that they would end up on the disabled list.

Roberts called several more players into his office and verified Adams' account. He understood the need for retaliation, but he also knew as a former player that intentionally throwing at a batter's head was taboo if it were done to cause serious harm. There could be no more serious harm than that suffered by Leyton. More from a moral imperative than from a public relations stand point, Roberts felt the need to take action.

In an executive meeting, the Phillies' brass decided to fire Sawyer. The prospect of their manager being vilified in the press for his role in the death would have distracted the team and cast the team as the indisputable bad boys of the game. Equally valid were their lawyers' concerns that management needed to "mitigate any potential lawsuit for negligent supervision of their manager and players." If Mrs. Leyton were to sue for the wrongful death of her husband, it would be the Phillies who had the deep pockets for any monetary damages. It was important to show the public that the Phillies took prompt action as soon as they learned of the facts.

They would not make public all that they knew. They would simply talk in terms of the need to make a leadership change to someone with a style more suitable to the players of today. Indeed, they tapped veteran Bobby Carson to be the first player manager in baseball since Pete Rose in 1984. Carson had the respect of the players and had a dogged determination to the game that was contagious. He was a quiet kind of leader that led by example. He knew the clubhouse atmosphere better than anyone, other than possibly Rowlands, but Carson was still an active player and held the edge. Roberts felt confident that Carson could handle both jobs and that he would be honored to take on the responsibilities.

The job to axe Sawyer fell upon Roberts, who called him up to his office. Sawyer assumed it would be a talk over the replacement for Charles.

"Buck, I'll make this short and direct. While we appreciate what you have done for the team as a scout and manager in the minors, we believe it's time for a change. We need to go in another direction. We haven't had the kind of manager here that related to the players since Charlie Manuel. We need someone like that, especially now, and we just don't think you fit into our plans. We're letting you go today. We'll continue to pay your salary, less suspension pay, for the remainder of the season."

"You can't be serious! After all I did for this team, and you want to throw me under the bus? Are you making me the scapegoat in this incident with Leyton? I didn't throw a head pitch at him. Why am I taking the fall? What kind of bullshit is this? You're worried that your Ivy League image is going to get a black eye with me at the helm, is that it?"

"Actually, I'm worried about the team's image. Let's just say I know what you ordered the team to do. Now it's true that in most cases you could get a pass for a retaliatory hit on a batter. But this is no mere hit in the ribs or on the rump. This order resulted in a death. That is an historical event that will haunt this park forever, and it can't help but have a lasting effect on our team. This is going to get out someday through the media or in a courtroom. I would advise you to go quietly, Buck. Anything you say to the press will only bring it up sooner, rather than later."

Buck sat stunned at the calmness with which Roberts delivered the devastating news. He had toiled his entire life in the minor leagues for this one chance at big money, and he was getting tossed out on his ass.

"Hey, at least let me resign. I'll say the stress is too much and I want to go back to scouting talent for the Phillies."

"Sorry, not even a scouting job. We need to cut ties. You're free to look for a job with any other club. I would suggest you do so. I'll call a press conference and break the news. If you want to issue a statement, that's up to you. Tell them that it's your health or you can't concentrate on the job because of the tragedy. But Buck, don't try to bullshit anyone or take a shot at us. It will come back and bite you in the ass."

A troubled Buck Sawyer left the GM's office with his tail between his legs. He had only done what any manager with balls should do in that situation, so he thought, and he lost his job for it. He was the victim here.

Next, the GM conferred with Bobby Carson, and as expected the veteran was honored to assume the dual role as player/manager for the team that had been his home since he began his career.

The press was assembled late afternoon when Roberts and Carson announced their decision regarding the departure of Sawyer and the plan for Carson to succeed him. When reporters asked whether Sawyer had been fired, Roberts did not play it close to the vest.

"Yes, Buck was let go. We want a different style of manager who can better relate to the modern player. We decided to make the change now because of the suspension of Sawyer. This is no reflection upon Terri Rowlands. He is certainly capable of running the team. We just felt an active player was the best course for us today."

Richard Hatfield from CSN Sports Channel asked if the firing was connected to the fatality on Sunday. Roberts didn't sidestep the issue.

"Let's just say that it was a factor in our decision."

That last answer fueled speculation in the press that Sawyer may have been the architect of the fatal retaliation, but no one knew any specifics. Their articles would merely opine about the culpability of the ousted team manager. Most writers assumed the hit came from the manager, so they chose to concentrate on the new managerial appointment and what it meant for the continued chances of the team.

In New York, however, the focus was on the Friday funeral. Fans had displayed their affection for Leyton at the first home game after his death. They would have to be content with that because Theresa had directed that the funeral be closed to the public. The only expression they could make was to send flowers to the funeral home in Morristown, New Jersey.

Theresa did not even want his teammates to attend, but she made an exception for Mike Zahn because he was her late husband's closest friend on the team. The remaining pallbearers were members of the extended family from both her and her husband's sides. Theresa also nixed any eulogy from the baseball fraternity. She would ask only Ken's brother and a representative from Ken's foundation for cancer stricken children to eulogize her husband. It was as if she wanted to deny the very existence of his occupation.

Reporters wanted to know if Tim Charles had shown up for the viewing that night. They were told by employees of the funeral home that Tim was accompanied by his parents, but was turned away at the door on instructions from Theresa Leyton. That image of a contrite Charles family being turned away from paying their respects had many in the public feeling sympathetic to their plight as well. At least that's what his legal team hoped.

Chapter 16

On Friday, Charles met with Jack Marino, a retired New Jersey judge who was Of Counsel to a large Philadelphia firm. He had the kind of earthy personality that Tim needed. Jack had nothing else to prove in the practice. He made his money by bringing in clientele. He was the rainmaker for the firm. While he had handled many criminal cases as a judge, he wasn't particularly comfortable in that arena as a practitioner.

"Tim, I've been thinking about your situation, and I think I have the right legal team for you. You would do yourself a favor by obtaining a local firm that practices criminal law in Camden County. There's a firm that's made up largely of former prosecutors that have worked in the Camden County office most of their legal careers. The firm is called Hunter, Cavanaugh, and Kemper. Now that doesn't mean that the current prosecutors are going to roll over for you just because you retain this firm. But it does mean that they know the players in the Prosecutor's Office and they have a special bond as former prosecutors. That gives them a bump up in terms of respect from that Office.

"I can help out and offer our firm for research and other resources that a smaller firm like the Hunter firm can't do. They also know the local judiciary and have a good working relationship with the court staff. They've been practicing before them for decades. That is a huge psychological advantage over a large out of state firm like ours that has little business with the local bar and judiciary.

"So, if you agree, I'll call and take you over for a consultation. That okay with you"?

"Sure, Mr. Marino, that sounds fine. Whatever you suggest is okay with me. I'm just a rookie in this area too, so I trust your opinion."

Moments later, the two were in Marino's car headed for the offices of the Hunter firm in Haddon Heights, New Jersey. It was a short ride to the Benjamin Franklin Bridge from the firm's Center City office. In twenty-five minutes they were sitting in a conference room with three of the senior lawyers in the firm. The partners had cleared their schedules for Marino because they knew a hefty fee was in the making.

Raymond Hunter took the lead in explaining the potential charges that the prosecution could bring, none of which sounded appealing to Charles.

"The key is getting to the prosecution as early as possible and convince them not to prosecute at all. Now, that may not be possible because there was a death. They may feel obligated to take the case to a grand jury, but we want to be in on this to help guide them to the correct resolution. So our first step is to try and avert a grand jury presentation.

Secondly, we might want to ask them to present some defense evidence to the grand jury. We may even ask to have you testify on your own behalf at the grand jury."

"I'd testify. I have nothing to hide."

"Well, let's not get ahead of ourselves here just quite yet. We're just spelling out the initial steps we could take, but that's good to hear."

"Exactly!" said Cavanaugh, "and what I'd like to do is talk to their first assistant in person if you decide to sign up for our representation."

"Can I ask you a non-legal question? I tried to go to the viewing but the family didn't want me there. I'd like to do something for the family or for Ken's memory. Can I send a card with a donation to his charity?"

"Certainly," said Kemper, "but let us read anything you write before you mail it. I want to be sure you don't say anything that could incriminate you. Limit it to expressions of sympathy and general words of that nature. Don't say anything about what you did before, during, or after the game."

They then decided to sign a retainer agreement that made the amount of the fee dependent upon each stage of the process. In that way, if Charles was never formally charged, the fee would be much less than if there was a full trial. The lawyers instructed their client not to discuss the case with anyone and to contact them if the Prosecutor's Office tried to talk to him.

"Look fellas, I'm not some murderer. I didn't try to hit him in the head on purpose. I felt an obligation to my teammates for what went down earlier in the series. The guys expected something of me. The skipper downright told us he expected me to put a hurtin' on one of their guys. I tried to throw him some chin music and shake him up a bit. Then I knew I would be tossed from the game. I was just hoping I could avoid the whole thing by getting ejected so I wouldn't have to hit anyone. You don't know me, but if you did, you'd know I couldn't live with myself if I had done what they're saying. You probably hear this all the time from your clients, but I swear to God it's true."

"I have a good feeling that what you're telling us is true," said Kemper. "You've never hit anyone since you came into the big leagues. We will do everything we can to prove to the authorities what we believe to be the truth- that this is a tragic accident and nothing more."

"What we'd like you to do is to write down everything anyone said during the past series with the Mets. Take your time and get it to us so we have some background and some names of potential witnesses," said Hunter."

"Can I go home to Florida"?

"Sure, there's no legal restriction at this point. Go home to your family and get yourself strong and healthy for the coming months. We need you well rested. Just make sure you're always accessible to us if we need you on short notice."

After Tim left, the partners summed up their reaction to their new client. Cavanaugh was impressed with the kid's earnestness, but thought he was a bit naïve about what the future held for him.

"Even if we agree that he threw that pitch up and in just to shake up Leyton and not hit him, when you throw a ball 95 mph from sixty feet away, a jury may very well believe that the risk he took in throwing so close to his head was reckless. That, in my view, makes a pretty good case for a reckless manslaughter case."

"Yes, and I think the kid would crap himself if he knew manslaughter carries a ten-year prison term, and that he has to serve 85% of the sentence before he's eligible for parole said Hunter.

"I just wish there was some applicable crime that we could negotiate, short of a charge that carries mandatory jail. I'll call Jaime and ask if he'll see me first thing Monday. I doubt that anything big will break before that time. I need to feel him out and see if there's room to negotiate," said Kemper.

The next day was a normal Friday for the law firm. They covered various motions and handled sentencing matters for clients in various counties. The Charles case, as big as it was to the firm, would be put on hold until Monday. The weekend would be a much-needed break from the tumult of the law practice.

In the meantime, Theresa Leyton was home in Morristown preparing herself for the church service and the unavoidable heartache that was awaiting her. The viewing was hard enough on her and she dreaded having to be strong for all of the friends and family that would pay their respects to her at the funeral home.

The funeral of Kenny Leyton was held on Friday morning with reporters pursuing the family of the famous ballplayer who was laid to rest after a private service in North Jersey. Jaime had kept his promise, and the coffin remained open for the family to pay their last respects. Theresa kissed her husband for the last time and told him that she would get justice for him for as long as it took. She would be alternating her time between her home and her parents' home until the day that she saw Charles carted away by police in handcuffs.

She would not have anything more to say to the press today, but she did plan to keep the pressure on the prosecutor as much as she could. That evening, as friends and family paid their respects, she was already gaining commitments from some of the Mets' wives and family friends to go to Camden City on Monday morning to protest out in front of the Prosecutor's Office. That would show them that she was not going away without a fight.

Chapter 17

On Monday at 10:00 AM, Hank Kemper parked his car a short block from the Prosecutor's Office. As he walked to the building, he passed an unusual sight. Several well-dressed, young, and attractive women were parading back and forth at the entrance of the Office. They weren't doing a runway-modeling event. Rather, they were holding signs that read "Justice for Ken Leyton" and "Arrest Tim Charles Now." He recognized Theresa Leyton among the group. He immediately felt queasy. *What a great start to the week*, he thought. He cursed himself for not getting to Jaime Brooks on Friday. Now the heat would be on the prosecutor to act fast and impulsively. It would just create a tougher climate for the defense to get a positive resolution to the case.

He tried to put the women out of his mind and hoped he could persuade Jaime not to prosecute, but he already felt that he might have missed the boat. He waited for Jaime in the waiting area that was used for both the First Assistant and the Prosecutor. As he waited, it brought back good memories of the hours he spent in that same area with his colleagues, anticipating the management meeting that was about to take place with the Prosecutor.

Then Jaime appeared and ushered Kemper into the office.

"Well Hank, how is it on the dark side these days?" This was a reference to defense criminal work that prosecutors often used to tease their adversaries for representing criminal elements.

"They're not *all* guilty. You know, it's amazing, but I seem to luck out and always get the clients that were wrongly accused Not one of my clients actually committed the crime.

They were either in the wrong place at the wrong time, or the victim accidentally backed into my client's knife six times."

"That sounds like an old Don Adams line from "Get Smart".

"Maybe, but it works for me, too."

"I read that you retained Tim Charles as a client. I assume that's why you've come."

"Jaime I have a great deal of respect for you, but I worry that those protesters outside and the media may cause you to make a bad decision on Charles' future. I know you've got integrity, and I mean no offense. I just want to hear it straight from you that you can do your job free from outside pressures."

"I've been in this job for nearly twenty-five years, and I've had my share of controversial and high-profile cases. I've always done what I believed to be the right thing. This will be no different. I'm dealing with the widow. She's a bit demanding, but I'm in control. I'll do what I think is right, even if it ruffles her feathers. But frankly, I believe that this is a legitimate case for manslaughter. Unless Charles was falling off the mound and his arm angle was thrown off, anyone that throws a ball 95 mph at a batter's head is taking an unjustifiable risk that serious injury or even death can result if the ball hits him."

"But that's baseball at its core. You're a fan. You know how the game's played. How many games would Randy Johnson have won if he hadn't hit so many batters? All of the greatest pitchers of the game, including Gibson, Clemens, and even Koufax, used it to intimidate."

"It ceases being just a game when someone dies. Then it becomes real life, and no one can wrap themselves around the cloak of innocence just because everyone does it. And not everyone does it either. I don't have the stats in my head but Robin Roberts did pretty well, and he wasn't a headhunter."

"Does that mean you've made up your mind?"

"I intend to investigate the matter through the grand jury process and let them make the call. It will be done fairly."

"We're very early in our defense case but if we wanted to have Tim appear and testify before the grand jury, would you invite him? I really have no idea whether we would let him testify or not, but I want that option available to us."

"I can appreciate that and the answer is sure. If you decide you want him to tell his version, I'll send you of an invitation to appear."

"Well, I'm disappointed that you're committed to a grand jury presentation because I think the right outcome is to divert this case from the criminal justice system and allow baseball to handle it. Let Mrs. Leyton sue for damages in civil court for her loss, but I don't want to spin my wheels trying to get out of a frozen pond. There is one request I want to make. If you do get an indictment, I'd want the courtesy of a call to us before you issue the arrest warrant. I'd like the opportunity for one of us to bring him in voluntarily rather than see a 'perp walk' on television. That would be humiliating to the kid, and unnecessary since he has counsel and we can produce him on demand. He's not going out of the country."

". I would probably be inclined to honor your request I'll let you know for sure in the coming weeks. This isn't going to be over in the near future."

"Fair enough-oh by the way, how's the love life going?"

"It's gone and left me watching old Bogart movies, but thanks for asking. I'm too busy now anyway. The right one will come along someday". But there was just a hint of melancholy in his voice that could not be mistaken. "Take care of yourself and give my regards to your partners."

Kemper returned to the office a bit disappointed but not entirely surprised by Jaime's reaction to his proposal. He told Cavanaugh that he almost convinced himself that his argument had merit. But reality was now setting in. This was not going to be easy, and the outcome could be devastating for Charles, and not just financially

Chapter 18

Jaime sent subpoenas to several players on the Phillies' team, the home plate umpire, and even clubhouse employees. The date to testify was not scheduled for another three weeks because the current term for the grand jury concluded at the end of June. New grand juries would be selected the first week of July and the jurors would have to sit once a week for the next sixteen weeks. They are made up of ordinary persons from the county who are selected randomly from a computer database from both the motor vehicle agency and the voter registration pool.

Unlike its name, there is little that is grand about their service. There are usually four groups or panels that sit and hear cases on selected days of the week in Camden County. For the most part, the work is tedious after the first couple of weeks because the cases all sound alike. There are twenty-three grand jurors for each panel. They exist as a buffer from the state, to act independently of the prosecutor, and their task is to determine whether probable cause exists that a crime was committed and that it was the person charged who committed the crime. It is similar to the standard needed for police to get an arrest warrant.

The jurors and witnesses in the Charles investigation would also be a bit shocked at the décor of the grand jury room itself. It didn't stir up pride in the justice system or put the fear of God in those witnesses who would have the temerity to challenge the prosecutor. Certainly from appearances alone, one entered the room a bit too comfortable for the seriousness of the process inside. There was a long metal table for the prosecutor and the clerk of the grand jury to sit. A wooden podium to the left of the prosecutor held a seat for the foreperson. Twenty-three plain wooden chairs surrounded the room while another metal table to the far right was used for coffee makers, the morning donuts, and bagels. An old school room chalkboard stood next to the witness chair adjacent to the foreperson.

The walls were barren of artwork or even photographs of persons in the justice system. The walls were yellowing from the lack of a fresh coat of paint. What was worse for the current panel was the fact that the room had two window air conditioners. One didn't work. The other one did work - all too well. The problem that Jaime and the jurors would have is that it made so much noise you couldn't hear the witness' testimony. The alternative was to open the windows in July heat which led to an inferno inside the cramped space. No, there was nothing grand about the surroundings of the grand jury area.

Unlike a petit jury that hears the actual trial of a criminal case, the grand jury merely hears some of the evidence that the state has against a defendant; namely just enough to enable them to determine the standard of probable cause. It is far from a full-blown trial. The rules of evidence are generally informal and relaxed. More importantly, a defense lawyer is never permitted to be in the room to advocate on behalf of his client. A defendant himself has no legal right to attend the hearing in which he may be charged. As a result, most of the routine cases are heard and voted upon within a five-to-ten-minute range.

With very few exceptions, the grand jury does not hear the position of the defendant. The focus is simply on whether the prosecution has shown sufficient evidence to formally charge the person with a crime. If the panel agrees to formally charge someone, they vote for a "true bill" and produce an indictment against that individual. If, on the other hand, they determine that the evidence falls short of a crime, then the grand jury votes to "no bill" the matter and the case is dropped.

Also, unlike the "proof beyond a reasonable doubt" standard at a trial, which must be unanimous for all twelve jurors, a grand jury needs only twelve votes out of twenty-three to return an indictment. The seemingly unfair advantage to the prosecution is based upon the fact that the indictment is merely a charging document that has the stamp of approval from ordinary citizens who sit on the grand jury. It is not evidence of the guilt of the defendant. In fact, the judge at a trial will instruct the jury of that fact. The whole process differs from many other states, such as Pennsylvania, where the DA can charge someone without going through a grand jury. New Jersey requires, through its constitution, that everyone that the prosecution wants to charge has a right to have his case reviewed by a grand jury before the prosecution can force a trial.

The assignment judge would be instructing the newly composed panels in those principles on the day they were sworn in as jurors. Jaime was happy that one of the assistant prosecutors would reiterate it the first week of the panel. He didn't want to come in to a grand jury that was totally clueless about their role. He wanted them to at least have a week or two of cases before he came in with his bombshell. So it was that on this Monday morning in mid-July, Jaime introduced himself to the panel.

"Ladies and gentleman, I will be presenting a matter to you that will be different in format from the cases that you have heard thus far. It differs because in virtually all of the cases you have heard, there has already been a complaint or arrest warrant filed by the police or a private citizen against someone and it has been your job to decide if there is a basis for that complaint.

"For the next few weeks, I will be dealing with only one case and there hasn't been a formal complaint filed by the police or anyone else. You will be utilized as an investigatory body to examine the death of an individual. Ultimately it is for you to decide whether that death was the result of a crime, and if so, what kind of a crime. You will be examining the circumstances behind the death of Ken Leyton, formerly a baseball player with the New York Mets."

With that, a young man wearing a Phillies' t-shirt on the panel perked up from his slouched position and said "how cool is that"? Several others clapped, smiled and generally expressed delight at the opportunity to hear a case with some pizzazz. One juror who had tried in vain to get off jury duty wanted to know if she should be excused because she was a lifelong fan of the Mets, but Jaime told her that was not a sufficient reason by itself to be removed from the case.

"I also need to stress what Judge Matthew Melucci told you at the start of your term. You took an oath of secrecy as jurors. That means everything, from whatever a witness says here down to the names of witnesses themselves, are to be kept confidential. This will be a high-profile case, and we don't want leaks to the press that could compromise our investigation. Also, unlike your other cases, I will read some applicable law to you after we conclude the testimony so that it's fresh in your minds. Remember also that there is no judge. If there is some legal question that you want to ask Judge Melucci, we can call him and go to his courtroom together for the answer."

With that said, Jaime was ready to call his first witness, Nick Falconetti, a homicide detective from his office. There was little testimony from the detective. He simply told the jurors that he had obtained the video discs of the recent three-game series with the Mets by subpoena from the CSN and ESPN networks, and they were authentic copies of what had been transmitted.

Jaime decided to play the relevant portions for the grand jury that included the hit-by-pitch upon Butterworth of the Phillies, the retaliatory hit by Adams of Luther Wynne of the Mets, the dugout tussle between Herrera and Adams, the hard slide by Leyton, and finally the deadly pitch and its aftermath in the Sunday game.

"We will hear testimony from other witnesses to explain what you have seen on the tapes, and we may revisit the discs in the future for your further review," explained Jaime. Several of the women jurors hid their eyes from the video as Leyton was plunked, and one was heard to say "that's outrageous." Jaime had to caution her from expressing her opinion this soon in the process, but she kept shaking her head in disgust. This did not bode well for Charles, thought Jaime.

Next, Jaime brought in the first eyewitness to the event. That was umpire Mike Kastle, who was the home plate umpire on Sunday, but who was also on the field for the first two games. Jaime was taking some witnesses out of order to accommodate their schedules. He wanted to establish some facts from Kastle that would be used as a portion of the circumstantial proof against Charles. After establishing his various roles during the series, Jaime asked, "Had you seen Charles pitch before this night?"

"Yes, I had seen him either behind the plate or from the field on two prior occasions."

"And how would you describe his control of his pitches?"

"He had very good control on every occasion that I observed. He walks maybe one batter a game if that. He has the ability to put his pitches on the corners or pretty much anywhere he wants."

"Why did you eject him from the game after he hit Leyton?"

"I had warned both managers before the game that any attempt to hit a batter would result in the manager and pitcher getting tossed?"

"Did you think that he hit him intentionally?"

"Well, I can't say for sure that he hit him intentionally, but I will say that I believe he threw at him intentionally."

"Fair enough, sir. My next question is, why did you think he threw at the batter rather than merely making a bad pitch? What goes into your decision making process?

"We aren't mind readers prosecutor, so we look for certain factors."

" Do you mean like using circumstantial evidence surrounding the game?"

"Yes, I guess you could look at it that way. We look at things like whether the pitcher has a prior history of throwing at batters. In Charles' case, he had no prior history of hitting batters, so that would be a factor that would suggest that he didn't throw at Leyton intentionally."

"So then why did you eject him?"

" I looked at the events that preceded the beaning."

"Please elaborate."

"Well, it was pretty obvious to me that the ball that hit Butterworth was intentionally thrown at him. Then you had Adams throwing his off-speed pitch that hit Wynne on the foot. That's not your typical pitch to use to throw at someone, but in the context of paying the Mets back for hitting Butterworth, it was still a deliberate pitch thrown at Wynne.

"Then you have the dugout incident between Herrera and Adams. In my opinion, that was a clear-cut argument over the fact that Herrera felt Adams didn't do his job in retaliating for the hit on Butterworth. Next, there was the cleats-high slide from Leyton into Colby Green. Now there's a right way to break up a double play, and then there's the spiteful way. That slide was meant to send a message.

"Combine those factors with a 95 mph fastball, thrown at the head of Leyton, by a pitcher who has uncanny control, then your intuition and common sense tell you that it was a *purpose pitch*. Now again, I'm not saying he tried to hurt him. I'm only prepared to say that he threw at him deliberately."

"Thank you, Mr. Kastle. Let me ask one more thing. Is there any rule book or anything else that you can direct me to which says that it is unlawful to throw at a batter?"

"That one is easy, prosecutor. Rule 8.02(d), which every ump knows by heart, says that 'the pitcher shall not intentionally pitch at the batter.' That's where we get our authority to throw people out of the game."

"Do the grand jurors have any questions for the witness?"

"Yes, I do have one," said a very attractive slim blonde who grabbed Jaime's attention immediately.

"We saw on the video of Sunday's game that you approached the pitcher at the mound and made that motion to eject him. It looked like you spoke to each other briefly, and I was wondering whether you can remember what was said?"

"I'm not so sure that's relevant, madam, because anything Charles said after the pitch would be a self-serving statement. In other words, he says something that makes him look in a better light after the fact," explained Jaime.

"That doesn't make sense ", said the juror. "What he said immediately after the pitch would seem to me to be the best evidence of what was in his mind."

"Yeah, that's right," said the young juror in the t-shirt.

"Well, I don't want to get too rigid about the proper role of this grand jury. We're simply looking at the state's evidence to see if there was a crime, but you may be right. It may very well bear on his motive, so let's hear what Mr. Kastle has to say." Jaime knew right away that he may come to regret that exchange.

Technically, he may have been right in trying to limit what Charles said after the pitch hit Leyton. He wasn't trying to hide evidence. He merely believed that it might not be admissible by the defense later at a trial under the evidence rules.

But there was a legitimate argument to be made for the opposite view. Now he had gone on record at the grand jury, a transcript of which would be made available to the defendant if an indictment were returned, as saying that "yes, indeed, the words of Charles were relevant to the case."

"When I tossed Charles from the game, he was sitting on his haunches with an anguished look on his face. The kid looked white as a ghost. Then he says to me, 'I didn't mean to hit him, Mike.' I didn't care whether that was true or not. The man got hit and that was enough for me to do my job.

"If there are no questions, and I see no hands, you are now excused Mr. Kastle.

Jaime felt a need to counter the statement of Charles with a piece of evidence that he had. He had received an unsolicited letter from one Clark Draper of Florida. In it, Draper wrote of a game in his senior year of high school when he was the catcher for Charles. Draper claimed that a batter hit a home run off Charles and took his time admiring and then showboated by trotting very slowly around the bases which embarrassed Charles. In his next time at bat Charles threw a fastball that broke the kid's jaw. Draper claimed that Charles later admitted to him in the dugout that he deliberately threw at the batter because he had shown him up.

Jaime knew it was a potential bombshell. He knew it wasn't a slam dunk to be admissible at trial, but he had a better than even chance to convince a judge that it was highly relevant. Despite being over two years old, Jaime would argue that it was other evidence which tended to prove that Charles deliberately threw at Leyton, and that the fatal beaning was no accident. The prior incident bolstered a scenario that Charles had intended to bean Leyton just as he had in high school. In other words Charles would pay back opponents by trying to bean them That would portray an entirely different portrait of Charles than the one described by Kastle. But Jaime hadn't had time to look into the allegation. Reluctantly, he decided not to read the letter to the grand jurors even though he would have been entitled to use the hearsay in the proceeding.

Jaime decided to call it a day. He would reconvene the following week with several witnesses. It was a short day for the jurors who had earned a hefty $5.00 a day jury fee. Yet today, nearly everyone wanted to mill around and discuss the events of the day. Jaime packed up his material and left before the jurors so he could scoot back to his office and return the massive number of phone messages he was sure would be on his desk.

As the jurors were leaving, the woman who had posed a question to the umpire approached Madeline Sarulli, the clerk of the grand jury. Immediately, Madeline feared that yet another juror was trying to get off of duty even at this late date. She was pleasantly surprised to hear the juror Barbara Jay ask about Brooks' marital status. Madeline had worked with Jaime for almost ten years and thought highly of him. If she weren't married, she would have been happy to date him.

"He's been divorced for quite a few years. I know he isn't seeing anyone."

"He seems nice, and he's not hard on the eyes either. Would you feel uncomfortable asking if he noticed me? I don't know what the protocol would be for a juror to date a prosecutor, so maybe I'm getting ahead of myself."

"I'd be happy to mention it to him. You two would make a nice-looking couple, but whether you hit it off is another story entirely. He's particular, but he's genuine, and likes down-to-earth women. He can't tolerate pretentious social climbers. That's not his style. If that sounds good to you, I'll follow up with him."

"That sounds almost too good to be true. Gee, it looks like I might enjoy performing my civic duty more than I expected."

"That would be sweet if it works out".

That same afternoon, as Madeline was about to leave her office, she decided to call Brooks and fill him in on her conversation with the juror.

"Jaime, do you remember the woman juror that politely took you to task on the question she posed to the umpire?"

Jaime didn't have to think too long. He still had her image in his mind. After Madeline filled him in, he wondered how old she was because she looked quite a bit younger than he.

"Look, I'll tell you, but you can't tell her I told you her age. She's forty-two, based on the jury computer sheets that show her date of birth. That sounds perfect for you-not too young, but still young enough not to look like me."

"Hey, what are you taking about? If it weren't for your husband, I'd be dating you. Actually she looks great to me, but she's a juror and I can't get around that. I'll speak with her, and maybe we can arrange something, but not now. Thanks for the tip. It would be fun to date someone that I met on a jury panel. It's the kind of thing that makes for a good dinner table story. I'll see you soon."

Chapter 19

Jaime leaned back at his desk and daydreamed. He wondered what he had gotten himself into. He was 49, single, and had no infringements on his free time. He had just a touch of grey at his temples but no other signs that he was nearing fifty. He stood just under six feet tall and his 170 pound frame added to his youthful appearance. His piercing dark brown eyes could intimidate defendants, but they also appealed to women who sensed his intensity and passion. He was in his 25th year as a career prosecutor, and he planned to retire at the end of that year. With his medical benefits and pension he would do fine. Sure he could supplement it, but it wouldn't be in the field of law. He wasn't in it for the money. Maybe if he had looked for the money he would still be married to his ex-wife, the former Bonnie Weil.

She had harped on him to leave the Prosecutor's Office after his third year to join a large firm in private practice, but he loved what he did. He had interviewed with some firms and had gotten substantial offers, but in the end he turned them down. As a consequence, she left him for greener pastures. Now she was married to some gray flannel-pin-striped-Brooks Brothers-looking lawyer in a megabucks Philly firm. The creep specializes in defending environmental polluters in federal class-action suits. How exciting is that?

He told himself he was better off without her, but he missed the fact that both of them shared a passion for baseball. He squirmed in his seat as he remembered the night he proposed to her at Veterans Stadium, twenty-four years earlier. Man did the guys at work bust his balls! It felt right at the time. He was a sucker for the game since he was seven years old. He thought of the time, a half of a lifetime ago, when his father and uncle took him to his first baseball game. He would never forget the adrenalin flow that overwhelmed him when his eyes took in the most beautiful green field that he'd ever seen. He didn't understand at the time that it was Astroturf. It looked fantastic to him.

He remembered his dad pointing out Tom Seaver, and he even saw Willie Mays, in what was his last year, in 1973. Sure the Phillies lost the game, and they would end up in the cellar with ninety-one losses that season, but he ate hot dogs and peanuts and cotton candy. To top it off, he still remembered that the clock displayed the time at 12:47 AM when he got home. It was the latest he had ever stayed up.

Jaime still rented "Field of Dreams" and "The Natural" every winter when he started feeling withdrawal symptoms from the game. He remembered with chagrin the first time he saw "Field of Dreams" with then-girlfriend Bonnie. In the final scene, when Kevin Costner plays catch with his father, he sobbed and heaved so loudly that he had to wait until the theater emptied before he got up for fear that someone would recognize him.

He knew he wasn't alone and that baseball was often the common denominator between fathers and sons. That was especially true with his dad. His dad had labored seventy-five hour work weeks, and the only real special time they spent together was in front of the television on a Sunday afternoon rooting for the Phillies, followed by dinner at a restaurant. Now both of his parents were gone, and he was essentially alone.

He pondered the possibility that the Charles case might not even be concluded by the end of December, the month that he intended to retire. Many lawyers would have eaten broken glass just to have the chance to prosecute such a high-publicity case. It could be the gateway to a big payday when private firms would seek his services after retirement. But he didn't want that.

He had nothing more to prove as a prosecutor. He had handled death penalty cases back in the days when it existed, and he was secure enough in his station in life not to feed off of high-profile cases. Instead, he would rather teach a course or two at Rutgers or Camden County College. He had his heart set on doing a little traveling and going to Clearwater Florida in March to follow the Phillies' spring training. He would supplement his pension by performing his other passion, playing piano and singing at a Center City bar. He loved the classic standards of Sinatra and Tony Bennett.

Jaime sang for fun at a piano bar in Center City when the professionals took their breaks. He couldn't get paid, because as a full-time prosecutor he wasn't permitted by law to earn money from a job other than his own. Now he looked forward to the day when he could enjoy singing and get paid as well.

That was a nice break from reality for Jaime. Now he looked forward to going home to watch the Home Run Derby at the All-Star Game. He checked his computer for the standings in the National League and saw that the Phillies were holding their own despite the loss of Charles. Scott Hill won two of his starts, and manager Bobby Carson had his team running the bases. The team had lost only two games in the standings since that fateful Sunday. Jaime anguished at the thought that he might ruin the team's chances at a championship if the grand jury indicted, but he knew that his duty to the rule of law had to prevail over his loyalty to his boyhood team. Yet knowing and feeling were not the same.

Misfortune still plagued the Mets. The second baseman who replaced Leyton was suspended for 80 games for using a human growth hormone. MLB had approved a new test for HGH in 2013, and the Mets endured another loss. They were now seven games out of first place. The Nationals were now the team to beat in the East.

Another article caught his eye about a statistic from Bloomberg Sports News. In the four weeks since the death of Leyton, only six batters had been hit by a pitch. In the prior month twenty six had been hit. Interestingly, not one batter had been hit above the chest area since the death.

The other stat that stood out during that same period was that runs per game had increased by almost a full run more than before the death. Jaime wondered, since pitchers were hitting fewer batters, maybe hitters were more relaxed at the plate and therefore were hitting better. Whether that was the correct conclusion was debatable, but Jaime found it interesting. It looked as if the death, and the criminal investigation, were having a deterrent effect on the game of baseball and perhaps even changing it. He knew Commissioner Wilson would see it too, and wondered whether the phenomenon would continue.

Chapter 20

In the second week at the grand jury, Jaime subpoenaed several of the Phillies' players to the grand jury. It was an off day on a home stand for the team, so counsel for the Phillies didn't try to fight their appearances. The witness list was to be secret, but not surprisingly, the press and cameras caught several of the team members going into City Hall with lawyers. There were too many places for leaks to occur, so Jaime decided not to waste his time trying to find the culprits.

Jaime called Doug Adams first because he wanted to explore the reasons behind the dugout blow up with Herrera. He suspected that there was a connection to the bean ball thrown at Leyton the following night.

Adams brought a lawyer with him, who was not permitted by law into the jury room. He waited in the hallway in case he was needed.

After the preliminary formalities, Jaime asked Adams if he was aware of any managerial or players-only meeting after the Friday night game when Butterworth was hit. Adams answered affirmatively.

"Who was involved in the meeting?".

"The manager Buck Sawyer called me into his office."

"Yes, please continue, Mr. Adams, and tell us what was said and by whom. Feel free to talk and not wait for my questions."

Adams described what his manager told him. He continued with the meeting with Bobby Carson in which he refused to put anyone on the disabled list.

"I told him I would make his feet dance or hit him in the rump."

"Did you nonetheless hit Wynne intentionally when the ball hit his foot?"

"Prosecutor, I respectfully request to speak with my lawyer before I answer that question."

"That's fine, please step outside."

Jaime waited a minute for Adams to talk to his lawyer. He used the time to check out Barbara Jay. He was impressed with her youthful look and long, straight, blonde hair. She was petite in height and frame but built proportionately for her size. In short, he was attracted.

Jaime went into the corridor and introduced himself to Adams' lawyer Todd Gelfand. He knew Adams and his lawyer were acting out of an abundance of caution by avoiding his question, so he chose to settle things informally.

"Look, I'm not trying to ambush your client. My question doesn't incriminate Adams in a crime, and he's not the target of this investigation."

"Well, I didn't know where you were going with this investigation. For all I know, you're looking to indict the whole team. If you assure me that my guy isn't in the line of fire, I'll let him answer."

"You have my assurance. Now let's get back."

Having assuaged the concerns of Adams' lawyer, Adams returned and admitted the intentional hit. More importantly for Jaime, he related in detail the confrontation with Herrera, the mocking response by Sawyer to him about the pitch, and the reasons why Sawyer was so hell bent on retaliating.

"Can you characterize the reaction of your former manager after the brawl on Saturday night?"

"I would describe him as determined and in a controlled rage. He lectured us about the customs of baseball; about the need to protect your team when they were hit or taken out, like what Leyton did on the slide to Green. He told us it was what the team expected of us, and he made a negative reference to my failure to seize the opportunity by merely hitting Wynne in the foot."

"Did he say anything specifically about what should be done in the name of your team or by whom?"

"He said it was a matter of self-preservation and he didn't care how it was done or to whom, but I remember him saying that he wanted one of the Mets taken out and put on the disabled list."

"Now, to clarify this for the grand jury, what happens when a player is placed on the disabled list, and how long does it last?"

"A player can be placed on either the 15- or 60-day disabled list. There was a 7-day list for players with possible concussions, but that was ended a year ago. They figured 15 days would cover concussions too. During that period, he's not on the official team roster. That allows the team to bring up a player from the minors, or trade for a player to make up for the loss. When you're on the disabled list, it means the team doctor thinks the injury is fairly serious enough that the player shouldn't play at the risk of injuring himself even more."

"Now Sawyer didn't say which list he wanted the Mets' player to be on, did he?"

"No, just that he wanted to level the playing field. Our guy Butterworth was placed on the 15-day list, but he could have been extended to the 60-day list if his injury didn't heal."

"What was the reaction from the players?"

"It was supportive- especially from Julio Herrera. I got hostile looks from some of the guys."

"Did anyone speak out against what Sawyer asked?"

"I wouldn't say that anyone spoke against it, but I did call him, if you'll excuse the language, an asshole."

"Did Sawyer say anything else that you deem to be important?"

"Well, there was this corny speech he made about the sanctity of the clubhouse, and that anything that was said here was to remain a secret from the outside world."

"Was it your impression that he wanted everyone to cover-up what he asked for at the meeting?"

"I guess you could put it that way."

"One more aspect I need to ask. Do you know what Tim Charles said, if anything, about the meeting?"

"I know the kid was troubled. He felt pressure from guys like Herrera, and I know he felt worried about letting the team down. He threw his guts up right before the game. I heard from Bobby Carson that when he took the mound on Sunday that Julio reminded him that he had to take care of business. I went over to him early in the game because I could see the strain on his face from the pressure. He was practically green in complexion. I told him that Sawyer wouldn't be around next year, and that he could satisfy the team by throwing some chin music at the Mets' batters."

"Did he respond?"

"No, I couldn't get a read on what he would do."

"I just remembered another question, Mr. Adams. Do you have any knowledge of why Sawyer was fired?"

"Well I wouldn't want to speculate on what was in the minds of the top brass, but I assume it was connected to my meeting with the GM. I went to see Roberts on my own right after Leyton died. I told him that Sawyer orchestrated the whole thing. Then the next thing I heard was that Roberts called in several more of my teammates and I guess they confirmed it."

The grand jurors were totally engrossed by Adams' testimony. The only questions came from a woman who wanted some of the baseball terms explained. Adams was excused, and Bobby Carson testified next. He largely corroborated the testimony of Adams, including the role that Herrera had played in instigating the retaliation. He would offer nothing meaningful about Charles' intentions when he threw the fateful pitch.

Then a male grand juror asked Carson, "What pitch did you signal for just before Leyton got hit?"

"It was supposed to be a slider, down and away."

"Did Charles shake off the pitch?" the juror wanted to know.

"No, I guess he just let it get away from him."

"Is that what you really believe?" asked the incredulous prosecutor.

"Look, I don't know what was in the kid's heart. I just know how he looked after he hit Leyton, and I'd bet anything that he didn't try to hit him in the head. I saw his reaction when Leyton went down and that was no acting job. Leyton didn't even try to get out of the way. He looked like he was frozen at the plate."

"He didn't have much time to see the pitch and react, did he?"

"No, but that's true of any fastball thrown at that speed."

"But the fact remains that you, as the catcher, called for an off speed pitch that was low and away from the batter. Isn't that correct?

Carson paused sheepishly, looked down, and replied "Yes.

"That will be all sir. You are excused", said Jaime."

Next on Jaime's list was Buck Sawyer. Jaime was hesitant about calling him into the grand jury because, the way the evidence was already shaping up, Sawyer could quite conceivably incriminate himself by testifying. Jaime wasn't trying to set a trap for him. Sawyer had not been the target of the investigation when it began.

Jaime deliberated whether it would look like he was deceiving Sawyer into incriminating himself, rather than merely using him to gain information about the circumstances behind the Leyton death. If a court believed Sawyer was deceived, any potential indictment against him would be dismissed. On balance, Jaime decided to call him because he felt that the true target, if any, was Tim Charles.

Buck entered the room and glared at the jurors. The foreperson asked him to sit in the witness chair and take the oath. Buck looked uncomfortably around the room at the jurors, who were dressed about as informally as anyone could be. Many wore jeans and t-shirts. They contrasted sharply from the suit, tie, and French-cuffed shirt that Sawyer wore. His lawyer prepped him on what to wear. *Who the hell were these people to be dragging me into court asking me about my players?* thought Buck. His face was tired-looking. His eyes had bags so dark that it appeared he was wearing make-up. His face was lined with crease marks from booze and years of smoking. Yellow stains had permanently tarnished his teeth, and his puffy face still carried a flushed red pallor.

After the preliminary questions, Jaime got to the point quickly.

"Did you have a one-on-one meeting with Mr. Doug Adams the night before he was to pitch in the last home series with the Mets?"

"I believe I did."

"Did you order, direct, or in any other fashion suggest that he retaliate against one of the Mets' batters?"

"Your Honor, on the advice of my lawyer, I will take the Fifth Commandment."

Many of the jurors smiled or laughed out loud and looked at Jaime, who tried to suppress a smile.

"What did I say that was so funny"? bristled Sawyer.

"First of all, you promoted me by referring to me as Your Honor. I'm the prosecuting attorney, not a judge. Secondly, you said you were relying on the Fifth Commandment. Did you mean to say the Fifth *Amendment*?"

"Oh, yeah, sure, that's what I meant to say. My lawyer doesn't want me to answer any questions. I take the Fifth on everything."

"Members of the grand jury, I'm afraid I have to temporarily excuse this witness so that I can call the assignment judge for a moment." At that point, Sawyer left the room while Jaime called Judge Melucci and explained the situation. Melucci referred the matter to the Presiding Criminal Judge Thomas Johnson. Jaime then instructed Sawyer and his attorney to meet him in Judge Johnson's courtroom to test the validity of Sawyer's Fifth Amendment claim. The law doesn't allow a witness to avoid testifying by merely claiming the Fifth Amendment without proof, so Jaime wanted to make sure there was a basis for the claim. The grand jury was given a thirty-minute break while the hearing took place.

The issue arose unexpectedly, so the press had no time to get to the courtroom, but it seemed like every law clerk in the building, as well as public defenders and prosecutors, showed up coincidentally for some bogus reason or another. The word spread from Johnson's law clerk within minutes. Unfortunately for them, Johnson cleared the courtroom of everyone except the parties and court personnel. The grand jury process had to be kept confidential.

Judge Johnson asked Sawyer to take the stand. His lawyer played virtually no role. It was up to the client himself to assert the Fifth; the lawyer could not do so for him. It was up to counsel to fully prep his client on the need to assert the Fifth whenever a witness at the grand jury claimed its protection.

Jaime asked Sawyer a number of questions all relating to the three-game series, the talk of retaliation, the meeting with Adams, the team meeting, and the last pitch thrown by Charles. On each occasion, Sawyer took the Fifth. Jaime argued to the judge that the witness was not giving a sufficient basis for refusing to answer. In other words, he argued, how could Sawyer incriminate himself if he merely acknowledged that he had a meeting with Adams or his team?

Judge Johnson questioned Sawyer's lawyer about whether his blanket refusal was too broad. Counsel for Sawyer explained that if the grand jury were seeking to assign blame for the death of Leyton, they might be looking at a conspiracy charge. If Sawyer were to admit saying things, he could be implicating himself in that conspiracy. Judge Johnson then asked counsel to go into his chambers.

In chambers, Judge Johnson asked Jaime to give him some background so that he could make a proper ruling. Jaime explained that there was a meeting between Sawyer and Adams. That was not new. It had made its way to the papers within days of the bean ball incident. He summarized the Herrera-Adams clash, the Butterworth hit, and the Leyton hard slide into Colby Green. None of that was secret information gleaned from the grand jury.

Judge Johnson felt he had heard enough. "Gentlemen, I will uphold the witness' refusal to answer any question about what he may have said to his players during the series as it relates to the issue of retaliation. That doesn't mean he cannot be asked whether he was present at certain events."

Jaime wasn't surprised by the ruling, and limited his questioning accordingly.

"Was there a team meeting Saturday night after the game, and did you call it?"

"Yes, I often have team meetings."

"Did you place a quotation on the bulletin board about the sanctity of what is said in the clubhouse?"

"Yes, and so did about ten other managers around the league!"

"Do you know what led to the argument between Adams and Herrera?"

"I object to that!" counsel for Sawyer said. "Again, Your Honor, if conspiracy is being contemplated by the grand jury, my client's knowledge of an unlawful agreement would be an issue, and if he admits some knowledge he could possibly incriminate himself."

"I'll sustain the objection, Mr. Brooks." Then, directing his remark to Sawyer, the judge advised Sawyer that he need not answer that question.

"Is that it, Mr. Brooks?"

"Yes, Your Honor, that's all I have."

Jaime knew that he wouldn't get much from Sawyer, but he was happy he got an admission about the team meeting and the bulletin board quote. That corroborated the prior testimony.

Sawyer was excused and a court reporter came back to the grand jury and read only the questions and answers that

Judge Johnson permitted. The jury was told that Sawyer was excused from further testimony based on his Fifth Amendment rights.

Jaime excused the jurors for lunch break. He took the opportunity to walk out with Barbara Jay. He asked if she were enjoying her service as a juror.

" I am, but I work at night quite often, and frankly I'm exhausted. I tried to get off, but the judge didn't think that was a good enough reason." She explained that she was a professional singer and was currently under contract with Bally's Hotel in Atlantic City, where she sang in the Blue Martini Lounge Friday and Saturday nights. She was formerly a middle school music teacher but burned out after fifteen years. She enjoyed putting on shows each year with the students, but the classroom experience got stale after teaching the same subject year after year. She supplemented her income by singing in a band on weekends at weddings or parties, and she taught piano privately on a regular basis on her off-days.

Jaime was impressed with her energy and shared her love of music. He wondered where she lived, and was stunned to hear that she lived out-of-county in Egg Harbor Township.

"What are you doing on the grand jury if you live in Atlantic County?"

"I moved after I was sworn in."

Jaime just shook his head. "You can't sit on this grand jury, Barbara. You have to be a resident of Camden County to be on our grand jury. Why didn't you tell the judge when you were sworn in that you were moving?"

"I didn't realize that I wasn't eligible to serve if I moved. I thought that as long as I lived in the county on the day I was sworn in that I was stuck. Do you mean I'm going to lose my five-dollar juror fee"?

"I'm sorry to be the bearer of such bad news, but yes, and I'm going to have to draft an order and present it to the judge to excuse you from further duty. Get me some proof of your new residence so I can submit it with the order."

"In that case, maybe you can come to the shore and listen to me sing some evening since there's no longer an ethical barrier. I hope I'm not being too forward but I think it would be fun."

"I would like that." As he looked into her hazel eyes, he felt stirrings in his groin that had been AWOL for quite a while. *Yes, he thought, I would like that very much indeed.*"

Chapter 21

After the lunch break, Jaime made his way back from his office to the grand jury room. Again he was greeted by Theresa Leyton and some other Mets' wives, carrying posters calling for the arrest of Charles. Theresa approached and told him about the letter of sympathy she got from Charles. She made it clear that it had had no effect upon her commitment to have him spend the rest of his years in prison. She asked whether the letter might somehow help in Jaime's case. He knew that there would not be anything useful because he presumed Tim's legal team had seen to that, but he took it anyway to appease her. He excused himself and walked quickly into the City Hall building.

That afternoon, Julio Herrera was sworn in as a witness. For the first time, the grand jury heard testimony that differed dramatically from prior witnesses. When Herrera was asked about the reason for his antagonism toward Adams, he provided an entirely new explanation. Julio exaggerated his speech with broken English in an apparent effort to suggest he wasn't able to articulate for the grand jury.

"Adams don't like the way I play too deep at third base. He yell at me to play up in case they try to bunt. My arm is strong enough and I am fast enough to play deep, so I tell him to worry about his pitching. When he hits Wynne, I yell at him for putting a man on base. We go back and forth so when I get to the dugout I let my temper get the best of me. That's all that it was. He thinks he knows it all because he's a college man. I don't like the guy, is all."

When he was asked about the team meeting held by Sawyer it was the same result. He denied that Sawyer ordered his team to retaliate for Butterworth's injury. He also denied that Sawyer reminded the team not to reveal to anyone what he ordered, or what was said at the meeting.

He did admit telling Charles to"take care of business," but insisted that it meant exactly that. He was urging his teammate to pitch effectively and to win the game for the team.

At that point, an exasperated juror raised his arm and asked Jaime whether they could indict Herrera for perjury. Jaime excused Herrera for the moment and then addressed the jurors.

"You are free to indict anyone if there is evidence of a crime, but please don't ask it in front of the witness. Let me see if I can get him to cooperate when I bring him back. Perjury is a tough crime to prove and it might be better to have him as a cooperating witness."

Herrera returned to the jury room at Madeline's request and Jaime asked him if he had a lawyer with him. "No" was the response.

"Mr. Herrera, I'm going to explain something for your benefit. At least one juror has asked about the possibility of charging you with perjury. I don't know how many others might join in that action. Let me ask you first if you have discussed what you have said here with any of your teammates before coming here today."

"No, I no have time to talk with them."

"Well sir, I want you to know that you have the ability to change your testimony before we end our grand jury investigation. There is in the law a defense to perjury if the witness corrects his testimony before it's too late. It's called retraction. I don't expect you to completely understand what

I'm saying, but I'm going to give you a week's continuance to enable you to get a lawyer and consult with him. You are to report back here again next week. Do you understand what I just said?"

"I understand I must get a lawyer and come back. Yes I will talk to a lawyer."

After Herrera left, Jaime explained that he didn't want to look like he was coercing the witness into changing his testimony so he wanted to give him a chance to consult with an attorney. The jurors nodded their agreement and the session ended for the week.

Back at the office, Jaime had Bea fax an invitation to the Hunter law firm for Charles to testify at the grand jury for 1:30 PM the following week. He believed he could very well end the case next week because all he had left was the autopsy, hospital records, and a few other witnesses.

When the fax was received at the defense firm, Henry Kemper convened a dinner meeting of pizza and sub sandwiches. If Charles were to testify, it would fall on Kemper to prep him and accompany him to the grand jury. The question for the meeting was whether or not to accept the invitation. There were grave risks for a lawyer to permit his client to testify at a grand jury without the presence of his lawyer. First of all, the defense had no idea what people were saying at the grand jury. They only had their client's recollection of the events. While they believed the kid, they weren't positive that they could totally rely on the word of their client. Who knew what things he may have said to other players, or people in general, about his intentions regarding Leyton? If they sent the kid in, he could end up telling a pack of lies that would be refuted later at trial by a number of witnesses for the state.

Hunter had serious doubts about the wisdom of allowing Charles to testify.

"Unless you almost have an assurance from the prosecutor that his case is weak, and that the defendant could sway the jury not to indict by testifying, it's too dangerous. We have no assurance from Jaime because he couldn't give us one even if he knew himself what the outcome would be. We are in unchartered waters in this case."

"I agree," said Sean Cavanaugh. "You would be committing our client to a defense version that boxes us in and may be a loser at trial because of contradictions by other witnesses. Then we're screwed and so is the kid. The other thing is the standard of proof at the grand jury is so low that it would take a brilliant performance by the kid to avoid an indictment. All they need is probable cause of a crime and he's cooked."

Kemper added another negative to the equation.

"The more serious problem that I see is that, if he testifies, he may actually end up admitting to a crime of reckless manslaughter. You have the kid saying that he didn't mean to hit Leyton, but if he admits to the grand jury what he told us, he's got trouble. If he tells them he threw the ball high and inside at 95 mph deliberately to give him some chin music, the grand jury could easily determine that the risk he took was grossly reckless, and therefore manslaughter. Then we don't need a trial because we're stuck with what he said. We can't claim the police coerced a confession. He did it in front of a grand jury for Pete's sake"!

"I say we save our options for trial and look at it when we see all of the state's evidence. Then we can all sit down with the kid and go over possible weaknesses in the state's case when we aren't so pressured to make decisions," said Raymond Hunter.

"Okay, but we have to lay it out for the kid so it's his choice. We can advise him but ultimately it's his life, and he needs to make the decision. We can have a conference call tomorrow morning rather than fly him up. If he wants to testify, then we can have him up and prepare him for the appearance," added Kemper.

Then the door to the office building opened and a young man wearing a Phillies' cap walked into the reception area. The secretaries were gone, and none of the lawyers had any clients scheduled. Hunter went into the reception area to greet the unexpected visitor and asked what he could do for him. He identified himself as Chris Meyer, and he was not shy about revealing his agenda.

Meyer was a twenty-two year old high school dropout who listed his occupation on the jury questionnaire as a mechanic. In fact, he worked about three days a week in a gas station pumping gas. The job clearly did not provide enough money to even pay for his rent in the two-bedroom apartment in Somerdale that he shared with another friend. He had no criminal record, other than juvenile offenses, so he was not precluded from sitting as a grand juror.

Meyer, like so many other aimless youths, found solace in crack cocaine. He saw an opportunity to bolster his purchasing power by selling some of the "product" that he routinely bought in Camden City. His source was a street-level dealer named Malik Marcus. They had an arrangement that permitted Chris to obtain cocaine on consignment. Chris would sell the coke, return the money to his supplier, and get paid with baggies of his chosen drug.

Meyer was one of those street punks that thought he could manipulate the best of them, let alone a small-time corner drug dealer. He faked a burglary at his apartment, complete with broken window and strewn property, and reported it to the police to provide a record of the event. He reported a loss of some jewelry and odds and ends.

Then he took the police report to Malik and feigned outrage that the perpetrator had stolen his unsold cocaine bundles. In all, the baggies had a street value of $3,500. His plan was, of course, to sell the baggies and keep the profits. The plan failed for two reasons. First it turned out that Malik worked for a lieutenant in the "Bloods" gang that supplied most of Camden County. This boss didn't care about reasons. He informed Malik that if he didn't get the money from Meyer that he would be found floating in the Delaware River.

Second, Meyer didn't have the foresight to expect that Malik and three of his cohorts would barge into his apartment and find the drugs concealed in a heating vent. It wasn't that Malik was thorough; it was more a consequence of the waterboarding that they used on Chris in his toilet bowl. Then, as a payback for his disloyalty, Malik and friends landed Chris in the hospital with internal bleeding and multiple fractures. If that weren't enough, Marcus told Meyer that his boss wanted $5,000 in retribution money. Thus Chris appeared at the offices of the Hunter law firm with his newest scheme.

"I think I may have a little something that you'll be very interested in seeing."

"That's fine, why don't you sit down and show us?" said Hunter.

Meyer took out a small piece of technology that he called a flip camera.

"Let me show you what I have on video to see if it whets your appetite. Then we can talk business."

Meyer proceeded to play the miniature camera that was about the size of a Blackberry. It had been easy for Meyer to sneak in the small camera. The guards knew he was a grand juror and merely waived him through security. The partners were astonished. They saw Jaime Brooks sitting at a table asking questions of Doug Adams. The camera turned to an angle and several other people could be seen sitting and watching. There could be no doubt; this was a recording of the secret grand jury proceedings in the matter of the Leyton death. Even more amazing was the fact that there was audio of the testimony.

"How in the world did you get this, Mr. Meyer?" asked the partners, almost in unison.

"It was easy. I'm a grand juror, and I took my camera to record everything that happened in the grand jury since day one. Everything you ever wanted to know about what they're saying about your client is right here for the taking."

"I see. And what is it that you had in mind in return for that?" asked Kemper.

"Hank, are you nuts? Let's throw this creep out now," said Sean Cavanaugh. "This is radioactive."

"Take it easy, let's hear him out."

Meyer surveyed the partners and felt confident that he had their attention.

"It's all good dudes. We all want the same thing. We want Charles to skate on this charge so he can go back to playing baseball. All I want is a small token of appreciation-

say about $10,000 for the camera. I'll even throw in a vote not to indict Charles as a bonus. Is that cool?"

"Get the fuck out of here you arrogant bastard, before I break your fucking face into pieces!" said an enraged Cavanaugh.

"Let's calm down and see if we can work this out," said Kemper.

Hunter was eyeing Kemper and recognized that Hank was playing the kid.

"What are you thinking, Hank?"

"I think the price is a bit high. I'm thinking $7,500 is the magic figure. The problem is we don't have the cash on hand, and I am certainly not going to write a check out to a sitting grand juror. We would be leaving an easy trace to convict us all. Let's say you give us until 4:00 PM tomorrow to get the cash, and you come back with the camera and we have a deal."

"Agreed," said Meyer, "but make it 6:00 PM because I gotta work tomorrow. I'll see you tomorrow right here." As he left, he grabbed a slice of pizza and thanked them for dinner.

The partners were astounded by the kid's balls.

"How many laws do you think the kid broke?" asked Hunter.

"That's Jaime's problem. I'll call him his cell right now and let him set this thing up," said Kemper.

"I'd like five minutes alone with that prick in my office. He wouldn't be able to eat for a week," said the six-foot, two-hundred-and-thirty pound hulk of a body that housed Sean

Cavanaugh. The call was made and Jaime used curse words that Kemper hadn't heard since college. Jaime was profusely grateful for their cooperation, and asked if he could wire one of the lawyers with a body microphone so that the prosecutor's investigators could record the next day's meeting with the suspect.

All agreed that it should be Kemper because he had the trust of the corrupt juror. Arrangements were made for two investigators to go to the office the next day at 4:00 PM to prepare for the trap.

Chapter 22

While disheartening to the process, Jaime was not shocked to read the lead story below the fold the next morning. Word got out that Sawyer took the Fifth Amendment. When asked for a comment, Sawyer's lawyer Fred Rosen took a shot at the prosecution:

"We refused to answer the questions posed to us at the grand jury because the prosecutor is on a fishing expedition. Everyone on the team is in jeopardy. Is it a crime to play hardball in New Jersey? This prosecution is looking to make a name for itself at our expense, and I was not going to let my client fall prey to that tactic. The fact of the matter is everyone has a right to refuse to answer, and the judge correctly upheld our position. No one should infer that my client has anything to hide, or that he has done anything illegal."

Writers and bloggers speculated about the legal theory that a prosecutor would rely upon against Sawyer. Was there a conspiracy by Sawyer and other players to get Leyton, asked a writer for Baseball News? Why else would Sawyer take the Fifth Amendment? Was Sawyer the target of the investigation, or Charles, or both?

Such publicity would not be helpful to Jaime if he were to get an indictment from the grand jury. The continuing press coverage of the story would potentially taint the jury pool when it came time for a trial. It would be hard for him and the defense to get an impartial jury with no pre-determined opinions of the case. He also knew there was nothing he could do about it. It was clearly a national story of public interest and the coverage would continue unabated until there was a verdict one way or another.

Now Jaime had to focus on the corrupt grand juror, and find out whether there were others on the panel also enlisted by Meyer to vote against an indictment for Charles. If so, he would have to ask Judge Melucci to dissolve the panel and start all over again. He gave instructions to Lt. Nick Falconetti and Investigator Evelyn Arroyo to bring the juror back to the office for questioning after they made the arrest. He prepared an order in advance for Judge Melucci's signature to remove Meyer from the grand jury for good cause. He also drafted one for Barbara and sent it through interoffice mail, along with proof of her new residence, so that she would be removed. That would lessen the number of grand jurors to just 21. That would make it even more difficult to get an indictment.

At the Hunter law firm, Kemper called Charles and explained the significance of the invitation to testify. He told him that defendants or targets of investigations have no legal right to testify, but that because of his relationship with the prosecutor, and the nature of the unusual case, Jaime agreed to let him testify. He summarized as best he could the conversation with the partners about the cons of appearing. Charles wanted to know whether he saw any pros.

"If you do testify, and you come across sincere, believable, as well as likeable, it is possible that the grand jury will decide not to indict you."

"Do you mean that would be the end of it? I would be cleared and it would be all over?"

"I can't even make that guarantee. Technically, the prosecutor could take your case to another grand jury panel and present some additional evidence to try to get an indictment again. But that's rarely done, and I know for a fact that Jaime Brooks does not believe in that kind of a practice. Still, in theory, it could happen."

"I'm not used to the law, Mr. Kemper. I've never even gotten a traffic ticket. I just don't feel right going in there without you. What do you think, sir?"

"We are all of the view that you should not testify. The chances are that you will be indicted either way, and we would rather not let the prosecutor have a shot at cross-examining you without my presence."

"That's fine with me. I'll pass on testifying and hope for the best. Thanks for explaining it all to me, and let me know if you need me up there. For now I'm just glad to be home enjoying the support of my family and friends."

With that issue decided, Kemper met with investigators Falconetti and Arroyo to go over the strategy for the Meyer kid. Falconetti told him to drop his pants and placed a wire apparatus around his lower waist that would record the conversations of Meyer and the partners. The investigators would be in another room with a recorder to capture everything on tape. It was all legal because it was done with the consent of the partners.

"Try to go back over what happened yesterday so any future jury will hear the whole crime. And don't try to raise your voice - the microphone will pick up everything very naturally," instructed Arroyo.

Falconetti gave Kemper $7,500 in marked $100 bills that came out of the Prosecutor's forfeiture funds, and instructed him to make sure that he gave it to Meyer before they arrested him.

At 6:10 PM, Meyer strolled into the office looking as cocky and confident as the prior day. He knocked on the door to the conference room and entered without waiting for a response.

"Well, dudes, hope you got the money because I've got the goods you need."

"We're ready to play ball, but we want more than just the contents of the camera for the $7,500," answered Kemper. "We want some assurance that you can get a few of the other grand jurors to join with you in voting against an indictment."

"Hey, we agreed on the price for the grand jury testimony and my vote. You didn't say nothing about any other votes. You want more votes, you pay me more. I'd say another $2,000 for every juror should do it."

Kemper looked at his partners and they nodded their approval.

"Okay, but I need another day to get the rest. Tell you what, let's make the trade today, and you come back again tomorrow and I'll have six grand for you."

"That suits me just fine. Let's see the green."

At that point, the exchange was made and Meyer left, but not after complaining that the partners hadn't provided him with dinner that night.

Outside in the parking lot, the two investigators moved in. They displayed their badges and announced that they were placing him under arrest. Handcuffs were placed behind the suspect's back, and he was searched for weapons. The only thing they found was their marked cash and a set of car keys. They orally advised the suspect of his Miranda rights and took him back to the homicide division for questioning.

The kid didn't look so cocky now, thought Falconetti, In fact, from the odor emanating from the back seat of the car, odds were he had crapped himself. They would have an enormous psychological advantage now that the kid couldn't hide it from them. He should be easy pickings. Falconetti began his interrogation aggressively.

"Meyer, you are literally and figuratively sitting in a load of warm shit. Now I'm going to read your rights again from this form, and I'm going to ask you after each question to answer yes or no and to place your initials next to each answer. Is that clear?"

"I can't go to jail. You gotta promise me I can go home after this if I talk, deal?" He looked at Arroyo.

"You're in no position to deal, my friend. We have all the cards. If you can't do the time, don't do the crime. Now listen to your rights and then we can talk about whether you can go home tonight."

After the formal reading of his rights, Falconetti asked if Meyer was willing to waive his rights and to speak to them without a lawyer.

"I got nothing to say. I know my rights. I'm a fucking grand juror."

"Then maybe you'll recognize some of the crimes that my boss, the prosecutor, is drawing up against you. Let me see if I can list them all. There's bribery by agreeing to take money as a juror, attempting to corrupt or influence grand jurors, conspiracy to tamper or corrupt a juror, obstruction of justice, hindering the prosecution of another for homicide, compounding a crime, and last but not least of all, contempt of court."

"Yeah, but I'm a first offender. I'll get probation."

"Not really asshole," said Arroyo. "Hindering a homicide will get you a state prison term, and we'll make sure you don't get an early parole. As a matter of fact, we'll piggyback every one of your crimes and get you consecutive time. You'll be looking at 20 years or more. Now, why not make it easy on yourself? We're tight with the prosecutor, and we can convince him to go easy on you. Be smart about this!"

"I want a guarantee that I go home when you're done with me, and then I'll talk."

"No guarantees and no promises, kid," said Falconetti. "It doesn't work that way. But if you cooperate fully, we'll ask Mr. Brooks to recommend that the judge gives you an O.R. bail. Do you know what that means"?

Meyer looked at them with a glazed look, so Arroyo explained that all he had to do was sign an acknowledgement that if he skipped out on bail, he would owe the county the amount of bail that was set. On the other hand, he didn't have to put up any money on an O.R. bail.

"That's an awesome offer Chris, but it goes away if we leave here empty-handed."

The kid was wavering, so they threw in a little incentive.

"You know," said Falconetti, "I don't even like to visit the Camden County Jail. I get the creeps when I have to interview somebody over there. They pack them in there like sardines. They got two and three people sharing the same cell. Last time I checked, they had 1700 inmates, and the capacity is 1200. That's a riot just waiting to happen."

"Alright, I'll give you a statement, but you'll go to bat for me, right?"

"We can certainly promise you that."

Meyer waived his rights on video camera and told a bizarre, elaborate, and totally fabricated story. He was in debt to a couple of local hoods because of gambling losses on various sporting events. It got to the point that he could no longer make the installment payments on the nearly three thousand dollars. When they found out that he was a juror on the Charles investigation, they made him the proverbial offer he couldn't refuse.

They would forgive his debt in return for his information and actions in dealing with his fellow jurors. He was to provide them with up to date information on the testimony and the chances for an indictment. If so, they were going to place a large bet against the Phillies winning their division. They would place another bet that the kid would be indicted. If it looked like Charles would beat the rap, they would place a large bet against an indictment.

"These days," explained Meyer, "you could place a bet on anything, and those guys were more than willing to wager on a sure thing."

Meyer maintained that he decided on his own to provide the defense with the grand jury information because he was a lifelong Phillies' fan and wanted to help the team. He forcefully denied that he lobbied any of the other grand jurors, or even that he made comments to them about the case. That would be something Falconetti would make sure got to Jaime immediately. If Meyer had tainted the other jurors, Jaime would have to start all over again with another panel, and that would be a nightmare.

After the statement was read back to Meyer, the investigators asked if he was promised anything in return for the statement. Meyer admitted that the statement was voluntary, and that the police merely promised to do what they could to convince the prosecutor to cut him a break by seeking an O.R. bail from the judge.

Nick Falconetti phoned Jaime and summarized the day's events, with special emphasis on the kid's statement that other jurors were not approached. Jaime, while relieved, explained that the whole panel still needed to be interviewed by a judge. It would most likely be Judge Johnson who would determine if any jurors were tainted by Meyer in any manner. He also told the investigator to tell Meyer to report to the Major Crimes Unit of the Prosecutor's Office the next day and seek out Captain Art Fultz.

"We own this kid now, and he's going to bring us the two hoods that corrupted the grand jury," said Jaime.

Arroyo finished printing out the charges against Meyer, but Falconetti told her to save them. They were not going to formally charge the kid now because if they filed complaints or if bail was set, those documents would be a matter of public record. The press would be on it before the Prosecutor's Office could nab the other suspects. They would have about five days to make arrests, because once the grand jurors were interviewed the next Monday, it would be clear to the hoods that their boy had been compromised.

Meyer was permitted to go home but was strongly reminded that, if he failed to show at the Major Crimes Unit, he would be arrested. He was assured that bail would be high enough that he would be a guest at county expense in their exclusive facility that was famous for macaroni and cheese.

Jaime called Judge Melucci at home and explained the situation. Melucci agreed to hold off dismissing the juror from further duty pending further arrests. He was firm, however, of the necessity to voir dire each grand juror individually next Monday morning before any further testimony was taken.

"I'm afraid my staff will have to contact Ms. Jay and ask her to join us one last time. I'll sign the order dismissing her from the grand jury, but we still need to interrogate her to see whether she was approached by Meyer."

"I agree with Your Honor. If you don't mind, I'll call her. She gave me her number in case I needed to talk to her about proof of residency. Sorry to interrupt your evening. Good night, Judge."

That was the only really good news that Jaime had. This would give him a legitimate reason to call Barbara and see her again. When he did call, he learned that she was off on Monday. He casually asked if she would like to go to dinner with him at the end of his workday. He knew it would be an inconvenience for her to wait around for him, but she assured him that she would visit friends in the area. Rather than wait in Camden, Jaime suggested that they meet for dinner at Duo Catelli's in Voorhees.

Barbara said she looked forward to their dinner, and Jaime thought it would be nice to have an evening together, unless, of course, the omnipresent Theresa Leyton showed up with her protesters.

Chapter 23

The following morning, much to the chagrin of Jaime and the investigators, Meyer failed to contact Captain Fultz. In the interim, they ran a rap sheet check on the two gamblers that Meyer named as coconspirators. Raymond "Red" Schultz had a record. The problem, he was currently serving time in Cumberland County. The other suspect turned out to be deceased. They were taken by a twenty-two year-old, and embarrassed themselves in the eyes of Judge Melucci and Grace Moore.

The first item on Jaime's agenda was to personally appear before Judge Melucci with criminal complaints that Arroyo had drafted a few days earlier against Meyer. Jaime requested a piggyback bail on the various charges that amounted to $35,000. Meyer would need to put up 10% of that amount to make bail. That was highly unlikely. The truth was, however, Jaime was not confident that his Office or the local Somerdale Police would find Meyer at his apartment or his place of employment. If that were the case, the warrant would likely languish amongst the other several thousand outstanding fugitive warrants until they got lucky. Law enforcement did not have nearly enough personnel or resources to adequately follow up on the daily issuance of fugitive warrants. Unless Meyer was arrested during a routine crime or traffic stop, he could evade police for years.

In point of fact, a search warrant at the fugitive's apartment revealed that Meyer took his property and left while his roommate slept. His employer hadn't seen him for several days, and there were no known associates that could be developed.

Melucci formally executed an order that dismissed Meyer from the grand jury. Both men agreed that the charges were now a matter of public record so Jaime could alert Grace Moore and ask her to call a press conference. There was no doubt that the charges, and the name of the grand juror, would lead to the press swarming upon the Prosecutor's Office. Jaime worried that having another story break in the case would only increase the risk of more pre-trial publicity. That would keep the story of the grand jury investigation front-and-center when and if a trial occurred. The continued publicity could damage the accused's rights to a fair trial, and that could delay a trial or even lead to a transfer of the case to another county.

Nevertheless, Grace Moore believed that the need to deter other potential jurors from this kind of perversion of the justice system was paramount. Consequently, she called her secretary, Karen Shull, to schedule a 3:30 PM press conference. That would be plenty of time for the media to get the story in that evening's news cycle. With Jaime at her side, Moore succinctly read the charges to the press, along with the maximum prison terms that Meyer could face if convicted. She reminded the public that Meyer was still presumed innocent until and unless convicted, but she also stressed that it was a sad day for the process.

Chapter 24

For Chris Meyer, a hot macaroni and cheese supper sounded damn good, provided it wasn't at the county jail. He'd live on the streets if necessary, but he wasn't going to go to jail. He was claustrophobic and got anxious just thinking of being caged up in a cell. He knew he needed to get away from his former hangout spots to avoid the police, but there were very few options. *The police, or a violent gang intent upon making him pay for his disloyalty? "What the hell kind of a choice is that?"* he asked himself. The answer came quickly. He needed his drugs. That was the only way he could deal with his predicament. Maybe, he thought, he could work out something with his dealer, Malik.

He headed for Camden City in his 1995 Maxima, driving with the paranoia of someone on the lamb. He found Malik at the drug production facility on Fourth and Vine Streets. It was essentially an abandoned row house that was partially rehabbed by gang members and used to manufacture various controlled dangerous substances. It was also used as a safe house for dealers or members too high to make it home. The windows and doors were reinforced with steel bars to delay police in the eventuality that they discovered the true use of the house. Ostensibly, the steel was to provide security to the homeowners from neighborhood thugs.

"Yo man, whatcha doin' at the crib? You come to make your payments"? asked an incredulous Malik Tillman.

"No man, but that's what I want to talk to you about. I'm runnin' from The Man and I need to hide. I thought I could work off some of my debt to you all. In exchange, you let me flop here 'til I get myself settled."

"Yeah, but I ain't paying you sheet, mutha-fucker. You wanna work? That's awright, but you workin' off the money you owe the Bloods. I gotta take this to my lieutenant first. If he say it cool, you can work."

"I figure I could help cut the heroin or coke. I could package the shit into baggies. I'd even deliver it or sell it on the street corner if he gives me the chance."

"He might even let you pick up the junk from Patterson with that piece-of-shit-ass car you got." That way, if you get stopped by cops, they ain't gonna bother trying to forfeit a brother's car."

"I'm cool with that. Can I stay for now?"

"Yeah, make yourself useful and start dividing the coke into baggies of ¼, ½ and 1 gram. I'll call the organization and see if I can get hold of my lieutenant."

And in short order, Chris Meyer had himself a new vocation. He would earn a mere $100.00 per week, which would be deducted from his substantial debt. Nevertheless, Chris was grateful to have a place to stay and food to eat. Indeed, he could even feel like he was an apprentice to an eventual membership into the gang itself. Perhaps someday, he thought, he would outrank Malik.

Chapter 25

On Monday morning, the remaining twenty-one jurors, as well as Barbara Jay, were asked to return to Judge Melucci's courtroom. There was a shared sense of shock, sadness, and alarm over the fate of their fellow juror. The group bonded early in the process and most of them liked the offbeat youth who vanished over the weekend. Each nervously wondered whether any other jurors would be caught up in the corruption probe.

Judge Melucci greeted them and told them that he would interview each of them individually in his chambers with Mr. Brooks about their interaction with Chris Meyer. Each interview was brief, and focused solely on whether Meyer tried in any fashion to influence their opinions or inclinations on the investigation of Charles. When Barbara entered, she exchanged warm smiles with Jaime that did not go unnoticed by His Honor. After she was excused, Melucci good-naturedly chided Jaime about how he became so chummy with a sitting juror. Jaime explained the circumstances and expressed hope that he hadn't jumped the gun by arranging a date this soon after her release from duty.

"As long as you don't discuss the substance of what goes on at the grand jury from here on out, I can't see any harm, Jaime. I'll grant you, I wouldn't want to wait another twelve weeks before I could see her again if I were in your position. She's not only a gracious young woman, but she's a looker to boot. You should be grateful to Madeline for her matchmaking skills."

"Thank you, Judge. It's still very early, but I feel a connection with her, and I could use someone in my life. It's been a long time since my divorce, and I've dated dozens of women but I never felt emotionally drawn to any of them. I was beginning to think I'd be single forever. But I'm getting ahead of myself. I think I better concentrate on this case for now."

After the process, Judge Melucci and the prosecutor satisfied themselves that no other jurors were tainted by Meyer. Everyone expressed incredulity at the thought that the kid would have approached any of them with a bribe. In fact, other than the normal chatter about the stale pastries and donuts at mid-morning break, the kid didn't say much else. His Honor thanked the jurors for their patience, and assured them that the integrity of their panel was intact. Melucci then carefully placed a detailed account of all of the preceding events concerning the Meyer escapade on the record for an appellate court, if that ever became a necessity.

The panel returned to the grand jury room to find Julio Herrera and his lawyer waiting in the corridor.

His lawyer, Ernesto Rivera, asked if he could speak with Jaime out of the jury's presence, and the two stood in the corridor discussing the legal realities that faced the third baseman. Jaime assured Rivera that he wasn't looking to have another sideshow by indicting for perjury. If, on the other hand, the witness insisted on his story, he couldn't guarantee that the grand jury would feel the same way.

Rivera countered that he would have his client take the Fifth and refuse to testify on the grounds that he faced a possible perjury charge. Jaime reminded him that all of the elements of perjury had already been placed on the sworn record by his client, and that taking the Fifth would only save him from further counts of perjury. That seemed to hit home with Rivera, and he excused himself to talk to his client. Rivera huddled with Julio for what looked like a contentious few minutes and then returned to Jaime.

"I think my client understands his situation now, as do I. I have urged him to retract his prior statements and to be truthful with the grand jury. I would hope that you will guide the jury away from any perjury charge should you find that he's truthful."

"I will do everything I can to explain the retraction defense to them and to advise them that if they find his second appearance to be truthful that there would be no viable crime."

That was acceptable, and Jaime returned to the grand jury room. He then called in Julio. Herrera looked uncomfortably at the jurors as he took his seat. Jaime repeated many of the same questions he posed in the earlier session. This time the answers were entirely consistent with those expressed by other witnesses and the video of the game. Julio explained that when he told Charles to take care of business, he was referring to the need to retaliate against a Mets' player. He was not, however, able to tell the panel what Charles said in reply because the young pitcher did not respond.

"Why did you tell us a completely different version of events at your first appearance?" asked Jaime. Julio looked out at the grand jurors and at Jaime with humility and quietly but sincerely explained.

"To be honest, I wasn't raised to be a rat. When my manager tells me that what's said in the clubhouse is secret, I take that to heart. I don't want to hurt nobody, 'specially my teammates. Baseball has rules too, and I want to be a good teammate to them. I realize that I should be honest, and I 'm sorry that I tried to cover up the truth. I ask for your forgiveness."

That one statement would prove to be fateful for Herrera. The jurors thanked him for his honesty and he was excused from any further questioning. Jaime told his lawyer that things went well and that Julio was no longer in any jeopardy.

Jaime filled in the remainder of the morning session with a few matters that didn't require live witnesses. Jaime called in an investigator who had made a copy of Theresa Leyton's 911 emergency call. Those bone-chilling few moments had a palpable effect in the room. For the very first time, the jurors were reminded that a family had been torn apart by what they were investigating. It was not just an academic civic duty that they were performing. They were witnesses to a tragedy that was brought home by a wife's desperate plea for help. Such calls were usually helpful to the state's case, and Jaime got a measure of just how effective the call would be at a later trial from the facial expressions of several jurors.

Next, as a courtesy to save the medical records keeper and the medical examiner from the inconvenience of a live appearance, Jaime merely placed into evidence the hospital records and a copy of the autopsy report. The latter reflected the opinion that the death was a result of a homicide rather than natural death. The medical examiner found no pre-existing condition that would have either solely, or in conjunction with the blunt trauma impact, caused death. In other words, the death was a result of the swelling of the tissues around the brain that ultimately strangled the breath and life from Leyton's vital organs. The records were distributed amongst the jurors to view for themselves.

At that point in the day, Jaime decided to let the jurors go for their lunch break and reconvene at 1:30.

Chapter 26

The afternoon witnesses were few in number, and their testimony went by in rapid fashion. Bradley Schofield was called because he roomed with Charles, and Jaime felt if anyone could add to the picture of the pitcher's state of mind, it would be Brad.

Schofield truthfully portrayed the conversation he had with Tim the night before the notorious game. Schofield characterized his roommate as tormented by both the manager's expectation of him, and by the divisive episode between Herrera and Adams that left the latter looking weak in the minds of his teammates. He also candidly admitted telling him that the Mets' fully expected retaliation- that it was all a part of the game. But he also told the grand jurors that he told Tim that he could pass and leave it to a veteran pitcher if he felt uncomfortable throwing at someone.

"What was his reaction to that choice?" asked Jaime.

"He was afraid the players would call him a wimp, and sort of ignore him."

He too was not in a position to tell the panel what decision Charles had ultimately decided to make.

The words of several other players were recounted by investigator Evelyn Arroyo, who took sworn statements from them in Philadelphia with the aid of the DA's office. Jaime was cognizant of the need not to overburden the team when statements would suffice. They included the statement of Bubba Mason, the bullpen coach who also exhorted Charles to honor the team by retaliating.

The Mets' Mike Zahn was called because he openly stated in some news accounts that Charles threw at Leyton intentionally. Jaime wanted to know the basis for that conclusion. The bottom line, however, was that Zahn's opinion was just that: a naked opinion with little evidence but for the circumstances of the entire series.

Jaime received a fax from Kemper in which the lawyer respectfully declined to have his client appear before the grand jury. There was no explanation, but none was necessary. Jaime knew that the risk was too great to a defendant to testify without the presence of his lawyer unless the charges were weak. In Jaime's view, that was not the case here. Jaime felt no need to even inform the jurors of the invitation because to do so might lead some of them to hold his silence against him as evidence of guilt. They never had a defendant testify before them, so they didn't expect it of Charles.

It was three in the afternoon when Jaime announced that he had no more witnesses or evidence to present on the case. He asked whether the grand jurors themselves wanted any other persons subpoenaed to be questioned, but there were no additional requests.

"I'm ready to vote right now," said a retired woman. She was joined by a few other older jurors.

"I think perhaps you need some guidance on the law before you vote," said Jaime, amidst light laughter from the panel.

"What are we voting on"? another wanted to know.

"Your task now is to decide whether there was a crime committed, and whether Charles should be charged with it. I'm going to read to you a short version of the law on manslaughter, which is a form of homicide. Then I'll take your questions.

"A person is guilty of manslaughter if he recklessly causes the death of another person. A person acts recklessly if he is aware of, and consciously disregards, a substantial and unjustifiable risk that death will result from his conduct. The risk must be of such a nature and degree, that, considering the nature and purpose of the defendant's conduct and the circumstances known to him, the disregard of the risk is a gross deviation from the standard of conduct a reasonable man would follow in the same situation.

"Lastly, you must find that Ken Leyton would not have died **but for** the actions of the defendant.

"Now I know you have had cases before where the term reckless was defined for you, so are there any questions on the law?"

"Yes, I have one. Why aren't we talking about murder here? To me, this is a clear cut case of premeditated murder, so why haven't you offered it to us?" This time, the question from the retiree was more in the nature of a challenge to Jaime's guidance. That was met with shouts of disgust and outrage from a few of the male jurors.

"What are we going to do, call it aggravated assault anytime a pitcher hits a batter? Murder! Are you kidding me? That's absurd." But a young mother on the panel agreed with the retiree, and joined in the demand that the definition of murder be given.

In truth, Jaime was a bit alarmed by the emotion generated, and by the willingness of some to consider a murder indictment. It was unheard of in this context. He would be vilified by the press and by legal experts who would suggest that the charge was an overreaction to the tragic event. They would argue that, if anything, reckless manslaughter was the appropriate charge. The public was of the perception that the prosecutor led the grand jury, and that he was the responsible party for an indictment. "A prosecutor could indict a ham sandwich" was the adage often used to describe the prosecutor's power over a grand jury.

Jaime, of course, was a veteran prosecutor, and he knew the truth. He was not permitted by law to even venture an opinion to the grand jurors about whether they should indict or not. It was his job to gather and present the evidence, explain the law, and allow the panel to vote. So despite his misgivings, Jaime had to tread lightly.

"If there is significant interest in a murder charge, I'll read the law. Can I see a show of hands?"

Several hands went up, and Jaime felt compelled to read a short form of the murder statute. "A person is guilty of murder if he either purposely or knowingly causes the victim's death, or knowingly or purposely causes serious bodily injury that then results in the death of the victim."

"Now again," said Jaime, "a person acts purposely if it is his conscious object to cause the conduct. Knowingly means he is aware that it is practically certain that the conduct will result in death or serious bodily injury that causes death."

"I, for one, don't see how Charles knew that by throwing at Leyton that he would kill him. Worst-case scenario, this is reckless conduct," said one man who was worked-up by the whole murder concept.

Yet another wanted more clarification. "Are you saying that you can be guilty of murder even if you didn't intend to kill the person?"

Jaime explained that the law only required that the suspect know that his conduct could cause serious bodily injury that then ultimately does cause death.

"Well, that's good enough for me!" said the young mother. "I make a motion for murder."

"Let's discuss this further before anyone seconds the motion," said the foreperson.

The various opinions fell into three categories. A solid, hardcore group felt that the circumstantial evidence surrounding the three-game series was enough to suggest that Charles intentionally threw at Leyton's head so that he would suffer serious injury. No one believed he tried to kill Leyton, but the definition given by Jaime convinced them that murder was appropriate. The second group, made up of all males except for one twenty-year old female, argued that the case called for a manslaughter charge and would not consider murder. Several equally adamant older jurors made it clear that they were inclined not to indict for anything.

The first group moved for a murder indictment. They were only able to garner eight of the twenty-one jurors, well below the necessary twelve needed. Manslaughter brought ten votes. One juror abstained entirely on the grounds that the process was too stacked in favor of the state, and he could not in good conscience vote. Jaime rolled his eyes and wondered why the juror hadn't said that before he was sworn in. The jurors argued and moved again for various votes, but none reached twelve in favor of or against anything. They seemed to be at a stalemate.

Then a juror asked "if we indict for murder and manslaughter, would that satisfy everyone?"

Jaime advised them that if they indicted for murder, the petit jury would be given the option of finding him guilty of manslaughter because it's a lesser-included offense of murder. In fact, he said, there was yet another form of manslaughter that was also a lesser included offense within the murder statue. He explained that aggravated manslaughter was similar to manslaughter, but had an added element to it. They would have to find that, under the circumstances, the defendant acted with extreme indifference to the value of life. The major difference between the two is that in the aggravated type, there is a probability of death, versus a mere possibility of death in regular manslaughter. In other words the jury would have a choice of murder, aggravated manslaughter, manslaughter, or not guilty of anything.

Most jurors felt that the aggravated charge was not applicable because they didn't feel that death was probable in a head beaning, but that it was possible. Ultimately, it came down to murder or manslaughter, and the group that favored murder successfully gathered five more votes to just barely get an indictment. The other group was persuaded that there existed enough evidence to suggest that Charles was aware that it was practically certain he would cause serious bodily injury when he threw the 95 mph fastball, and that that injury led to death. Secondly, they felt better that the jury at trial would have the benefit of finding merely manslaughter.

Jaime was a bit unnerved by the vote because he felt reluctantly that manslaughter was the only appropriate charge. He was about to thank the jurors and leave for the day when the retired woman who led the fight for murder threw another monkey wrench into the pot.

"What about the manager? We're not going to leave without discussing him, are we? This shouldn't just fall on the shoulders of the Charles boy. This Sawyer character is as much to blame. I think we ought to do something about him, too."

Jaime was beginning to worry that he had a runaway grand jury on his hands and it may already galloped away. He could hear Grace Moore's voice imploring him to "say it ain't so."

"Just what did you have in mind, madam"?

One quiet and frail looking juror who hadn't opened his mouth for three weeks said in a polished manner that he quite agreed with the lady's view. In his mind, there should be no distinction between the principal actor, in this case Tim Charles, and the aider and abettor, Sawyer. He would agree to vote to join Sawyer in the indictment. It turned out that this juror was a retired law professor who didn't want the others to defer to him merely because of his profession, so he had taken a back seat in prior discussions.

Most of the jurors did not respond. They seemed to be mulling the idea over in their own minds. One asked Jaime if that were legally possible. Jaime told them that the law punishes not only the principal but the accomplice as well. He told them that they would have to believe that Sawyer solicited Charles in the commission of the murder as it had been defined, that it was Sawyer's purpose to promote that crime, and that he shared the same state of mind of acting knowingly or purposely with respect to the fatal pitch.

Jaime tried to keep his composure but he envisioned the headlines if Sawyer were included in the indictment. His mind, in the course of a few moments, imagined the Attorney General's Office making a formal investigation into his handling of the case. He could see his career going down the tubes at a time when he was so near retirement. Why had he agreed to take this case? Why hadn't he been more adamant with Grace and told her to let it be the DA's headache?

And then, as suddenly as it appeared, the panic was gone. He realized that the juror arguably had merit in his position. Hadn't Sawyer not only stirred the pot, but actually ordered that the action be taken? In a sense, wasn't Charles merely the surrogate for the manager's plot? If Charles could be charged with murder, wasn't it morally justifiable to condemn Sawyer as well? In Jaime's mind the answers were all affirmative.

There was very little discussion. The jurors were in a feeding frenzy and Sawyer's vote was almost unanimous. Even two of the jurors who voted not to indict Charles voted to charge Sawyer. He would share top billing in the indictment for the murder of Ken Leyton. Jaime cautioned the jurors about the secrecy of the vote, and the fact that the indictments would not be made public until the following week. With that done, he headed back to the office before his date with Barbara.

He felt an obligation to call Hank Kemper and alert him to what just happened. Technically the indictment was not a matter of public record until next Monday, but the vote was a shocker, and he wanted to give Kemper as much notice as he could so they could make arrangements for their client to get back to the Philly area. As he imagined, Kemper thought the call was a joke. It took a few minutes to convince him that it was the truth. Kemper was shaken by the news. He couldn't believe this could have happened.

"There is no secret about what the testimony is in this case, Hank. I didn't propose the murder count, one of the jurors raised it, and there was plenty of support for it. It surprised me as much as you. You've got company too, because Sawyer was indicted as well on a complicity theory."

"I could give a rat's ass about Sawyer. I don't know how I'm going to make that call to Tim. He's already a basket case. His career may be over, and now he could face life in jail for doing his job. Jesus, I hope to heaven that we didn't give him the wrong advice by not sending him in to testify."

"You can't second guess yourself, Hank. No one can ever know what the right call would have been. In my opinion, it wouldn't have made a difference."

Kemper was grateful for that remark, although he wondered if it were true. Now he had to address the issue of bail for his client. He knew it was out of the question to ask for an O.R. bail on a murder charge. Yet he also knew that Charles was low on funds, because he was not getting paid while on suspension.

"Jaime, you know this kid is not going anywhere. He's not the type of guy to flee to another state, let alone another country. He's recognizable from all the publicity, so he's no risk to become a fugitive. Can we agree on a bail figure that you can recommend that is reasonable? I don't want this kid spending time in jail pending trial."

Jaime explained that the normal guidelines for murder called for bail in the range of $250,000 up to $1,000,000. Jaime said he would feel comfortable at a figure in the middle of the range because the kid was a first offender.

"I can't go too low, Hank, because I have to deal with Leyton's widow, and I don't want to give the impression that I'm giving a break to Charles because he's a celebrity."

"I was hoping for less, but I can appreciate your position. Thank you for the heads-up on the indictment. I'm dreading the call to the kid. Get ready for plenty of motions and a trial because we'll fight this charge vigorously."

"That's what I would expect, Hank."

Next, Jaime had to pay a visit to Grace Moore and break the news to her. He tried the humorous approach.

"Well Grace, you're going to like shopping for new outfits because you'll be all over the network shows starting next week. I envy you."

"Do I take it we have a manslaughter case in Major League Baseball to prosecute?"

Jaime mimicked Don Adams' "Get Smart" character and replied "No, but would you believe a murder prosecution?"

Grace's eyes closed and she put her head on the desk. "Why did I let that DA talk me into this? She's off the hook, and we'll be the fall guys for the press. They'll make us the story. 'Out of control publicity-seekers indict for murder.'

"No, they'll make us the fall guys for two stories."

"What's that supposed to mean?"

"Would you believe two murder cases? They also indicted Sawyer as an accomplice."

"Sweet Lord, what have we gotten ourselves into?"

Jaime briefed her on the bail recommendation he would make on Charles. Sawyer's lawyer hadn't been in touch so he would wait for the indictment before discussing a figure, but he would likely recommend the same amount.

Now he wanted a vodka martini, but he would gladly opt for a glass of wine rather than risk the "loose lips syndrome" that hit him after a martini. This first date was too important to him. His gut told him that Barbara Jay was someone worth getting to know.

Chapter 27

When he got to the restaurant, he found her sitting outside at a table for two. She looked dazzling in a peach silk dress with a white sweater wrapped around her shoulders. What was it with women? It was still 80 degrees and she had a sweater. Was she preparing for an early autumn? When she rose to greet him, he stole a glance at her snakeskin-colored high heels. Oh man did she look hot. He felt his cheeks getting bright red, especially when he bumped heads as he leaned in for a kiss. As he kissed her cheek, she smelled of a summery peach scent that matched her appearance.

"I hope you don't mind me choosing a table outside, Jaime, but I just loved setting here."

"Not at all, I never get tired of this place, and the outdoor seating makes me feel like I'm in an Italian trattoria. Of course, I'd prefer to be in Tuscany, but this will have to do for our first date."

They spoke of their mutual desire to spend more time in every region of Italy when they could get the time to travel. They engaged in typical small talk until they felt comfortable enough to gently probe their respective relationship histories. Jaime's end of the conversation was humiliatingly short. Barbara's story was sobering. When Barbara was just thirty two her husband contracted ALS or Lou Gehrig's disease. He lived for four years but died died at the age of thirty eight. They had no children because her husband wanted to concentrate on his career, but that chance never materialized. She quickly moved on to lighter topics and soon they were both laughing about the horrors of the dating scene and the lengths to which people went on internet dating sites to attract a "soul mate".

They lingered over coffee so that he didn't have to leave her so quickly. The conversation flowed with no hint of forced effort. He felt at ease with her, and he seemed to get the same vibes from her in return. She smiled in a lovely and genuine way, and she laughed naturally at his attempts at humor. He was really enjoying himself. He couldn't remember the last time he was so relaxed on a first date, and he hoped it was mutual. He was already looking forward to their next meeting.

"So, are you ever free on the weekend?" he asked her.

"I'm usually free Sundays, because the wedding and Bar Mitzvah circuit is slow in the summer. I would love you to come down and keep me company some weekend and listen to a couple of my sets. I finish at 10:00 and we could get a light bite to eat and a beer."

Jaime cast aside the risk that he would sound too anxious and replied "I do happen to be free Saturday, if that's okay with you."

"That sounds wonderful. Now I'm dying to ask about the case. Wasn't it terrible about that young grand juror? Will you be able to find him, and how much longer will it be before there's a vote on the case"?

He couldn't tell her about the vote because it wasn't public, and despite his rising feelings for her, he would not take the risk of letting out the secret vote to anyone other than the defense team. He told her he could talk more very soon, and that she would know before anything became public. Barbara told him she felt conflicted when she sat as a grand juror because she believed that Charles was a young and innocent kid who threw a tragic pitch without animosity. She saw it many times before in games, only this time the consequences were so permanent; but she felt for Theresa Leyton and her son as well.

" I didn't hear all of the evidence, but I would not have voted to indict. Even if Charles was trying to brush back Leyton with a hardball up and in, it's a risk that batters know that they have to expect."

"Are you suggesting that there's no crime because the players assume that there is always the risk that they could get a fatal bean ball to the head?"

"I think what I'm saying is that unless you have a smoking-gun-like statement by Charles to someone that he intended to bean Leyton, I don't think it should be prosecuted. Let Mrs. Leyton sue Charles or Sawyer for the loss of her husband, but don't make a criminal out of the kid just because he did what any pitcher would do for his team. I saw the pain on his face after Leyton was hit, and it seemed real."

"Well, I guess it's unfortunate for him that you were removed from the panel, because he could use your advocacy. I'm not as forgiving as you. A young man died that night because of a team's vendetta. To me that calls for punishment. Frankly it should send a message to ballplayers in general that conduct such as that will be reviewed by law enforcement should it happen again." Jaime heard his words, but a part of him felt conflicted. He loved the game that had existed for so long, and feared that his prosecution would change the way the game was played. Still, he had a dead player who may have died as a result of an unwritten code that necessitated accountability.

"Let's agree to disagree. I respect your opinion. Whatever the outcome, it will be difficult to get twelve people to unanimously agree. On a lighter subject, it sounds like you follow baseball, am I right?" asked Jamie.

"Yes, I'm a big Phillies' fan. My dad took my mom and I to the last game of the 2008 World Series. He paid a bundle, but it was worth it to him. I will never forget Lidge falling to his knees as Ruiz jumped on him at the end of the game. Some things stay with you forever."

"How about I take you to a game this season? Maybe we can go on a businessman's day special, and I'll take half a day off."

"That sounds wonderful! It all depends on your calendar, because I should be fine. By the way, it's getting late and I should be getting back. It's been a long day, and I still have about an hour ride ahead of me."

As he stopped by her car in the parking lot he had that teenage panic come over him about whether to kiss her or not. Was it too soon, too public? He looked at her hazel eyes and longed to pull her close to his body. She seemed to read his face and made it easier for him by pulling him close and kissing him tenderly. The kiss ended with Jaime wanting more. Maybe that's what she had in mind.

Chapter 28

Kemper had the unenviable task of calling Tim and giving him the nightmarish news. He couldn't grasp it himself, and he wasn't the one facing prison, so he could only imagine the toll it would take on Tim and his family. As expected, the kid was flabbergasted and at a loss to say anything. Finally, he simply said, "I'm no murderer Mr. Kemper. I made a mistake in throwing near his head, but how does that make me a murderer?"

"Tim we'll have plenty of time to explain the law to you in the weeks that follow, but first things first. I need you to get back to the Philly area no later than this coming Sunday. The indictment will be released on Monday and a warrant will be issued for your arrest at that time. We want to walk you into court and surrender you before you are actually arrested."

Kemper went on to explain that he would contact a bail bondsman that worked with them in the past to set up bond so that Tim could stay out of jail pending the pre-trial or subsequent stages of the process. Then he dumped the second bit of bad news; namely that Tim would have to pay 10% of the bail to the bondsman as the fee for making himself liable for Tim's appearances at every court proceeding. He would not get that money back, even if he attended every court date.

"I don't know how I'm going to get that kind of money, sir. I'm low on funds, and I've spent a good deal already. I'm going to have to scrape together the money."

"Do everything you can, even if it means taking out a loan with your parents' home as collateral. I wish there was another way, but whether we like it or not, the charge is murder and the bail amount is not unreasonable. And Tim, do not tell anyone except your family about the charge, or the fact that I got the prosecutor to agree to a bail amount before arresting you. We don't want to make the prosecutor look bad to the public after he did us a favor."

Kemper told Charles to be at his office at 8:30 AM on Monday. Then he made preparations with a bail bondsman so that he would be ready with the bail contract.

He then got together with Hunter and Cavanaugh and shared the news. Their immediate concern was to keep their client out of jail for the present time. It would be his decision to accept a plea agreement, but the prospects didn't look good because they would involve some serious prison time. Hunter suggested that they set up a defense legal fund and ask for contributions in the media so they could help the kid pay his legal team. Hunter agreed to establish the fund and initiate radio and television ads during Phillies' games to attract contributions from fans. It was also agreed that Cavanaugh would handle a trial if it came to that. Kemper and Jack Marino's firm would handle the motion work and legal research so Sean Cavanaugh could concentrate on trial strategy.

Back in Sarasota, Tim could not hide his emotions from his family. It was a blow that he was unable to shield from them. Tim reluctantly revealed the fact of the indictment and the need for a bail bond. But he told his parents that it was his responsibility, and if it meant staying in jail pending trial, he would do that rather than collateralize the home. Tim meant what he said but hoped there was another option.

"Nonsense", said Lois with stoic determination. "We are in this as a family. Your father and I have no doubt whatsoever that you will walk out of court a free man. Then you can play ball again. When you get enough money to pay us back, you'll do it. I'll not hear another word on this subject. Your father can borrow from his pension and we have enough cash in savings to help make your bail." Lois promised to be with Tim throughout the trial, no matter the cost in lost wages. Jeff assured Tim that he could go to New Jersey next Monday and give him support, because he was not working during the summer recess. It was no small comfort to Tim that his family stood by him in this his only life crisis. He promised himself that he would find a way to repay them no matter how long it took.

The family felt no animosity towards the prosecutor or their own lawyers. They understood that outside of their Sarasota community, many people believed a homicide charge would be brought. The family, however, refused to believe that the ultimate outcome would be anything other than an acquittal. In the interim, the family would have to share the secret that they knew would rock their community when next Monday's news hit the airwaves.

For Jaime Brooks, there was little for him to do on the case before Monday. Virtually all of the evidence that he would have to turn over to the defense - in what is called discovery was in the form of grand jury testimony. That would be available to the defense within a couple of weeks after the indictment was returned. He would have his staff copy any statements that the homicide investigators took from doctors or other witnesses, and they would include a copy of the television video that he played for the grand jury.

There were three important items that he would need to take care of soon. The first was to have a discussion with Gary Slater, and then to consult with Grace Moore about a plea offer. It was mandatory to include such a plea agreement offer in the discovery. If he insisted that Charles plead guilty to murder, it would be an empty gesture because it would give Charles virtually no incentive to plead guilty. The minimum sentence for murder was thirty years without parole, and the maximum was life imprisonment, so there wasn't much in the way of an incentive to plead to murder. If he offered a plea to a lesser form of murder, the number of years involved would drop greatly.

Slater was astonished by the grand jury vote and warned Jaime that there was little chance that a petit jury would find Charles guilty at trial of the most serious of charges.

"I'd say there's as much chance at acquittal as there is for manslaughter. You could be looking at a hung jury" said Slater "If they're hung, do you really want to go through another trial?"

"I don't disagree with your analysis, but I do believe I would have to try the case again if they were hung. I think the principle is worth giving another jury a shot at it. In any event, what would you offer?"

"There will be a lot of sympathy at play here because of the pressure put on a 20 year old by his team and manager. I'd offer him the lower end of the scale for reckless manslaughter, something like six years. He would get paroled in roughly five years."

"I think that's about right, but I was thinking of offering an initial plea of ten years. I would be negotiating from a position of strength because they're facing a lot more if they get convicted of one of the higher offenses. If they want to roll the dice, they're playing a very dangerous game. Ultimately I think I would accept a plea to manslaughter for seven years.

That won't satisfy the widow, but it will satisfy me and most of the unbiased public."

Jaime then ran it by Grace, who was satisfied with Jaime's reasoning and approved the offer. She also asked about Sawyer, and Jaime expressed the position that he felt no moral or legal obligation to forewarn Sawyer's lawyer about the imminent indictment. He would ask for a bench warrant from Melucci on Monday. On the issue of the amount of bail for Sawyer, Jaime was thinking of asking for a higher bail than Charles on the grounds that Tim was substantially influenced by the more mature authority figure of his manager.

"That is a decent argument to put forward, Jaime, but I doubt you will succeed. In any event, it will make for interesting reading in the papers and on social media. Good luck with it, and rest assured I'll take any heat thrown your way about over-indicting the case."

The second item was to send detectives to Sarasota Florida to interview Clark Draper and try to find the batter to corroborate the broken jaw incident. Jaime assigned two other homicide members to that task.

The third caretaking item that Jaime had to address was a courtesy call to Theresa Leyton. He wanted to let her know in advance that there would be a proceeding Monday because he felt she had a right to be in court during the bail hearing. His concern was that, if he told her before Monday morning, she would leak it to the press and stories would appear over the weekend.

She was calling his office virtually every day and he passed her off to Linda or Diana Baker another victim/witness coordinator. Her phone messages seemed to be getting more urgent and more frequent each day. Moreover, she was becoming increasingly more strident with the staff. He was aware that she had a two-hour ride from her North Jersey home, so he decided that he would call her Sunday evening.

With those two items finished, Jaime would spend the rest of the week on the in-house issues that, as First Assistant, he needed to address.

Chapter 29

On Saturday evening, Jaime made the ride down the Atlantic City Expressway to Bally's Hotel. He got there about an hour before Barbara was to begin her first set. They sat in the lounge and caught up on the workweek. He wanted to share with her his ideas for the plea offer, but realized there would be time enough for that after the weekend.

Instead, he told her that he had tickets for a ballgame on a Thursday afternoon in twelve days. The Phillies would be playing the Washington Nationals in a battle for the division lead. She looked genuinely excited, and that pleased him. Was he looking for someone like his ex-wife, Bonnie? Hell no! But it would be great to share the love of the game again with a lovely woman.

She had to slip away to finish getting dressed for her set, so he let himself relax and be in the moment. Any thoughts of the case were taboo this evening. Instead, he "people-watched" as the lounge began to fill with casually dressed couples taking a break from gambling or enjoying a drink before dinner.

When Barbara came out on stage his body parts came to attention. She was alluring in a silver sequin dress with one shoulder bare. The dress came a bit above her knees, and her platform shoes made her legs look strikingly shapely and supple. She smiled broadly when she saw the deer in the headlights look on his face, and he felt the blood rising in his face. She blew him a kiss and he felt like a million bucks. The couples in the lounge were a bit loud for his taste, but when she began to croon "Beautiful" by Christina Aguilera, several men in the lounge leaned back in their seats and seemed to forget their dates. She followed that with a Sade classic, "The

Sweetest Taboo," and she had the rapt attention of all in the audience.

Then she sat at the piano and played a medley of Norah Jones hits. Jaime was in awe of her range and talent. She had the small audience in the palm of her hands. She followed with a series of songs by Alanis Morissette, and before he knew it, she was coming off the stage and sitting next to him. Wow, he thought, what did I do to deserve this? It was in those moments of her break that Jaime first told her of his plan to sing in a piano bar after he retired from the active practice of law.

How wonderful for you to be able to do something you really love. I had no idea you sang. You look like a gangsta hip hop artist to me, am I right?" she said facetiously.

"Actually, I dig the old standards, but I love the selections you sang too."

"Wonderful! You can sing a song while I accompany you at the piano in the next set. That should be great fun."

"Actually I don't think your audience wants to trade in a hot babe who sings sensual songs in a slinky dress for a middle-aged amateur wanna be. Thanks, I'll pass, but I promise you that some night I'll sing for you on my home turf. Deal?"

"Deal! Now let me finish my last set and we can go for a bite to eat.

When she finished to the steady applause from the near-capacity lounge, she quickly changed into casual clothes and asked if he liked deli. In a flash, she was pulling him towards Pickles, the deli restaurant at the hotel. That was a perfect option for Jaime. They spoke energetically about music while sharing a pastrami sandwich and a large salad, which they washed down with Brown's Black Cherry Diet Soda for him and an iced tea for her.

An hour later she made an offer that panicked him.

"Would you like to stay over? I live about seven miles from here, and it's late for you to drive home at this hour.

In the split-second that he mulled over whether to be a gentleman and decline, or to satisfy his lust and accept, she added "I have a second bedroom with a queen bed that I'm sure would be comfortable, and if you want we could spend the afternoon on the beach."

"If you have an extra toothbrush and a feather pillow, how could I turn it down?"

As he entered her rented townhome, he was pleased to see that she had no cats or dogs. It wasn't that he didn't like animals. It was just that they limited one's mobility. .

She gave him an extra set of pillows and wished him a good night, but he brought her close and kissed her longingly for several seconds before he broke. "I better stop now or I won't be responsible for my actions."

"Now counselor, you know that's not a legal defense. Anyway I had a great time. Let's end the evening with our expectations still intact until our next date when we can sample each other for dessert, if you know what I mean."

That night, Jaime tossed and turned for several hours, and it wasn't because of the new bed.

On Sunday, after breakfast, they drove to the end of Ventnor City and parked. They wore their running clothes over bathing suits. They walked to the beach and ran a mile-and-a-half towards Atlantic City and back. It was a gorgeous day with hardly a cloud visible, and the humidity was modest for the end of July. They both felt they could have gone longer. They were barely able to find a spot on the beach because sunbathers were everywhere. Jaime's vision of Barbara in a two-piece was accurate. She was put together like a cartoon figure out of Playboy come to life. Jaime was a bit intimidated by her physique. He joked that he too was fit, but his genetic make-up made it impossible to have that kind of chiseled body, despite his workout routine.

They spent a few wonderfully relaxing hours soaking up the sun. Barbara warned him that she didn't like to go into the ocean beyond her ankles so they contented themselves with walking at the edge of the water.

It was a fantastic day, but Jaime wanted an early dinner so he could get at least an hour of work done before the morning. Barb picked a local Italian restaurant because it was near her place. Before they went out, Jaime felt the need to call Theresa Leyton and give her notice of Monday's events. The day would get even better because no one answered her home phone. He left a detailed message, and told her that if she wanted to be there, court would begin shortly after 1:30 PM.

Now he and Barbara could enjoy their veal saltimbocca and shrimp scampi respectively, with a small carafe of Chianti - without the worry of Leyton hanging over their evening.

"I may need to wear a girdle to get into my suit tomorrow," groaned Jaime. "I ate like I was on death row this weekend."

"I hope that doesn't mean you wear women's undergarments when you make love, because I'm not into that kind of behavior."

He assured her that he would keep his kinkiness to the bare minimum when and if the time came.

" I feel certain that the time is fast approaching."

On that promising note, Jaime kissed her goodnight and thanked her for one of the best weekends he had had in years. Barbara echoed his feelings and kissed him again for good measure.

On the ride home, he had the top down on his much-abused 2008 Saab, and he savored each moment of the last twenty- four hours. He already missed her.

Chapter 30

On Monday morning it was back to business. Jaime alerted Judge Melucci that the grand jury foreman would be handing up an indictment to his court clerk at about 11:00 AM. Jaime and the foreperson walked the two blocks to the judge's courtroom in the Hall of Justice. They handed the clerk the historic documents that would formally charge two Major League ballplayers for crimes committed on the field during a game. Jaime then asked that bench warrants (arrest warrants that originate from the judge's bench) be issued for the codefendants because of the nature of the crime. He did so despite the fact that Charles would voluntarily surrender himself after the lunch recess, but he would have his investigators execute the warrant. It was legally necessary, so warrants were issued for both men.

It didn't take long for the news to become public. A local print reporter, Renee Winkles, made it a practice to go through the indictments, which were public information, to discover any newsworthy matters. She alerted her editor as well as her friend at the AP desk. Within minutes local television affiliates were broadcasting news of the murder charges against the former hometown heroes. Grace Moore scheduled a press conference for 2:30 PM that afternoon. Conspicuously absent would be Nancy Artis, for obvious reasons.

At 1:00 PM, Theresa Leyton and her parents, Donald and Elizabeth Cox, showed up at the Prosecutor's Office asking for Jaime. They had heard about the charges on the news and were ecstatic. Jaime asked Linda Margarita, as the victim/witness coordinator, to sit with them and accompany them to court. Jaime didn't want to have to explain to them his decision to alert Charles' attorney in advance so that they would be in a position to surrender him. He had done nothing legally or ethically wrong. He was merely doing what he thought was the appropriate approach for what he considered to be a reckless manslaughter case.

At 1:30 PM, Jaime and investigators Falconetti and Arroyo arrived in Melucci's courtroom. The Leyton family was already seated. The press called the Hunter law firm for a comment on the indictment, but the team plan was to avoid a circus so the secretaries told them that they were unavailable for comment. As a result, the attendance was normal for a Monday afternoon when Tim Charles and Sean Cavanaugh entered the courtroom. The firm secured the bail contract in advance, and had the necessary money for the bondsman.

Judge Melucci's demeanor was all business when he called for order, asked the parties to place their names on the record, and asked for Jaime to describe the purpose of their appearances. Jaime asked the court to set bail on defendant Tim Charles, and the judge asked whether Jaime had a recommended amount.

"Yes, Your Honor, the State asks for a bail in the amount of $500,000 cash or bond to secure the appearance of Mr. Charles.

"What do you have to say, Mr. Cavanaugh?"

"Judge, if it pleases the court, I believe that is a reasonable amount requested by Mr. Brooks. As you may be aware, my client is a first offender with no prior history of police involvement. Although he is a permanent resident of Florida, he does have roots in this area. He is employed by the Phillies organization and still rents an apartment in Center City. The risk that he could successfully flee is extremely low because he is highly recognizable.

"Furthermore, with respect to the State's case, we will fight the charges vigorously, and we believe that the evidence towards gaining a conviction is not compelling. For those reasons, we ask the court to accept the recommendation of the State."

"Can I say something, Your Honor?" It was Theresa standing in the front row, shouting to the judge.

Judge Melucci recognized her from the various protest marches and calmly told her no, she could not speak to the issue of bail. Chagrined and angry, she reluctantly sat down again.

"Bail is not a form of punishment to keep defendants incarcerated while they await their trial. It is merely a mechanism to provide them with a monetary incentive to appear at all stages of the criminal process. In my opinion, based on the State's recommendation and for the reasons stated by counsel for the defendant, I will set bail at that amount. I will also set the date for the status/arraignment for two weeks from today. Mr. Brooks, please forward discovery and your plea offer to the defense by that date. Now, Sheriff's Officer Washington, please handcuff Mr. Charles and remand him to the county jail."

Tim's knees buckled as the officer placed him in custody. Cavanaugh placed his arm around him and told him that he would be out as soon as the jail fingerprinted and processed him in the jail. A wailing sound came from the back of the courtroom, where Lois Charles crumbled to the floor when she saw the guards take away her son. Judge Melucci was touched, and did not admonish her. Jeff Charles gave his son a thumbs-up that belied the pain and fright that he felt. As the grieving parents left the courtroom, Theresa Leyton glared at them with a look that was callously indifferent to their plight. Then she turned her attention to the prosecutor.

"Just what makes you think that $500,000 is enough bail for a murder case? That's an amount I would expect for manslaughter. Why wasn't I even consulted?"

" You have made yourself palpably clear to me on various occasions, but this was my call. He has a right to reasonable bail. In my humble opinion that amount falls in the mid-range for a factually unique homicide in this State, or any other, for that matter. Now if you will excuse me, I have some business back at the office."

"I'm not finished with you yet. What's this business about a plea offer?"

"I'm obliged to make an offer to him if he's willing to plead guilty to a charge. When I'm ready to do so, I'll listen to your input and take it into consideration."

"Well I would hope that you're going for murder, so if he wants to plead, that's fine with me. You just better not give my case away in some plea bargain."

Jaime assured her that he would call within a week with his draft proposal of an offer and hurried away before she could lean on him any further. He wanted to delegate the task of explaining the reasoning behind his plea offer, but he couldn't do that to Gary. He'd make sure Gary sat with him as a witness to the event, for his own sake and protection.

Theresa was not mollified, and her display of anger deeply worried her parents. Her mental state had begun to hit the wall. She hadn't even taken time to grieve before she took up her crusade for justice. That task had left her parents as the chief caretakers for their grandson.

The anxiety and stress were leaving her looking warn and older than her years. She was sleeping sporadically, and it was more common than not that she would get only three or four hours of sleep per night. Donald and Elizabeth offered their total support, but their daughter stopped listening to their advice years ago. All they could do was care for their grandchild while Theresa devoted herself to her cause.

Grace stood at the podium of the office library that doubled as the pressroom. Jaime stood to her left. Her statement was short and direct. She merely read the contents of the indictment to the press. She told them of the maximum sentence exposure for the two accused, and explained the concept of accomplice liability as it related to Sawyer. Then she ended with a statement that the indictment was not evidence of their guilt, and that they were presumed innocent, unless and until proven guilty beyond a reasonable doubt.

Naturally that didn't satisfy the room full of reporters. "Where is Buck Sawyer, and will you be seeking the same bail?" asked a reporter of Jaime. Grace nodded to him and Jaime merely replied that he was unaware of Sawyer's whereabouts, and that he would make his arguments in court and not in a press conference. To the countless questions about who testified to what at the grand jury and what would the plea offer be, Jaime replied that it would be unethical for him to comment on those issues. When the reporters soon realized the futility of their questions, they departed for more fertile ground. They found it in Theresa Leyton, who was waiting on the steps of the Prosecutor's Office.

"What is your reaction, Mrs. Leyton?"

"I am pleased that the people, in the form of the grand jury, got it right. I'm not so sanguine about the appointed representative of the County. It disheartens me that the bail was seemingly set low enough for Mr. Charles to get released. I'm also distressed at the very thought that the prosecutor might be considering any plea offer other than to murder." At that point, her father took her hand and led her away from reporters.

The press conference and the scene outside of the office were shown on television networks across the country. It would be the beginning of a seventy-two hour news cycle dominated by America's favorite pastime.

Grace Moore made the talk-show circuit the next day. The hosts questioned whether she or Jaime had political ambitions as their motive for the indictment. One wondered aloud if this was just an example of a runaway grand jury. None could absorb the meaning of a murder indictment from a baseball game.

More of the same criticism and skepticism was expressed by the media pundits. The prosecution was crucified for its excessive zeal in dealing with the tragedy. They argued the prosecution had abdicated their discretion to an aberrant grand jury. Some suggested that Theresa Leyton's constant pressure led prosecutors to buckle under the strain. It was claimed that they had reacted too swiftly and emotionally to a unique situation that was unlikely to occur again. What was the value of deterrence when this was only the second death in baseball's history? It wasn't as if batters were open targets for frothing-psychopathic pitchers out to win at any cost.

Moore and Jaime were virtually helpless to defend themselves because ethics rules severely limited what they could say. Fortunately, many former prosecutors did explain the likely scenarios on various evening talk shows, but public opinion was running five-to-one against the murder charge. Those opinion polls placed a heavy burden upon the already anxiety-ridden widow of Ken Leyton.

A higher percentage, 39% of the public, would have approved a manslaughter charge. In the baseball community, the chilling effect that one could face criminal charges for hitting batters led some pitchers to threaten early retirement. An anonymous survey, conducted by respected pollster Ted Feld, found that of the 750 surveys mailed to professional players, 600 replied. Of those, only 4%, or 24 players, believed that the indictments were meritorious. Many speculated that the Mets made up the bulk of that support.

Another by-product of the publicity was the occasional death threats that the Office started to receive from a few crackpot fans in the Philadelphia vicinity. Most of them were directed at Jaime. He merely shrugged them off as coming with the job, but Grace was more circumspect. She asked Nancy Artis to call in a favor. She explained that Jaime often went to a Center City piano bar to sing, and she asked that the DA send a pair of undercover detectives to protect him when he frequented the bar. The DA was more than happy to get off the hook that easily, and accepted the request without hesitation.

In other news, MLB Commissioner Wilson issued a statement modifying his prior suspension order. Wilson suspended the pair for the remainder of the season. He also indicated a willingness to revisit the issue of a potential lifetime ban if either a guilty plea or verdict were rendered. For Sawyer, it was a token gesture because no club had any interest in his managerial or coaching skills. For Charles and the Phillies organization, it was an entirely different situation.

Financially it would be a crippling blow for Charles, and for the Phillies, it meant losing their number-two starter.

The Commissioner added another item on the agenda for the policy team he appointed to study the bean ball issue. He wanted the committee to include trainers and physicians in addition to baseball personnel. Their task was to determine, if longer suspensions were given out for bean balls, would there be a corresponding effect on the balance of power in favor of hitters? If so, what countermeasures could be taken to even the playing field? This committee had the capability of radically changing the game if their suggestions were approved by the commissioner.

Chapter 31

Buck Sawyer heard of his indictment on a fishing and whitewater rafting trip on the Salmon River in Idaho. He was there just one weekend before word got to him via the lodge keeper. He hadn't fully decompressed from his grand jury drama, and now he was being sought for murder. What the fuck was happening in this country? Had everyone gone bat-shit? He called his agent and lawyer, Fred Rosen, who was licensed to practice in several states, including New Jersey.

"Who the hell is out to get me Fred? And why I'm out of a job? I may end up in some single-A league in Oklahoma making squat just to survive. I'm too old for this shit now."

"Buck, you're going to have to come up with $50,000 in cash for a bail bondsman quickly. There is no way around it. Then get on a plane and we'll surrender you to those out-of-control Jersey lawyers. In the meantime, I'll let the press know we're prepared to fight this nonsense every step of the way."

Having squandered much of his savings on his second divorce, Buck called his stock manager and placed a sell order so that he would have enough to post the bail. That night he drank himself to sleep, alternating shots of bourbon with his favorite lager.

Rosen placed a call to Jaime Brooks to discuss surrender terms and bail, but Jaime would not agree to the same bail as Tim Charles. Rosen was not known in the Camden County Prosecutor's Office, so his repeated pleas fell on deaf ears. Rosen felt a surge of dread pass through his stomach, because if he didn't convince Judge Melucci to grant the same bail, Buck would spend some unhealthy days and nights in jail.

After four days scrambling for money, Sawyer and his lawyer entered Melucci's courtroom to seek bail. Media were everywhere because Rosen had issued a statement assuring the public that his client would surrender forthwith, and fight the "alarmingly bogus charges brought by the local authorities." Jaime sought $750,000 bail, largely on the contention that Sawyer actively ordered a much younger and naïve codefendant to inflict serious injury upon Leyton which ultimately caused his death.

Rosen, playing to the press and public, remonstrated dramatically that the indictment would prove to be without merit, and that he was confident the court would find the case fatally flawed and ultimately dismiss the indictment. The argument was so over-the-top that Melucci reminded Rosen that there was no jury present, and therefore no need for his melodramatic histrionics. In concluding remarks, Rosen asked that the bail be set at $200,000. His hidden agenda was to pocket the difference between the bail sought and the bail figure requested to cover part of his fee.

Judge Melucci analyzed the factors he considered for assuring the appearance of Sawyer at trial and ruled that a higher bail for Sawyer would pose Equal Protection problems under the Constitution. Therefore he set bail at the same figure as that for Charles. He also gave him the same return date for his arraignment.

Sawyer shared the same anguish and fear felt by Charles when he was handcuffed and taken to the jail to be processed. Unlike Charles, the process did not go smoothly. There was a foul-up with the paperwork between the bondsman and the court clerk. As a result, Sawyer sat in a holding cell for six hours before his lawyer was able to rectify the confusion.

That didn't sit well with his already angst-ridden client, who had to be taken to the infirmary during the wait to be treated for a blood pressure reading of 195/110. The long delay, and the unwelcome tour of the jail facility, left Buck in a sour mood that led to some verbal abuse towards his lawyer, whom he blamed for "the royal fuck-up that landed me in the hospital."

That evening, Barbara phoned Jaime at home because she hadn't spoken to him since the day before the indictment and bail hearings.

"You promised to let me know the news. I was shocked by that vote, and my only fear is that the grand jury put you in an untenable position. I'm sorry the media has been so tough on you, but at least your boss has stood by you. I have confidence in you, Jaime, and if you want some company, just ask. By the way, you looked like a million dollars in your suit on TV."

"Well, thanks, but it was a $220 Joseph A. Banks suit, on sale. That's all my budget will allow. I'm doing fine but busy, and I apologize for not calling sooner. Issues at the office are taking up more time than I would like, but let's get together Sunday so we can spend the whole day together and talk about the case."

"I like Saturday night into Sunday better. See you at the same place?"

"You drive a hard bargain ma'am, but I'm in."

Unfortunately for their budding relationship, Jaime had to cancel the Saturday night commitment because of his on-call duties. Grace left Friday for a District Attorneys

Association meeting in Denver, which left Jaime Acting Prosecutor until her return on Thursday.

Jaime regretted the missed Saturday night opportunity with Barbara, but drove down on a rainy Sunday to spend the day with her. He was tired so they agreed to take in a remake of the Maltese Falcon that was playing at the Frank Theaters in Egg Harbor Township. There was only one Humphrey Bogart, but the new cast gave creditable performances to the updated version, which was still shot in black and white.

They brought Chinese food back to her place and washed it down with a bottle of pinot grigio. It was a perfectly satisfying day considering the weather. After some heavy duty breathing on the couch, just shy of the goal posts, Jaime headed back home for the night. They would see each other midday Thursday for the baseball game and dinner afterwards.

Chapter 32

For his part, managing partner Raymond Hunter established a defense fund for Tim Charles. Events in the Philly area were planned in several venues to rally support. Likewise, in Sarasota, Tim's old high school planned a barbeque and fish fry. Local merchants that included microbreweries and pubs would donate the food and beer, and the admission fees would go to the defense fund. Even some of Tim's elementary and high school papers and uniforms were set to be auctioned off to raise money.

Hunter also asked Jack Marino to assign a young lawyer to prepare for a motion to change the venue or location of the trial out of Camden County, on the grounds that pre-trial publicity on the case was so pervasive that Charles would not be able to get a fair trial. The legal argument would be uncomplicated, but the effort to prove the extent of the publicity would be daunting. Hundreds of articles, broadcasts, editorials, tweets and blogs would have to be researched and copied for the brief on the issue.

Meanwhile, Cavanaugh and Kemper were busy sifting through the discovery that the prosecution turned over in an effort to find holes and vulnerabilities in the state's case. They requested an expedited transcript of the grand jury testimony so that they could discover the extent of the evidence, and in hopes of finding some legal arguments to defeat the murder count.

They knew, at a minimum, they would file motions to change the venue and to dismiss the indictment. They realized they had little chance of success on the latter motion but they felt compelled to try. At best, it would allow them to find out the prosecutor's thinking on the facts, as it related to murder, because Jaime would have to lay out a road map of his strategy to rebut the defense motion.

They would also have to bring in their client to discuss the plea offer that Jaime promised would be faxed to them by the end of the day. A meeting was scheduled for Tuesday to provide Charles with all his options.

At the same time, Jaime Brooks had his hands full on Monday because he arranged for Theresa Leyton to come in for an explanation of his plea offer. They were joined by Gary Slater and Linda Margarita. He gave her essentially an hour-long seminar on the law of homicide and broke down what he thought were the weaknesses in the case.

He explained the role that sympathy would play in the trial for the 20-year-old professional, especially if he testified and came across remorseful and naïve. Jaime reiterated the relative percentages he and Gary had given for a murder verdict as well as the other prospects. He summed it up by telling her that he would be offering the maximum sentence for manslaughter, which was ten years. Jaime made it clear that under New Jersey law, Charles would have to serve eight-and-a-half years before he could be paroled. Given the risks of an acquittal, he reasoned that the plea was fair and the prison time substantial.

"Weak case, Mr. Brooks? Who do you think you're talking to? Hundreds of thousands of people saw the murder with their own eyes. I don't see how a competent prosecutor could lose this case under any circumstance!

"Sympathy for Charles"? "What about sympathy for the Leyton family? Fair, you say? To whom? Maybe to Tim Charles, but eight years for the murder of my husband is not acceptable. I won't go along with it."

"I'm going to make that recommendation to both defendants, but conditioned upon both of them pleading guilty. If I have to try one of them I may as well try them together. Unless both accept the terms, there will be a trial. If they plead, you will have your chance to voice your views to the judge before they're sentenced. That's your right, but frankly you have no right to veto my offer."

"Then I'll go directly to Grace Moore," said an increasingly agitated Leyton.

"I've already gotten her approval for the plea offers, but you can call her if it makes you feel better."

"Then I'll make an appointment with the Attorney General if need be, but I won't allow your office to tarnish my husband's life with a corrupt plea bargain."

Jaime felt he had done all he could to explain himself, but there was no middle ground for Mrs. Leyton. He had no concern that the Attorney General would intervene and question the discretion of a county office. She left more determined than when he first met her. She wanted a public trial of the issues, and he sensed that she might get what she wanted because he doubted that both men would plead guilty. Next, he had Bea fax a formal plea offer to Sean Cavanaugh and Fred Rosen. He realized that the lawyers would be unable to convince their clients to plead to such long jail terms this soon in the process. The likely day of reckoning would probably not occur until the final pre-trial conference.

Chapter 33

Tim Charles and his father Jeff, sat in their lawyers' conference room with skeptical looks on their faces.

"Are you saying my son should plead guilty to manslaughter, Mr. Hunter? Because if that's what you mean, I think we have the wrong lawyers."

"No, no, that's not what I said. Let's slow down and go over this again. We're merely advising you of what the prosecutor has agreed to recommend to the judge as a sentence if you decide to plead guilty rather than take the risk of going to trial. You know what a conviction for murder would mean. So this is Mr. Brooks' way of offering you an incentive to avoid that potentially catastrophic outcome. You're under no obligation whatsoever to accept his offer. We can counter-offer and see if he would consider taking less time."

"That's my point, sir! My son isn't going to plead guilty to anything, let alone go to jail. He's going to go back next season and do what he does best, and that's winning ball games."

"Dad, let's hear what Mr. Cavanaugh has to say. I'm the one who will have to do the time if I lose at trial."

"Tim, this offer is something that you need to carefully consider. We aren't able to give guarantees of a certain result. You never know what twelve strangers on a jury will think. Obviously at least twelve of the grand jurors felt there was enough in the case to charge you with murder. Now do I believe you will be convicted of that? Probably not, but I can't rule it out completely. We are more than capable and ready to take this to trial, if that's what you want. But if I can get Jaime Brooks to come down to maybe six years rather than ten, is that something you would consider?"

"If I did that, my career might be over. I need time to think it through. I know it's my responsibility for what happened, and I feel like I should pay somehow. But spending five years in jail for something I didn't want to happen? That's just not right either. Can't I do community service or house arrest? It's hard enough to know that I killed a man. I have to live with that guilt and shame for the rest of my life. I can't believe this is happening."

"The prosecutor can't really come down below five because that's the minimum for manslaughter. His offer is actually very reasonable, given the fact that a jury could compromise at aggravated manslaughter. That carries up to a thirty-year prison term.

"My biggest concern is that you have told us that you intended to throw at his chin. If you admit that to a jury, you may very well be admitting to at least manslaughter. Now you don't need to decide this today, or even in the next few weeks, but it's something you need to think about. I wish I had better news to give you, but we're all working in unchartered area with these facts."

Jeff Charles wanted to know what else the firm planned for his son's defense, and he was assured that motions to dismiss would be filed. Kemper wanted the two to provide a list of potential character witnesses who would be willing to testify at trial about Tim's character for honesty and non-violence. He explained to them that a jury would be entitled to acquit Tim just on the basis of his character witnesses, if the jury was impressed with them. That evidence alone was enough to cast a reasonable doubt on the indictment.

Hunter told them that there was one more item that he wished to discuss. He had hired a pollster to track public sentiment in several New Jersey counties about whether the indictment was legitimate in their minds, and whether they watched Phillies' baseball games. They would use that information to decide which counties would be more favorable as locations if they chose to make a motion to change the venue or location of the trial out of Camden County based on the pre-trial publicity.

Ordinarily, it was the very rare case that lent itself to such a motion. The defendant had the burden to prove to the judge, by clear and convincing evidence, that a fair and impartial jury couldn't be had in the original county because of pervasive, inflammatory emotions sparked by publicity.

"This may be one of those cases that would get us a change in venue. The problem we have is the admonition to be careful of what you wish for, because you may get it," said Cavanaugh.

Kemper added that he checked and found that SNY, which carries the Mets' games, is seen in 10 of the 21 counties in New Jersey. "Those counties are largely in the north, but it is also seen in Mercer, Ocean, and Monmouth. We can therefore eliminate those counties from our wish list because presumably they would be Mets' fans and unsympathetic to you, Tim. That's what Sean meant earlier. We don't want to find ourselves in a position to fight for a change in counties, only to have the prosecutor push the judge to move it to a county that is in Mets' territory."

"It's the old double edged sword quandary," said Hunter. "We could be worse off if we win. That's why we 'll wait for the pollster's results, but I'm inclined to move forward with the motion because we can always withdraw it later".

"Okay gentlemen, I feel more assured that you have a strategy for my son and aren't just looking to have him plead guilty. His mother would not survive it if he had to go to prison. Do you need Tim for anything else?"

"Not at the moment, but I will want Tim to be there when we present our motion to dismiss in a few weeks. It will give you the benefit of insight into the murder statute and what facts the state will rely upon to prosecute you. Don't look so terrified, Tim, you won't testify. You can only watch and listen to legal arguments. There won't be anyone to testify; it's based solely on the grand jury transcript," said Kemper, reassuringly.

Hunter returned to his office to greet a new client, while Sean and Hank did a postmortem on the meeting.

"It looks like the kid's father will pressure him to go to trial, and I'm not very optimistic about his chances to walk out a free man, even the great Sean Cavanaugh is trying the case" said Kemper. "Will you ask Jaime to come down on his offer?"

"No, because I know he'll say that he isn't going to negotiate against himself. He'll wait until we come to him with an ironclad promise that our client would plead to a lower number. Besides, we need to find out what Sawyer plans to do when we see them at the arraignment. I think we better get ready for a trial, but I would rather we stay in county. Aside from the lost travel time if we move, my gut tells me that Camden County is closest in proximity to Philly and likely has the most supportive fan base of any other county for the Phillies. We need that advantage."

"I hope, said Kemper, there's something in the grand jury transcript that gives me a credible argument to dismiss the indictment, but knowing Jaime as we do, it's unlikely. I'll probably be left with boilerplate arguments that have no chance of success. Maybe that will get the attention of the father and start them thinking it's time to plead. It's a good deal for him given the alternatives, but it ultimately is the kid's decision. I won't push back hard if he says no."

Chapter 34

Jaime advised Grace while she was at her conference that he planned to take the afternoon off to go to the game with Barbara. Grace would be back at the office by then, so she wished him and the Phillies well. Jaime, however, was second-guessing his decision to take a half-day off. He was swamped with personnel issues. He spent the better part of the morning at an administrative hearing for a young investigator who was arrested for DUI.

He had to excuse himself early from a meeting with an Assistant United States Attorney, federal drug agents, and his own Narcotics Unit about gang violence in Camden so he could pick up Barbara at the Collingswood subway station. As much as he looked forward to seeing her, he felt embarrassed that it necessitated him leaving an important joint venture. The competition among rival drug gangs had reached epic proportions in the City, resulting in a twenty percent increase in the murder rate for the same time period as the prior year. Federal assistance was needed to curtail the rising tide of violence, so a special task force was charged with the responsibility of using all of the tools and resources of the federal government to aid in the fight.

Nevertheless, he had already broken one date, and he wasn't about to do it again. He changed at the office into a polo shirt and golf shorts, and took a clean shirt with him to change for dinner. He found her standing outside the station, wearing a Phillies' cap, shorts, tank top, and a pair of Sketchers. She held a small bag that contained a sundress and sandals for dinner. She looked like she was in her late twenties, and Jaime set aside any guilt about leaving the office. She hugged him tightly and kissed him eagerly. He was instantly aroused.

"It's good to see you. I've missed you, Barb."

"I know, I can feel you've missed me. Maybe we should skip the game and go to your place. I'll walk in front of you so you don't attract attention."

Jaime could feel his face turning red, but he laughed along with her. They were getting to that point where they felt comfortable trading sexual jibes and double entendres. They walked holding hands to Jaime's car and caught up on the news in their lives. It was all so natural that Jaime felt he had known her for years. He left all thought of the office in the recesses of his mind and drove to Citizens Bank Park. The tight division race with the Nationals and the Dollar Hot Dog Day translated into a-capacity crowd.

Jaime did allow for one precaution because of the prior threats. Although he didn't think anyone would recognize him, he wore sunglasses and an old Phillies' hat to shield his appearance. They both decided to lunch on hot dogs and beer rather than eat a heavy steak sandwich from Tony Luke's, because they would be eating a nice dinner afterwards.

The game was totally satisfying. Ron Barkowsky had the Washington hitters look like minor-leaguers. He relied less on his renowned high heat (hence his moniker "The Barber"), perhaps because of the Charles case, but stymied them with his floating knuckle-curve. Meanwhile, the offense scored seven runs, largely as a result of a pinch hit grand slam by Jim Lynch in the seventh inning, which put the game safely in the win column. The Phillies retained their first place status, but the Nationals sat only two back, followed by the Braves at three-and-a-half. The luckless Mets were nine back and were all but finished in the minds of the experts.

After the game, he took her to the Zinc Bistro on South Eleventh Street, a cozy and romantic French-style restaurant. Afterwards, Jaime surprised Barbara by bringing her to a bar a few short blocks away. He got a warm reception from some of the regulars and the bartender, and Jaime explained that this was where he came to sing during the intermissions from the live group.

"Sing for me tonight won't you?"

"That's how I intend to get into your boudoir, madam."

"That may depend of how well you sing Let me hear you first, and then I'll let you know if you can score "

When the trio took their break, the leader introduced Jaime to the audience. He sat at the piano and winked at her. She hadn't known he played. True to himself, he started out with "Fly Me To The Moon," then changed moods a bit with "Girl From Ipanema." Lastly, he sang directly to Barbara with the classic Sinatra version of "The Way You Look Tonight." She couldn't have been more excited by his sexy upbeat rendition.

"You've been holding out on me. Why didn't you tell me how good you are? And you play piano too? We could become the new Faith Hill and Tim McGraw."

"Not so fast sweetheart. I think the wine just hit you."

"No really, you were so sexy. I wanted to climb on the piano. I had such seductive thoughts, it even made me blush."

"I think it's time we headed to my place so I can make your wish come true."

As they made their way to the front door, two drunken mugs stood in front of them blocking their exit.

"Aren't you that asshole prosecutor I saw on television?" asked one guy who looked like he played linebacker for the Eagles.

" Yeah you're that dude that wants to put Tim Charles away. I've seen you too. You think you're a hot shot don't you? Why don't you step outside and leave your little honey with my pal. I'll teach you something about *Philly* justice."

Jaime made no move to go outside so the linebacker type guy grabbed Jaime by the neck and pushed him towards the exit. Thoughts quickly passed through his mind. He thought of how impotent he felt, and how he would look after this mule beat the crap out of him. He wondered if he would even be in condition to try the Charles case. *How long did it take for broken legs to heal?*

Jaime was hoping against hope that Barb was going to kick off her sandals, assume a karate position and proclaim that she had a black belt in the martial arts. If not, it looked as if he was going to end up at Jefferson Hospital rather than in a boudoir. Shockingly, Barbara made no move other than to grab his arm. He was grateful she hadn't held his hand because it was beading up in pearls of sweat. The hulk picked Jaime up by the throat and opened the door when a calm but firm voice interrupted.

"There a problem here?" Jaime glanced to his right and saw a younger version of Clint Eastwood standing next to an attractive blonde at the bar. Barbara noticed them come in after Jaime and Barbara had arrived.

The two clowns seemed to relish the chance to add this Good Samaritan to their list of assault victims when Clint pulled out the largest gold badge that Jaime had ever seen.

The words HOMICIDE DETECTIVE were clearly visible from anywhere in the restaurant.

"This is Detective Beth Glenn, and I'm Detective Neal Dingott These people are friends of ours. Now I strongly suggest you two call it a night, unless you want to be taken in to meet some of my brothers and sisters at the Department". Detective Dingott pulled back his linen sports jacket to reveal his police-issued revolver as if to emphasize the futility of rebuffing his request.

The two dirtballs sobered up pretty quickly and their machismo shrunk like testicles after a cold dip in the ocean. They meekly left the bar without even a glare towards Jaime. Glenn and Dingott offered to walk Jaime and Barb to his car. Along the short walk, Jaime learned of Grace's call to the DA for help. He was grateful that he had told Grace of his plans, because the detectives had followed them from the ballpark and thereafter to the restaurant and piano bar.

"We're happy to act as your security Mr. Brooks anytime you get the urge to spend time in our City. Just make sure you call me." With that, Beth gave Jaime her card and wished him well in the future. As Jaime and Barbara got in his car, Barbara asked,

"Had enough excitement for one night?"

"Actually, that was a big turn-on for me. I like getting scared out of my mind before sex."

"I was hoping that didn't spoil the mood. I'm still up for a late night snack."

That night Barbara slept over Jaime's. At least she stayed in his bed. They didn't get much sleep, but it was the best case of insomnia either of them ever had.

Chapter 35

The arraignment of Charles and Sawyer had taken place three weeks earlier. The lawyers had entered "not guilty" pleas to the indictment and waived the right of the judge to read the charges against the defendants. Judge Thomas Johnson was assigned to try the case by Judge Melucci.

Judge Johnson was a former Deputy Attorney General and was well respected. He granted a joint request by counsel for a four-week continuance of the status conference because the grand jury transcripts had just arrived. Briefs were to be filed in two weeks, and the motions were to be argued on the fourth week. The time had come for a critical test, especially for Buck Sawyer.

On this late September Friday afternoon, Kemper had the task of arguing the motion to dismiss. Sawyer's lawyer joined in the motion but filed a separate brief. In the courtroom Jeff and Lois Charles sat as did Theresa Leyton amidst the capacity audience. Tim went over to his former manager before the start of court and wished him well.

There was no animosity felt by Tim towards Buck. Tim knew that he had made his own decision and would have to live with the consequences. But Tim was astonished by Buck's appearance. In the last few months, it seemed that he aged years. His stomach pulled at his suit jacket with the extra inches around his waist. His face had a yellow pallor that Tim never saw before. Buck was clearly unnerved by the ordeal, and his eyes looked bloodshot and tired. Both men stood as the judge entered the courtroom.

"Mr. Rosen, I'll hear your argument on your motion as to the legal sufficiency of the murder indictment", said Johnson.

Kemper knew he had little chance to win this preliminary battle, which was purely a matter directed at the legal sufficiency of the murder charge.

Fred Rosen was confident in his argument that there was insufficient evidence presented to the grand jury to support a murder charge, and that therefore Sawyer could not be an accomplice to murder. While conceding that the state presented evidence from several witnesses of Sawyer's expressed intent to seek retaliation, he argued that did not translate into a purpose to cause serious bodily injury. To be murder, the defendant must have shared the purpose that serious bodily injury should occur and that death ultimately resulted.

"Your Honor, there is simply not enough evidence to draw the conclusion that my client had any knowledge that serious bodily injury would result, much less that death would result from that injury. As Your Honor fully knows, serious bodily injury means 'injury that creates a substantial risk of death or which causes serious permanent disfigurement, or a protracted loss or impairment of a bodily organ or member.' It's our contention that, even if a jury finds that my client called for retaliation from his players, throwing a baseball at a batter is not practically certain to cause serious bodily injury. In fact, I ask this court to take judicial notice that only a fraction of the injuries to a hit batter lead to any serious injury.

"Therefore, since there was no purpose or knowledge on Mr. Sawyer's part that serious bodily injury should occur when he directed retaliation, he could not have shared a purpose to cause serious bodily injury and thus cannot be found guilty of murder."

It was an interesting argument that many observers believed had some merit, but Jaime was ready for rebuttal.

Jaime pointed to several portions of the grand jury transcript in which Sawyer had specifically said to Doug Adams that he wanted a Met player placed on the disabled list for what happened to Butterworth and Colby Green. There were also statements that he wanted to even the playing field for the loss of Butterworth.

" Your Honor, on page 24 of the testimony, Sawyer said at a team meeting that he wanted an eye for an eye, and I quote 'I don't care if he gets beaned in the head.' Later he says 'I hope that someone sticks the ball in his ear.' If that isn't calling for serious bodily injury, I don't know what further proof anyone could want."

"Even if he said that he wanted to put a player on the disabled list, that doesn't equate with serious bodily injury," shot back Rosen. "Look at Butterworth's injury. A broken finger may hamper a ballplayer and put him on the DL, but that isn't the same as serious bodily injury. A player could tweak his back ducking out of the way of a pitch and be placed on the fifteen-day DL."

"But the DL can be as long as sixty days, not just for fifteen. Sawyer didn't specify the length of the stay on the DL," said Jaime. "Certainly any injury that could put a player on the DL for sixty days could be considered serious bodily injury. Look how long Justin Morneau was disabled by a concussion. He missed most of the seasons in 2010 and 2011."

"Gentlemen, I have heard enough, and I'm ready to rule," said Judge Johnson. "The circumstances surrounding the beaning, including Mr. Sawyer's stated dissatisfaction with the initial retaliation by Adams towards Mr. Luther Wynne, and the words of encouragement, if not flat-out orders to retaliate by placing a Mets' player on the disabled list, convinces this court that the grand jury had at least some evidence from which they could conclude that Sawyer was seeking serious bodily injury. I am satisfied that even if Leyton had been placed on a fifteen-day list, the loss of work due to an injury for fifteen days from a thrown fastball would be enough in my mind to satisfy the statute's terms. Accordingly, the motion as to Sawyer is denied."

Theresa Leyton sat ramrod tall and nodded her head in earnest agreement with the court's ruling.

Sawyer's heartbeat, as reflected by the rapid pulsations in the arteries of his neck, seemed to be pounding out of his chest. He felt like he would faint. He shot his lawyer an angry and disgusted look. Rosen, for his part, would not accept the decision.

"This court has made a grievous mistake and placed my client in jeopardy of facing a life sentence. I ask that the court reconsider its decision and permit further argument."

"Sir, if the Appellate Division is willing to halt these proceedings and issue a stay of the trial pending your appeal, more power to you. Until then, we will continue."

A chastised Rosen resumed his seat and tried to reassure his client that this was only the first battle in a long war, but Sawyer wasn't buying. For the first time, he actually began to consider the plea offer. If he could get the prosecutor down to six or seven years, he would still have some decent years left in his life. He asked Rosen to get the judge to take a recess so he could talk to him. Judge Johnson granted the request because Kemper had not yet begun his second argument.

"I want you to ask the prosecutor if he'll take five years. I can't take the risk. This is killing me. I'd rather do the five years and still have a life left than risk a murder conviction. I can't believe I'm saying this shit, but you haven't done dick for me yet, and I don't expect anything different at trial."

"That's gratitude for you. Didn't I keep you out of jail?"

"Yeah, it only cost me $50,000 that I'll never see again, and that's beside the legal fees. I don't know if I can afford a trial. Just ask him, will you? Tell him I'll testify for the state against the kid if I have to."

"You're crazy, Buck. If you are convicted of anything, it will be reckless manslaughter and the most you can get is ten years."

"Just do what I tell you," spat Buck, "or I'll get a lawyer that does what I ask."

Rosen approached Jaime, and the two went into the judge's hallway to talk. Rosen conveyed the counter-offer from his client.

"Look, it's an admission of guilt that will make your victim happy, and then you only have one defendant for the jury to focus on. Your case will be stronger with Buck, too."

"Sorry Fred, it's a non-starter. First of all, he has nothing to offer in the way of what was in Charles' mind when he threw the pitch. Secondly, I would have no credibility with a jury if I were to go into court and ask them to convict Charles of murder while at the same time recommending just five years for Sawyer on manslaughter. I would rather try them together and let the jury decide their relative degrees of guilt. I appreciate your client's offer, but I said I would only let the case go if both pled guilty."

"You're screwing me over here but I get it. Do me a favor and don't broadcast our offer. I wouldn't want the press, or even Charles, to know.

"You got it."

Lois Charles sat in the first row praying with her rosary beads. She saw how defeated Buck Sawyer appeared by the decision from the judge, and she worried that her son would soon share the same fate.

Theresa Leyton was concerned when she saw the prosecutor and one of the lawyers go into the hallway. Her instincts told her something was brewing. When Jaime returned, she approached him and asked what the talk was about. She had a right to know if Jaime intended to make a new offer, so he explained the substance of the talks and his unequivocal rejection.

"Good! I'm glad he's sweating it out. You must not give in for any reason, do you understand me?" she asked quite heatedly. Jaime was alarmed at her tone and demeanor but knew that any further discussion would be counter-productive. He merely nodded and walked back to the courtroom.

Court resumed, and it was time for Kemper to make his effort at eviscerating the murder charge. He knew it was for naught at this stage, but he advocated as if he were preaching the indisputable truth. He argued that there were no direct statements attributable to Tim Charles concerning any murderous intent. If anything, his actions and words after Leyton was struck demonstrate there was no purposeful or knowing attempt to strike Leyton in the head region.

"Your Honor, my client immediately fell to his haunches and placed his glove over his head in anguish. That was the testimony. He immediately told umpire Mike Kastle that he didn't mean to hit the batter. He said it within seconds of the event. There was no time to fabricate a defense. It was an honest gut reaction that he expressed, and it should not be ignored. Where is the evidence that my client caused the death on purpose, or that he threw the deadly pitch with a practical certainty that it would kill Leyton? There is none. I respectfully ask the court to dismiss the murder count, or, alternatively, we would consent to an amendment of the charge to reckless manslaughter."

Lois almost crushed her beads in her fingers as the judge began to discuss the law. The members of the press took copious notes. Sawyer's crimson face was in sharp contrast to the pale pallor of his codefendant who waited for the decision that would determine his fate.

"While there is no direct evidence of the intent of Mr. Charles, this court finds abundant circumstantial evidence for a jury to find that he knowingly caused serious bodily injury that resulted in death. The circumstances of the first two games of the series, the fight between Herrera and Adams over the failure to satisfactorily hit Wynne, the peer pressure that Charles felt from other players as well as the manager, the fact that he threw up before that particular start, the closed door club meeting that excoriated the failure to retaliate and the need to honor the code of the team, in conjunction with the most compelling fact of all, namely the fact that Charles shook off the slider signal and threw a 95 mph fastball, all taken together could lead a grand jury to infer that Charles thought about retaliation in advance and executed the deadly pitch knowing what the result could bring.

"In short, there was a *prima facie* case for murder presented against the defendant Charles at the grand jury. The motions to dismiss are hereby denied. If there are no further items on the docket, court is adjourned."

The press battled each other to get out of court and pass the story on to their producers and editors. The Charles family stood somberly with Tim at Kemper's side, while Hank gave the best pep talk he could to keep the client upbeat about the future. It didn't seem to have the desired effect on Lois, who seemed not to comprehend what was happening. She stared at Theresa Leyton with eyes devoid of anger, but rather as if she were appealing from one who was about to lose a loved one to one who had already lost one. If she were expecting an empathetic response, she found none in the eyes of Theresa. Instead she saw a look of fiery disdain and utter contempt.

Kemper pulled Tim aside and assured him that he expected to lose the argument at this stage. Tim was shaken and practical.

"Do you think I should take the plea offer while it's still open?"

"I think it's something to discuss with your family. We may be able to get Mr. Brooks to come down a year or two on his offer. Take the weekend to think it over and let Sean or myself know."

Outside the Hall of Justice, a camera crew caught up with Leyton and asked for her reaction.

"I'm gratified that this judge will permit the murder charge to go forward. Both Sawyer and Charles will ultimately face a jury for what they have done. Mr. Brooks has already turned down Sawyer's request to plead guilty to manslaughter, and I look forward to the day when a jury hands down a guilty verdict to murder. Anything less would be a slap in the face to me and my husband's memory."

Needless to say, those words would cause a storm of protest from the defense lawyers. The words would be spread in newspapers and Internet articles throughout the country, and be read by even those who lived in drug houses in Camden City.

The fate of Chris Meyer did not improve in the several weeks since he fled the authorities. His fantasy of moving up in the ranks of his gang fell flat. He was at the nadir of his young life. Instead of reducing his debt to Malik and the organization, he found that he still owed virtually the same $5,000. The gang members turned him into a virtual indentured servant. Rather than reduce his obligation by $100 per week, upper management deducted room and board. That netted him $25 a week. This was going nowhere real fast, and Meyer knew he must use his creativity to find a way out of his abyss.

Chris kept abreast of the Charles case since his days at the grand jury. He had read the papers, including articles that concentrated on the efforts of Theresa Leyton to influence the outcome of the case. He was struck by the intensity of her mission. She was quoted as saying that the conspiracy to kill her husband by the manager and pitcher were worthy of the death penalty. She railed against the New Jersey legislature that abolished the death penalty, and vowed to campaign for a state constitutional amendment to reinstate it.

Chris was also aware that odds-makers were betting on an acquittal for Charles at trial. He wondered just how far Mrs. Leyton would go to seek revenge, especially if the courts turned their back on her. The kernel of a pathway to financial freedom was growing in his mind for several days. He boldly ignored the risk of arrest and traveled to the Hall of Justice in Camden. He got there early Monday morning after reading about Leyton's impromptu press conference the prior Friday. He sat in his car waiting for Theresa to arrive.

She drove into an outdoor parking lot across the street from the courthouse. He waited until she entered the building, and then walked over to her car so he could write down her license tag number. Thus he committed the first overt act towards his new venture.

Chapter 36

Bright and early on Saturday morning, Fred Rosen broke his golf plans and went to the office. He saw the Leyton interview and was outraged. He sat at his computer and prepared a motion for a gag order to prevent any future highly prejudicial statements from Leyton, or anyone else, from tainting a future jury. Were potential jurors to know that a defendant tried to plead guilty, it would be very difficult to wipe that from their minds. How could the presumption of innocence be maintained if a jury knew in advance that a defendant wanted to plead guilty? He also asked that any trial date be set months in advance to diminish the lasting effects of Leyton's prejudicial remarks. He faxed the motion to the court and the litigants.

At Hunter's firm, the three criminal lawyers met for a working breakfast. They independently decided to ask for a gag order, but when they saw the continuance request, they questioned whether that was their best strategy. Unlike most defense lawyers, who try to delay trials in hopes that the state's witnesses will move, disappear, or have their memories fade, Charles' legal team wanted a speedy trial. He was banned for the current season. If he were acquitted, he wanted the verdict quickly so that the commissioner would have time to consider reinstating him for the next season. The legal team agreed to join in the gag order but oppose the continuance requested by Rosen. In addition, they decided not to file a change of venue motion.

The pollster hired by Hunter provided her results. A higher percentage of Camden County residents felt the murder indictment was unwarranted than did the other counties polled. While Atlantic, Burlington, and Gloucester Counties heavily viewed the Phillies' games, Camden still had a significant advantage in viewer percentages and in terms of antagonism toward the prosecution. While the lawyers considered filing the motion to protect themselves against any possible legal malpractice claim, they felt that the poll gave them a sound basis to forego the motion to change venue.

The following Friday, the parties returned to court. Conspicuously absent was Buck Sawyer, who waived his right to be present at the motion. Rosen explained to the court that Sawyer's blood sugar level was at the 170 mark, which made him too tired to come to court for the motions. His doctor advised that he rest, since the stress and lack of exercise were likely contributors to his diabetes condition. There was no legal necessity for Sawyer to attend, so the argument ensued without him. Judge Johnson needed very little in the way of legal argument to agree to a gag order preventing any of the parties from discussing any of the court proceedings or plea negotiations with the press.

"The term 'party' shall include the family of the defendants as well as the victims. And let me admonish Mrs. Leyton specifically for her conduct. Mrs. Leyton, I can appreciate that your zeal and emotion can sometimes cloud your thinking, but making statements to the press such as the ones you made last Friday can only hurt your cause. I may have to continue the trial and keep you from getting the closure you want if there are additional prejudicial statements made by you. Do I make myself perfectly clear?"

"Are you saying that you can prevent me from talking about my case? That is a violation of my rights!" shot back Theresa.

"I'm saying you can talk to your family and friends, but not to members of the media. And yes, I can order you to refrain from speaking to the media. Please don't try to test my order, Mrs. Leyton, because I can hold you in contempt of this court."

"That would be perfect! Make me the victim twice. Isn't it enough that my husband was murdered?"

"Mr. Brooks, please take Mrs. Leyton into the corridor and explain my ruling and report back to me."

"I don't need him to explain anything to me, Judge. I'll do what you say, but under protest."

"That's fine, as long as you obey my order. Now let's proceed."

On the argument to postpone the trial for several months, the Charles legal team found themselves on the same side as the prosecution. Jaime wanted to move the trial along, as did Cavanaugh. Rosen presented a packet of news media articles, tweets. newspaper articles, blogs, and magazines concerning Leyton's statements to support his motion to delay the trial.

"Your Honor, there are literally scores of articles that have permeated this county over the last week. There is no way my client can get a fair trial in the foreseeable future, and I suggest that the matter be carried until after the New Year to monitor the level of publicity."

Jaime argued that there would never be a perfect time to schedule the case because of the nature of the defendants and the continual press interest. While he conceded the current flap would pose a problem in selecting an unbiased jury, he argued that in a month it would be old news. Cavanaugh agreed with Jaime's view of the publicity and urged the court not to delay the trial. A further delay would not necessarily lead to a jury pool free of opinions on the issues in the case, he argued.

"I am concerned about the prejudice to Mr. Sawyer, but I am in agreement with the State and defendant Charles," said Judge Johnson. "There is no guarantee that time alone will remedy the danger of prejudice. I am of the opinion that a meticulous jury selection process will enable the court and attorneys to weed out any juror who may have preconceived notions about the guilt or innocence of these defendants. All of us will provide questions to the jurors, and then we will interrogate them individually to test their knowledge of the case as well as any fixed opinions that they may have. Now, is there anything else before I set a trial date?"

"Your Honor, we will have some evidentiary issues to discuss, as well as our request for certain jury charges that we want the court to give the jury at the end of the trial," said Cavanaugh.

"That's fine. How does November 2nd look as the day for argument on those issues? We'll have an off day for elections on Tuesday. We can begin to pick the jury on Wednesday the 4th. That should leave ample time for trial of the case before the Christmas holidays."

"That is fine with Mr. Charles," agreed Cavanaugh.

"The State will be ready, Your Honor," echoed Jaime.

"I respectfully dissent, but we will be ready, Your Honor" said Rosen.

Chapter 37

County Detectives briefed Jaime on their visit with Clark Draper. He was a college student at Florida State with a baseball scholarship. He seemed credible to the detectives and was willing to appear voluntarily at a trial against Charles. With the assistance of the Florida authorities they had obtained the medical records for Bart Thompson the player that was struck by Charles' pitch. The record did reflect a broken jaw. That was the good news. The other news was ambivalent at best. His detectives had also found Thompson from the address on his medical records.

He still worked in Sarasota and lived at home. Thompson told the detectives a slightly different story. He confirmed the fact that Charles had been the pitcher. He even admitted some showboating on his part after the home run. But Thompson said he had always been fed a steady diet of inside pitches because he couldn't hit them. When he connected he was so startled he just gazed at the ball until it reached the stands for a home run. So in Thompson's next at bat, he expected Charles to throw him something outside Thompson said he may have been leaning over the plate as he got ready for an outside pitch when he was struck in the jaw. Thompson said he couldn't be sure if Charles had tried to hit him or whether he got hit because he leaned into the pitch.

Jaime was torn. He had a key cooperating witness in Draper who could be very helpful to prove that Charles intended to hit Leyton based on the Thompson incident. On the other hand, he had the recipient of the broken jaw accepting partial responsibility. Still, Jaime reasoned, he had an admission by Charles to Draper of his actual intent versus Thompson's opinion. Jaime knew he could keep out that opinion based on the rules of evidence. On balance he decided he'd use Draper at trial. As a result, he faxed the statements over to the defense teams as was his duty.

Upon receipt of the potentially damaging information, Kemper called his private investigator Harry Cain to arrange to go to Florida to interview Draper and to dig up anything to use to impeach his credibility. Cain was working on another case but promised to do so before jury selection.

The weeks flew by for the defense, and the day of pre-trial arguments on evidentiary issues was upon them. Cavanaugh sat in his office waiting for Tim to arrive. They had two hours before court arguments at 10:30. Kemper took a second seat to Cavanaugh because the trial would fall on Sean's shoulder. Despite their collective belief in Tim's character, the Draper letter gave them pause. Most of their criminal clientele swore they were innocent until the day they got the plea deal they wanted. Cavanaugh wondered if Tim fell into that category. No one had confronted Tim about the issue. They were waiting for Harry Cain's findings. In fact, they had not even told Tim about the letter from Draper.

But then Harry Cain sauntered into the office with a broad smile. "I've got some goodies from Florida that you might like".

"Good timing-Tim's due any minute so let's have it."

"I had a little chat with Mr. Draper after I did some digging in town. I spoke to some former teammates, and the baseball coach. It seems that the coach and the high school administration found out about Draper's homophobic directive to the team over summer break. They all agreed that Draper's conduct was a poor example for someone who was the team captain. Not only did they strip him of that honor, but they made Tim the captain. How's that for a motive to fabricate against our client"?

"That's very good news. You have more?" asked Cavanaugh.

"Actually there is. I asked Draper how it would look if the whole country learned about his homophobia on national television. See it turns out that Draper wants to go to law school. I suggested that the news might not help him in his career goals.

"And"?

"Well, let's just say he might feel differently about coming all the way to Camden, New Jersey. Oh, one more thing.-that kid Thompson? Turns out the next time he faced Charles in a summer league, Tim wouldn't throw the ball anywhere close to him-all outside pitches. "

"I'd say the first report 'makes my day'. I'm not quite sure what to make of Thompson's statement. But good job! I'll fax Jaime Thompson's name as one of <u>our</u> witnesses. That should stir things up a bit and neutralize Draper. There's no legal duty to tell Jaime about Draper's motive to lie about our client. We'll keep that to ourselves."

Tim arrived just as Cain was leaving and Cavanaugh summarized the Draper scenario. While Thompson's testimony might neutralize Draper, Cavanaugh realized it could work both ways. The jury could either believe Charles threw outside pitches because Thompson had homered off an inside pitch previously, or they could believe he did so because he was afraid of hitting him again. The latter option would help the defense but the former would be useless. So if Draper did testify, the trial would be more complex and it would impact on the most significant item that Cavanaugh needed to discuss with his client: whether Tim would testify on his own behalf.

Typically with a client who had no record of convictions, there would be very few reasons, if any, not to let him testify. Tim was a nice looking young man who would present himself well to a jury. He was sincere, modest, and he had not made any statements to the police that were of an incriminating nature. Most importantly, he needed to humanize himself for the jury. He was not merely a kid who threw a baseball. He was a brother, a son, a churchgoer, a teammate, and a fine young man.

"Tim my biggest concern for you, if you testify, is that you could be putting a nail into your own coffin. I'm not as concerned that the prosecutor will hurt you on cross-examination as I am that your own testimony could bury you if you tell the jury what you told us in the past. If you admit that you deliberately threw a 95 mph fastball at Leyton's head - because of Sawyer and peer pressure - you may very well be admitting you are guilty of reckless manslaughter. That in itself is conduct that the jury may find was so risky that there is simply no justification, in the context of the series, to shield you from criminal liability. All I will have left to argue is some form of jury nullification: forget the law and show sympathy. Legally, the law prevents me from doing that. I'd have to somehow ask the jury to disregard the evidence without telling them outright to nullify the law and the facts."

"I kinda understand what you're saying, Mr. Cavanaugh, but I won't lie. I screwed up enough already, and while I sure don't want to go to jail, I don't want to make things worse by committing perjury. That pitch to Thompson just got inside too much. Draper's version is bull. I'll look the jury in the eye and tell them so. But If you think it's better not to testify, I'm all for it. I'm not that keen on the idea of testifying in front of all those people anyway."

"I'm really torn by this decision" said Cavanaugh," but what happens later this morning may help me decide the best course. If I can get into evidence what you told the umpire *after* you hit Leyton, we'll have a defense to argue without you having to take the stand. We point out to the jury that what you said immediately after Leyton got hit is the best evidence of what was in your mind *before* you threw the pitch. Then you can avoid the prosecutor's questions about whether you felt peer pressure to do something for the team."

"Let's make our way over to Camden so we don't get off on the wrong foot," said Kemper.

In the courtroom, Sean Cavanaugh addressed his most pressing evidentiary issue to Judge Johnson. He showed film of the moments after the ball struck Leyton. Then he quoted from umpire Mike Kastle's grand jury testimony regarding Tim's demeanor when he uttered the words *"I didn't mean to hit him, Mike."*

"Your Honor," said Cavanaugh, "this is a textbook example of the excited utterance exception to the hearsay rule. The statement occurred literally within a few seconds of the pitch striking Mr. Leyton, as Your Honor can see on the film. It occurred immediately after the startling event, and my client certainly had no time to deliberate a defense or to fabricate one. It was a statement from his heart and not said by someone who was anticipating that judicial proceedings would ensue from the beaning. Because it is a classic exception to the hearsay rule, it should be admissible as evidence regarding the state of mind of my client at the time of the event."

Sawyer's lawyer also joined in the motion. If Charles had no intention to hit the batter, Sawyer could not be an accomplice to an act that was not done on purpose, and therefore could not be guilty of murder.

"Prosecutor, what is your position?" asked the judge.

"As Your Honor is well aware, the law regards statements by defendants outside of the courtroom offered in their own defense as inherently unreliable. It does so because a defendant can say anything to other people after a crime that puts him in a favorable light, and he simply disavows any criminal intent. It's notoriously unreliable, and there's no way that I can cross-examine him on that statement if he doesn't take the stand."

"Didn't you essentially agree with Mr. Cavanaugh at the grand jury, when you allowed Mr. Kastle to testify to what the defendant told him at the time?" asked Johnson.

"I did so because a grand juror asked the question, and I didn't want to make hard-and-fast rules with the jurors. This is different Your Honor because it is at trial, where the rules of evidence strictly apply."

"That is true, but the rules do recognize certain reliable hearsay statements, such as the exception Mr. Cavanaugh relies upon. Frankly, I can think of no better example of an excited utterance than the one before me this morning. In this court's opinion, the statement by the defendant has all the earmarks of reliability, and I will allow it to be introduced by the defense for the jury to consider its worth as reflective of his state of mind."

Sean patted Tim on the back and Tim turned to his mom and gave her the thumbs-up sign. It was a significant victory for the defense and it was eagerly appreciated. Now Tim would have a legitimate defense without the necessity of him testifying and exposing himself to cross-examination. On the prosecution side of the courtroom, Theresa shook her head in disgust but kept quiet.

The second legal ruling that Sean and Rosen sought dealt with a subject that the defense team of both men worked on for several weeks. It dealt with the defense plan to introduce expert testimony, in the form of former baseball players or managers, on pertinent issues in the case. The legal fund enterprise created by Raymond Hunter would now come in very handy because part of the funds would go towards paying the expenses and fees of those baseball experts.

Hunter had asked Arlene Gantz, an associate who handled civil cases, to coordinate those efforts. Rosen wanted to demonstrate that it was an accepted custom in baseball for managers to order their men to protect their players from perceived injustices by the other team. Those included running up too many runs, stealing a base when the lead was more than ample near the end of a game, showing up the pitcher during a home run trot, sliding needlessly hard into a fielder, or throwing at a hitter.

Both he and Cavanaugh also wanted to demonstrate that throwing inside pitches was a necessary part of the game. They would explain the continuous battle between the pitcher and batter for domination of the plate. Whomever won that battle usually won the game as well. Thus they argued, they should be allowed to call baseball personnel to testify that whatever risks were involved in winning the battle of the plate, they were inherent in the way the game was played.

"More importantly, Your Honor, it is our position that by agreeing to play Major League Baseball, every player is impliedly giving his consent that, should an injury occur, he has assumed that risk and cannot seek damages in the courts," argued Cavanaugh.

"Are you suggesting that the assumption of risk doctrine is relevant in a criminal case?" asked Judge Johnson.

"Yes I am, Judge. I can cite multiple state and federal cases in which ballplayers in the minors or college were seriously injured by a so-called bean ball. They sued for damages against the opposing school or pitcher, and the courts all ruled against them. They ruled that the players had assumed the risk of injury by playing in a game where the bean ball was an accepted custom of the game. We want to prove it by experts, and we want a charge to the jury on the doctrine of assumption of risk."

"But surely, Mr. Cavanaugh, you can appreciate the difference between a civil damages case and a criminal case. In the criminal law we don't allow people to consent to serious bodily injury or death. The state has a say in the matter and prosecutes regardless of whether the parties agreed to fight or to play outside of the bounds of the rules."

Rosen chimed in with "we are suggesting that it can't be murder where it's an accepted part of the game, even if we concede, for purposes of argument, that this was a bean ball case. It's a tragedy that has happened only once before, but it's still an inherent risk of the game."

"Judge, our defense depends upon Your Honor accepting the doctrine. The jury does not have to be told that it is a legal defense unless they find from the testimony by the experts that in the baseball culture players accept the risk that they will be beaned. I draw the court's attention to the model charge for reckless manslaughter. The instructions advise the jury that the reckless risk that the defendant disregards must be 'substantial and unjustifiable,' but it goes on to say that even 'substantial risks may not be reckless when the defendant is seeking to serve a proper purpose.' That's what we are contending, Judge. The game of baseball is being served by brush-back pitches. That purpose is what a jury needs to hear about from the experts," said an impassioned Sean Cavanaugh.

"That is quite an interesting argument. What's the State's position in response to this novel approach?"

" With respect, this court has no authority to create a new statutory defense to a crime. That is the responsibility of the legislature. Secondly, I contend that there is no need for expert testimony in this case. Experts are needed only when the topic is scientific or technical so that ordinary jurors would not understand its complexity. Here there is no complexity. This is a murder case with motive, intent, and opportunity. Jurors are perfectly capable of understanding why Charles threw at Leyton and why Sawyer ordered it. They're merely trying to create some sensationalism in the trial and distract the jury with celebrity, rather than confront the issues in the case."

In truth, Jaime had been partially surprised by the defense argument. Although he had the names of some baseball celebrities in discovery and a summary of what they intended to say, he did not think of it in terms of how it was expressed by Cavanaugh. It was a fascinating argument, and Jaime worried that it may have some merit - at least as it pertained to reckless manslaughter. He was disappointed that he didn't see it coming, and hoped the judge was not buying it.

"Gentlemen, I'm going to combine the morning break and lunch into one long recess so I can do some serious thinking about the requests by counsel. I'll see you back here at 1:30 PM."

Reporters and the public were all dying to learn the names of the proposed experts. They would speculate all day, but the answer would come only if the judge permitted their testimony.

Chapter 38

Judge Johnson decided to give something to both sides, but his decision was based on sound legal reasoning.

"I see absolutely no basis for an assumption of the risk defense to a murder charge. For me to create one would violate my function as a trial judge. Such a defense must come from our state legislators or from a recommendation to the legislature by our Supreme Court. Accordingly, I will not instruct the jury that they can acquit if they believe that Major League ballplayers have assumed a risk of death by playing the sport.

"Now, as to reckless manslaughter, I do find some basis for that concept in an instruction to the jury. Once again, I am not creating a legal defense of assumption of the risk. But I do believe that the concept can be argued by the defense. In essence, the jury must make a value judgment of whether the risk of death that the defendants are charged with disregarding, by throwing a bean ball pitch, is unreasonably reckless.

"To assist them, I believe it is relevant for them to know whether ballplayers have indeed voluntarily assumed the risk of potential serious bodily injury or death when they are at bat, given the "battle for dominance of the plate" theory that has been discussed. If the jury finds that the risk taken by the defendants was not reckless, in that it was reasonably justifiable in the context of a ball game, they may acquit the defendants. In other words, I am not creating a new defense in the law. I am merely providing *a factor* for the jury to consider in their analysis of the question of whether the risk taken was unreasonable or not."

The packed audience did not immediately appreciate the consequences of the ruling until they saw Rosen and Cavanaugh embrace their clients. This indeed was a major victory for the defense. It was the second triumph of the day and would give the defense a legitimate chance to succeed at trial. At counsel table, Jaime packed up his legal papers and congratulated Sean on his clever argument. Jaime reminded him that his plea offer would no longer be on the table once the jury selection began. Sean said that, in light of the court's ruling, he doubted that there would be a guilty plea, but would call if Charles felt differently.

Over at the other defense table, the ruling did little to alter Sawyer's pessimism. He appeared to be a broken-down old man. By his demeanor and physical presence, he looked a decade older than when he was fired from the team. The pressure of a criminal conviction exacerbated his medical problems, and he worried that the trial itself would create an even greater strain on his constitution. On the other hand, he thought maybe it was best to get it over with rather than have it postponed, as his lawyer had argued. He sat shaking his head and asked himself what he had done that was any different than what hundreds of managers before him had done. He couldn't come up with an answer.

On the way out, Theresa Leyton asked Jaime about the consequences of the ruling. For the first time since Jaime met her, she seemed less assured, almost on the verge of despair. "Is this as bad as I think?" she asked.

"It gives them more of a chance than they had coming in, but this is not a game changer. The jury still has a dead young man to deal with and a vendetta that caused his death. I wouldn't be disheartened by this ruling. I still remain convinced, as I told you long ago, that this is a classic reckless manslaughter case. Maybe if you could adjust your level of expectations downward, you would feel less anxious."

"I won't compromise, Mr. Brooks, and neither should you. No amount of legal chicanery by those paid mouthpieces for Ken's killers changes what they did. I want murder convictions and nothing less."

"I can assure you that I have and will continue to give it one hundred percent, but lawyers can never make guarantees when you're dealing with twelve jurors who come with their own life experiences."

As she left court for the day, she couldn't help but notice Lois Charles who sat in the front row silently praying the rosary. She didn't know exactly why, but she felt a profound sadness suddenly envelope her. For just a fleeting moment she felt empathy for the woman. She had an urge to speak to her, but the feeling subsided as quickly as it came, and the fire in her belly for retribution returned.

As she made her way to her SUV in a parking lot across from the courthouse, a young man, sitting in a battered Maxima, watched. On her windshield, covered by the wiper blades, was an envelope that contained a handwritten letter from Meyer. She sat alone and read the crudely written note:

> *You don't know me but we have something in common. I want those fuckin' bums to fry just like you do. What they did ain't right no matter how you look at it. I grew up in Manhattan and I been a Mets fan all my life. I greeve for you and your kid. If the jury don't do there job I will. I can put them*

in there graves for $15,000. It's a
good deal!!! Call me on my cell
phone 856-627-1447.

Chris was street smart enough to use a prepaid, untraceable phone that the Bloods gave him for his work. He could renew the agreement every thirty days, in case the offer took longer for her to accept.

Theresa's initial reaction was to crumble up the note, which she thought was the work of a psychopath. She shuddered at the notion that this creep knew her car and possibly even where she lived. She wondered whether to take it to Jaime but decided against it. She tossed the note and envelope into her glove compartment and drove home. During the ride, she fantasized about the offer and the mechanics of how it would happen. After indulging herself in this cathartic outlet, she scolded herself and rejected the idea. Still, it gave her comfort to know there could be a final solution.

Chapter 39

Wednesday, November 4th was a huge day for the defendants because jury selection was to begin. It was also big for the baseball community in the nation's capital. The world of baseball crowned its newest champion after what was an incredibly tight National League Champion Series between the Phillies and the Washington Nationals.

The series was notable for two extraordinary reasons. Historians of the game would claim that the series turned primarily not on what happened on the field, but rather what was happening in a courtroom in Camden, New Jersey.

In game six, the Phillies had a three to two game advantage at home. The Phillies brought in starter Nolan Albright to relieve in the eighth inning with the home team holding a one run lead. The "Nats" had men on first and third with one out when Bobby Carson went to the mound to discuss strategy.

At bat was the power-hitting fifth batter in the Nats lineup, Tommy Cottler. Carson wanted Albright to pitch inside and move the batter off of the plate. Then he wanted a teaser outside so the batter would lunge for the pitch and strike out or hit a harmless ground ball. On the first pitch Albright threw a fastball low and in, but the pitch did nothing to move the batter off the plate. Carson again signaled for a high inside fastball. Instead, the pitch was high but right over the heart of the plate. Cottler hit a line drive that reached the stands in a nanosecond, and the Nats took the lead. It was a lead they held onto for the win.

In the clubhouse, reporters asked Albright about the pitch.

"To be honest, I wasn't focused. When Bobby asked for a high inside fastball, all I could think of was Tim. I was afraid of hitting Cottler in the head in that situation. I know I let the team down. I guess I just let other things distract me from my job."

Perhaps the Phillies were snake-bitten that year, but game seven proved to be disastrous as well. The Nationals were leading 5-4 going into the bottom of the ninth. With Colby Green on second after a single and a sacrifice bunt, Butterworth came to the plate with two outs. On a 2-2 pitch he got jammed but powered the ball over the second baseman into shallow right field. Green, who had good speed, took off with the pitch and took a wide turn at third past the propeller-like action from his third base coach.

The wide turn seemed to cost the runner a fraction of a second that observers sensed would make the costly difference at the plate. The throw was on target, but Green's slide was adept, and it clearly looked like he was safe at the plate. The umpire hesitated but called the runner out. The call was so bad that even Washington fans were stunned by the egregious mistake. Phillies' manager Bobby Carson stormed out of the dugout and used his final challenge of the day to contest the call. Television replays showed the controversial play from multiple angles and most fans expected a quick reversal. Shockingly MLB officials in their central offices in New York reviewed the video and could not agree that there was clear and convincing evidence to overturn the plate umpire.

It was a remarkable ending to a series that may have robbed the Phillies of their chance at a third World Championship. The ensuing World Series was anti-climactic after the controversial seventh game. The people of the City of Brotherly Love would not parade down Broad Street. Some writers and fans opined that the baseball gods had judged the team's responsibility for the death of Kenny Leyton and rendered them guilty.

And baseball fans continued to debate the merits of a replay system that still lacked clarity Fans and analysts questioned the efficacy of officials in New York making calls rather than a crew chief. The public still waited for more news from the commissioner's office about another crucial aspect of the game's future. The panel's report was due after the series, concerning whether there would be fundamental changes to the game as a result of the Charles case.

Chapter 40

Jaime's face was flushed with anger as he spoke with Clark Draper over the phone. On the eve of trial, Draper was refusing to voluntarily come to New Jersey and testify. As a Florida resident, a New Jersey prosecutor did not have the power to force him because the subpoena would not have validity. Jaime had been lulled into a false sense of security. He had relied on Draper's word that he was happy to testify. Now it was too late for Jaime to go through a complicated legal battle in Florida to force him to testify. Surely, he thought, if the jury believed Draper they would see a different side of Charles: one that would contradict the video of him looking remorseful after he had plunked Leyton

Jaime accepted the blame. It was a big blunder, and the verdict could be impacted by his omission. He should have filed papers in Florida ordering Draper to appear in New Jersey well in advance of the trial. He tried to assuage his guilt by acknowledging to himself that Draper would have been demolished on the stand over the homophobic issue. Also with Draper out of the case, the defense would have no reason to call Thompson Jaime also realized that Judge Johnson may have prevented Draper from testifying about an incident that happened two years earlier on the grounds that it was too inflammatory. Jaime had no choice but to go with the original evidence. He still believed that the evidence supported a guilty verdict to some form of homicide.

At the courthouse, seating in the <u>State v. Sawyer & Charles</u> matter was at a premium. Judge Johnson dealt with the numerous media requests for seats and camera locations by limiting it to one network that would run a closed-circuit feed to another courtroom. In that manner, the press and general public could watch the proceedings on a television monitor. There would be few seats available while dozens of prospective jurors were led into the courtroom and seated in the several rows of benches in the courtroom. Judge Johnson's court clerk would start the process by randomly calling names from a wooden box that she would rotate, and then pick out a number that was assigned to each juror.

That process would continue until fourteen potential jurors were seated in the jury box. Although twelve were needed, the judge usually had two other potential jurors sit as alternates in case some unanticipated problems arose during the trial. When the clerk finished calling numbers, Judge Johnson addressed them and asked that the remaining pool of jurors in the rows listen closely to his general instructions. Because this was a murder case, each of the parties had a greater number of juror challenges than in an ordinary case. Both defendants could exercise ten challenges of jurors that they didn't want on the jury. The State was entitled to six challenges per defendant, for a total of twelve.

As the jurors took their places, Buck Sawyer's pallor turned from a patch of red to full-blown tomato red. The artery in his neck pulsated at a furious pace. His lawyer leaned over and asked if he was okay. Buck told him he was nauseated and felt dizzy. He also complained of weakness in his right side, but he was slurring his words and was barely intelligible to his lawyer. He sounded drunk.

"Jesus Buck, have you been drinking this morning already?"

"Need to go to bed."

"Buck get your act together, you're not funny. That's all I need - a sauced client on the first day of trial."

In the interim, Judge Johnson explained that this was a criminal trial, that the defendants were presumed innocent, and that the presumption remained throughout the trial unless and until they decided that the defendants or one of them was guilty beyond a reasonable doubt. Finally, he reminded them that their verdict had to be unanimous.

"Now, I would ask Mr. Cavanaugh to rise and turn and face the panel. He represents Tim Charles in this matter. He practices in Haddon Heights with a firm called Hunter, Cavanaugh, and Kemper. Have any of you been sued or represented by Mr. Cavanaugh?" Johnson asked of the panel. When there were no hands raised, he repeated the procedure with Jaime Brooks and Fred Rosen. Next was the introduction of the defendants themselves.

"Would you have your client stand Mr. Rosen so that the jurors may see Mr. Randall Buck Sawyer?"

" Buck stand and turn so they can all see you."

But Buck had difficulty standing up, and when he did stand upright he held his head, moaned, and fell face first onto the floor. Gasps rang out from the jurors and court personnel. It seemed as if everyone could do nothing but stare at the lifeless looking body until a sheriff's officer bent down and felt for a pulse. Sawyer did not appear to be conscious, but he was breathing heavily and loudly. Another officer used his radio to call for 911 help, and, within a few minutes, Buck Sawyer was being carted off by paramedics on a stretcher to Cooper Hospital just a block away. It was a frightful scene, even for Jaime, who experienced his fair share of courtroom seizures and fainting spells from defendants. But he had never witnessed anything life-threatening.

The unexpected collapse of the defendant unnerved the jurors as well as Judge Johnson, who politely thanked the jurors and asked them to return to their gathering room until further notice. He needed to think this through before he could decide how to proceed. He called counsel into his chambers for a strategy session.

"I'm inclined to postpone the trial until next week to see whether Mr. Sawyer can stand trial. This may just be a high blood pressure or diabetes condition that can be alleviated in the short-term. By that time, if we have a poor prognosis, I would draw a jury so we can conclude with the Charles case before the Christmas break. What do you gentlemen think?"

"Your Honor", said Jaime" it's not easy getting any witness - let alone pro ball players - to come to court, especially since they are all ready to go now. I would be in a position to seek a severance of Mr. Sawyer and just proceed against Mr. Charles as soon as we can."

"I 'm in agreement with Jaime," said Sean. "My client wanted a speedy trial from the outset, and we have our experts ready with plane tickets. I suggest that we start next Monday, and maybe we'll have a better idea of Buck's condition."

"Your Honor, I really can't take a position at this point until I get some preliminary reports from the hospital. Buck doesn't really have family. There is a son from his first wife and that's about it. I will report to Your Honor by Friday with any news I can get from his doctors," offered Rosen.

"Okay, let's go out there and place what we discussed on the record. I'll set next Monday as the tentative trial date." Judge Johnson then excused the jury pool from further service.

Later at his office, Jaime assigned Gary Slater and Investigator Arroyo to help track down and reschedule the witnesses. This task was a nightmare and Jaime was grateful he could delegate it to his trusted staff. Jaime needed to focus on the consequences of trying Charles alone. He had to map out the legal arguments that would arise without Sawyer.

If Sawyer were not a party in the trial, how would he be able to get into evidence all of the statements made by Sawyer to Adams and to the team about retaliation and honor? Technically it was an out of court statement and was therefore hearsay. He would have to write a brief for the judge explaining just how and why the manager's words were admissible as exceptions to the hearsay rule.

Jaime called Barbara and told her of the disturbing turn of events in the case. Their exclusivity as a couple meant that they spent every weekend together, usually at her place, because she worked Friday and Saturday nights. Their ease with one another grew exponentially with each passing week.

He was enjoying November very much, despite the stress of trial, because of the court holidays in the month. He spent Election Day with her going to a movie and dinner. She listened attentively over dinner as he tried out his ideas for the opening statement to the jury. Barbara had good people instincts and he appreciated her input. Now it was almost a certainty that he needed to modify his opening because of Sawyer's illness. He needed to build a circumstantial case to complement the video of the fatal beaning.

Chapter 41

The legal brief Jaime submitted in anticipation that Sawyer was unable to attend the trial proved to be a prescient move. The condition of the former manager was clearly not one that would permit him to be tried along with his codefendant.

The following Monday morning, a Cooper Hospital agent hand-delivered a current report from Dr. Mark Sharon concerning Buck's medical condition to Judge Johnson. The judge's secretary made copies for the attorneys, who read the very detailed and informative report in chambers. According to Dr. Sharon, Buck Sawyer was still in intensive care but was now stable. A series of tests and CT scans reflected that Sawyer suffered an ischemic stroke. Dr. Sharon explained that his stroke was from a blood clot called a thrombosis, which completely blocked an artery that was previously narrowed due to Buck's lifestyle abuses. His smoking, overeating, drinking, and high blood pressure caused fat and cholesterol to collect on the wall of the artery, causing plaque to form. Ultimately blood could no longer flow to the brain, and the blood clotted.

Sharon pointed out that Sawyer was a classic example of a stroke in the making. He had all of the most common risk factors including high cholesterol, high blood pressure, diabetes, and he was at an age where the risk of stroke greatly increased. He was prescribed heparin for the first five days, and was receiving blood thinners such as anticoagulants. He would remain on an aspirin and Coumadin regimen.

The stroke occurred on the left hemisphere of his brain, which controls movement on the opposite side of the body. As a result, Buck was presently paralyzed on the right side of his body. More pertinent for the trial was the description of his communication skills. Sharon called it aphasia, which affected his ability to speak as a result of muscle weakness. He also had memory problems, and the nursing staff described his difficulty in learning new information. He was also reported to be in a highly agitated and impatient mental state.

The current plan, according to Buck's son, was to transfer him to the Magee Rehabilitation Hospital in Philadelphia. In Dr. Sharon's opinion, the duration of the stroke, which halted the flow of blood to the brain, would mean that the rehabilitation would be long-term. Even then, there could be no guarantees about the patient's ability to communicate adequately with counsel in the foreseeable future.

"Jaime, do you wish to have another opinion from a doctor of your choosing?"

"No Judge, I think we should go on with the trial, and we should look at Sawyer again in the future, after he has gone through rehab."

"Yes, Judge, that would be my judgment as well, but frankly I envision making a motion to dismiss the indictment as to him sometime down the road," said Rosen.

"Well let's not go there yet, we aren't going to dismiss a case at this juncture. Let's go out on the record and I'll summarize the report and Jaime can move to sever Sawyer."

In open court, Judge Johnson explained to the public the contents of the report, and on Jaime's motion Johnson severed Sawyer from the trial. He went to great length to explain that this severance did not mean that the case was over, but only that it was in a state of limbo for a period of time.

"Every defendant has a constitutional right to effective assistance of counsel. If Mr. Sawyer cannot communicate with his lawyer, there cannot be a defense mounted against the charge. We call this competency to stand trial. We are all in agreement that Mr. Sawyer is currently not competent to stand trial. What I will be doing is periodically getting updates from doctors who will evaluate Mr. Sawyer's competence. These psychiatrists and neurologists will provide me with an opinion as to Mr. Sawyer's capacity to understand the proceedings against him and to assist in his own defense. If the State wishes, it can hire experts to challenge the opinions of those doctors.

"In three months, if the reports suggest that the defendant is still not competent, I will hold a hearing to decide whether the charges will be dismissed with prejudice, meaning for all time, or whether I will hold the charges in abeyance. There is a legal presumption to hold the charges in abeyance, but every six months thereafter if necessary I will hold another hearing and address the same issue. I hope that is clear to the parties, the victim's family, and to the public at large. Now I think we are ready to bring in another jury pool."

Judge Johnson began anew with his general instructions to the jury pool. This time, however, the sole defendant Tim Charles was permitted twenty peremptory challenges while the prosecution was given twelve. They could dismiss up to those numbers for any reason that wasn't based on a discriminatory basis, and often defendants used most of their challenges to try and seat a jury most favorable to their side. The judge would pose several questions to the prospective jurors to determine whether they had any general bias for or against either side, as well as some personal background questions of the jurors, so the attorneys would be in a better position to gauge the attitudes of the individual jurors.

The lawyers played a secondary role in questioning the prospective jurors, unlike the extensive personal questioning done in some other states. The parties submitted some supplemental questions that they wished the judge to ask, but the lawyers would not get the chance to personally address the jurors in Judge Johnson's courtroom, and consequently the process would move more quickly.

Johnson denied a request by Cavanaugh to ask the jurors their position on brush-back pitches because it was essentially asking them for their verdict in advance. But he did allow a question from the prosecution about whether any of them would be more swayed by the testimony of an expert merely because the witness was a celebrity. He also permitted questions about whether they were fans of a particular baseball team, and whether they attended games.

Nonetheless, the extensive pre-trial publicity would, of necessity, cause Judge Johnson to ask a series of questions of the jurors to find out how much of the case they had heard or read about, and whether they had discussed the merits of the indictment with family and friends. All of this was an attempt to find out whether the publicity was so pervasive that the juror had a fixed and rigid opinion of the case that could not be swayed by the evidence. If that were the case, the judge would dismiss that juror for cause and the lawyers would not have to use one of their precious challenges.

An overwhelming number of potential jurors were familiar with the story and consequently the process was ponderous. The task was to sort out those who merely knew of the facts versus those who had formed an inflexible opinion. It took three days for Johnson just to find enough jurors who would be initially acceptable as free from pre-conceived outcomes.

Now the lawyers got their chance to dismiss jurors they found unacceptable. Some jurors were excused by the court for physical disabilities such as hearing problems or inability to sit for long periods. There were the usual numbers of jurors who wanted off, and would use any justification that their friends used in the past. For the most part, however, the panel was eager to stay and participate in what the press dubbed "Baseball Custom on Trial in Tim Charles Case."

For Jaime's part, he would have been anxious and willing to accept the first fourteen people in the jury box. Jury selection was nothing close to being a science, and all he wanted was a jury that would follow the law. As such, he got Judge Johnson to question the jurors on whether they would accept the dictates of the law even if they personally disliked the legal doctrines. That gave him some insight into a potential holdout juror.

The last thing he needed was a hung jury. He and the Office needed to move on. This wasn't a case where police were involved, so he wouldn't have to worry about juror bias against the police based on any previous confrontation they may have had. In his mind, the facts were not really in dispute, and the verdict would come down to a value judgment on whether the pitch was worthy of condemnation in a criminal court.

He only challenged three jurors. One was a woman who said that her beliefs prevented her from passing judgment on another human being. When pressed by the judge to elaborate, she essentially admitted that she didn't want to sit on the jury because of her job. Jaime didn't want a reluctant juror who might blame him for her stress at work, so he used a challenge to get her off. He struck another male juror who actually came to court wearing a Mets' hat. Jaime didn't care whether or not the guy said he could be fair. He was a high-risk juror, pure and simple, and couldn't be trusted. Lastly, he reluctantly struck a young woman with small children, someone he would have preferred, because she worked in the public relations department for the Phillies.

As for the defense, the legal fund supply was drained on experts and legal fees so there wasn't money left for a jury consultant. Sean was left with his experience and instinct to help him select a jury that would be sympathetic to his cause. Sean believed he had a better chance with men, especially those who were middle-aged or older and who were baseball fans. He hoped they were aware of a long history of bean ball incidents in their lives and would accept it as an integral part of the game.

More importantly, they were the kind of jurors who would be more likely to accept the concept of the assumption of risk, which Sean would argue throughout the case. He was also betting that young, unmarried women would be a safe wager, given Tim's good looks and humble demeanor. Absent those groups, he was unsure of what he wanted. He knew one thing for certain. He didn't want any young mothers, either single or married, who would empathize with Theresa Leyton.

Sean and Tim worked as a team in evaluating the prospective jurors. They did what they could with the little information available to them. They looked for hostile or unwelcome body language, whether the juror made eye contact with them when they answered the judge's questions, and whether they had strong opinions about the case. Sean dismissed one juror when she said she believed that an indictment was evidence of guilt even though she claimed she could set aside that false notion. There was no reason to take a chance with so many available challenges. He used several of his challenges for young, stay-at-home mothers with small children in the same age range as James Leyton.

After several hours and a total of nine challenges, the lawyers found an acceptable jury. Of the fourteen that were seated, eight were men. Cavanaugh managed to keep off all but one young mother, whom he did not challenge because she was divorced and was smiling at Tim during the jury selection process. It was simply a gut feeling, since he was at trials in the past where a juror smiled at the defendant literally right before they uttered the guilty verdict. In any event, it was still a jury with a majority of men, and several of them were baseball fans.

Chapter 42

The prosecution always opens first in a criminal trial in New Jersey because they have the burden of proof, and Jaime wasted little time in getting to the facts.

"Ladies and gentlemen, this trial is a bit unusual because you will see with your own eyes the actual crime take place. There is no doubt who the killer is, no risk of misidentification or coerced confessions. There will be no battle of experts from both sides over the meaning of, or lack of, scientific evidence. You will see virtually everything that happened from direct evidence.

"You will likewise see the events leading up to the murder of Kenneth Leyton which will convince you beyond a reasonable doubt that this defendant, Timothy Charles, had a clear motive to cause serious injury to his victim. You will learn of the animosity that existed between the two ball clubs in June of this year, of the pressure exerted upon this Phillies' pitcher from his manager, and to a lesser extent from peer pressure, to retaliate against a member of the Mets.

"You will hear circumstantial evidence from members of his own ball club that will paint a picture of what was in Charles' mind when he threw his final pitch of the season. You will learn that the defendant rejected a signal from his catcher to throw a slider, a pitch that would have broken away and down from the batter. And then you will see that the defendant armed himself with a deadly weapon, a five ounce baseball, and..."

"I object, Your Honor," said Cavanaugh.

"On what grounds, Mr. Cavanaugh?"

Cavanaugh knew he had little support for his objection, but he didn't like the way the jury was mesmerized by Jaime's opening, and he wanted to break the spell and throw Jaime off his stride, so he argued anyway.

"Judge, a baseball is not a deadly weapon. It is a piece of equipment that is a necessity of the game. It can be purchased by children in any sporting goods store in America. For the prosecutor to refer to it as a deadly weapon is pure melodrama meant to inflame the passions of the jury, and is thus prejudicial to my case."

Judge Johnson cut off Jaime, who was about to respond.

"Mr. Cavanaugh, you have practiced for many years in this county so don't tell me you are unaware of the definition of a deadly weapon. A deadly weapon can be any object, which in the manner it is used or intended to be used, is known to be capable of causing death or serious bodily injury. As you are fully aware, baseball bats, beer mugs, golf irons, and even pens have all been held to be weapons in past cases. A baseball certainly could qualify as one if the jury believes it was intended to be used as a weapon by your client."

"Yes Judge, but in an opening statement, where he's limited to laying out what he expects to prove, labeling the ball a deadly weapon is argumentative at this stage. He can argue it in his summation, but it is premature now."

"Objection is overruled. You may continue, Mr. Brooks."

Jaime continued, but the distraction broke his momentum. He went on to describe the fastball and its impact upon Leyton. Then he took the jury through the last hours of

Leyton's life with a promise that it would hear it from the lips of his widow, and the doctors who attended to the victim. It would hear the 911 call, and finally from the medical examiner who autopsied the body.

He ended by telling the jury that it would have no doubt that a crime had been committed in this case and that, aside from the fact that it occurred on a baseball field, it was still called murder. His opening took just twenty-five minutes, but the jury was charmed and captivated. Cavanaugh now had to change the momentum, because he knew that first impressions in a trial were powerful and lasting.

He began by thanking the jury for their service and by asking them to recall the judge's instructions about the presumption of innocence and the fact that an indictment was not evidence.

"Tim Charles is an innocent, twenty-year-old man who has been caught up in an event that we can all agree was tragic, but that doesn't mean someone must be convicted for it. Sometimes tragic accidents occur, or events take place that were unforeseeable. The grand jury did not hear from the defense, they only heard the viewpoint of the State. Now, for the first time, we have an opportunity to give meaning to the video that the prosecutor has promised to play for you.

"We will explain the dynamics of the game in a way that will raise serious doubts in your mind that a crime was intended, or acted upon, in this case. You will hear from several well-regarded experts in the game of baseball that what happened here was an accepted custom in the strategy of the game of baseball. You will learn that the culture of baseball accepts that there is a risk of serious bodily injury to batters whenever they step up to the plate. Nonetheless, they play because the risk is remote in the history of the game.

"As important as the expert testimony will be, the fact is that my client's greatest flaw as a Major League pitcher was his inability to throw balls at batters to move them off of the plate. It was not in him to do it. You will also hear from multiple people who know him best that he is a man of honest character, and has a reputation for non-violence in the baseball community, as well as his home environment."

Sean concluded with a reference to their duty to seek justice and not vengeance.

"I will ask you at the conclusion of the trial not to condone the overreaction of a grand jury panel that heard only one side of a viewpoint. I am confident that by the end of this trial, you will have no doubt that Tim did nothing criminal. I am confident that you will see through the legalese and bring home a verdict based on your own common sense, and that is a verdict of not guilty."

Sean purposely left vague any reference to whether Tim would take the stand in his own defense. They still hadn't fully decided, and he didn't want to promise the jury something that he couldn't deliver.

Chapter 43

The following morning began with Sean Cavanaugh making a motion to exclude anything that Buck Sawyer said to Doug Adams or to any other members of the team. The legal basis was that Buck was no longer a party to the case, and therefore anything he said would be inadmissible hearsay. Once more, the evidentiary ruling would have severely negative consequences if he lost. The result would mean that the jury would hear the crux of the plan to retaliate, and the orders given by the manager to his team.

"Your Honor," responded Jaime, "I submit that the words of Sawyer are admissible on the grounds that all of the statements were made as part of a conspiracy, and in furtherance of a conspiracy to commit a crime. As such, any statement by one of the conspirators is admissible against all of them."

"Judge, there isn't even a conspiracy count in the indictment," said Cavanaugh.

"There doesn't have to be one, Judge. Conspiracy is always a lesser-included offense, and the jury could find them guilty of it even if it isn't formally charged."

"That is correct, Mr. Brooks. Now lay out for me the basis for your conspiracy theory."

"Judge, it is clear from the grand jury testimony that Sawyer instructed Adams in a private meeting to throw at and hit a Mets' player. He told him he wanted an eye for an eye, and he wanted to equal the playing field. It is also clear that Adams told him he knew what to do, would do his job, and then later discussed the conspiratorial plan with his catcher, Bobby Carson. Carson later assures Herrera that action will be taken. Then we have the ruckus between Julio Herrera and

Adams in the dugout because Adams fell short of the conspiracy's objective. That leads to the team meeting in which Sawyer demands from his team that a Mets' player be put out of action and onto the disabled list. He exhorts them to adopt baseball's honor system to protect one's own players by retaliating in kind, and several players applaud his speech.

"Then we have the testimony of the defendant's roommate Brad Schofield that the defendant mulled over and deliberated over the conspiratorial objective. Clearly, that is sufficient proof of a conspiracy that should permit all of the statements to come in."

"What say you, Mr. Cavanaugh?"

"Judge, there is no criminal object for this to be a conspiracy. Even if we accept what Sawyer said to be true, Adams did not sign on to commit a crime. He merely said he would 'take care of his job.' He tells Carson that he will not do what Sawyer asked. Thus he never joined a conspiracy, and he never had a crime as his object. As for Tim, he is never once quoted as agreeing to any conspiracy to commit a crime. Their purpose was to throw at the batter, and at most strike him, but not to cause injury that rises to the level of a crime. For those reasons, and because we cannot cross-examine Sawyer, I ask that the statements be barred from the trial."

"Gentlemen, statements made in furtherance of a conspiracy have always been an exception to the hearsay rule. I find more than ample evidence of a conspiracy. Even if Adams did not fully enter into an agreement to commit a crime, our law recognizes that there can still be a conspiracy since two or more people agreed to participate.

"Moreover, Mr. Cavanaugh, I have already ruled that there is sufficient evidence for a reasonable jury to conclude that there was a plan to cause serious bodily injury, which is a crime. It is for the jury to ultimately decide if your client had a purpose to do what Sawyer wanted, but my job is to determine whether any reasonable jury could find a conspiracy. I have no doubt that they could so find. Therefore all of his statements will be admitted into trial."

It was not an unexpected result for Cavanaugh, and he certainly wasn't banking on the ruling to save his client. But it was an essential ingredient of the State's case, and Jaime felt like he had jumped another hurdle successfully.

Jaime then began the prosecution of the case against Timothy Charles. Unlike some who began with the cause-of-death-type witnesses like the medical examiner, Jaime preferred the chronological approach. To him, the best evidence was the video of those portions of the games themselves that led to the fatal pitch. He would follow up with live witnesses who would describe the events and put the video in perspective for the jurors.

After the game clips, Jaime asked Judge Johnson to read to the jury a stipulation or an agreed upon set of facts that Sean and Jaime wrote to save some time for the jurors. The stipulation said *that if a representative from the Rawlings Company testified, he would say that his company produces baseballs for the Major Leagues. Further, he would explain that they are made pursuant to the specifications of Major League Baseball Rule 1.09, which call for a circumference of between 9 and 9.25 inches and a weight of between 5 and 5.25 ounces for every ball. The balls are constructed around a cork and hard rubber core that is dipped in a rubber-cemented compressor and then covered by a tightly sewn, cowhide exterior.*

Jaime then placed into evidence a stamped official baseball without objection from the defense, and he asked that the jury be permitted to pass it around to one another. Jaime wanted some of the jurors, who had not touched a ball in decades, to realize how hard an object it was, so that he could justifiably refer to it as a deadly weapon.

Then Jaime called as his first witness Doug Adams. It was the first time that a celebrity personally appeared, and the jury unsuccessfully tried to hide their exuberance at the sight of the handsome star pitcher in a business suit raising his hand and swearing to tell them the truth. In the adjacent courtroom, it was standing-room-only where the monitor was carrying the network feed to those lucky enough to squeeze into one of the benches.

Jaime led Adams through the bad blood that had developed between the two clubs over the last several years, and had him explain the injury to Butterworth's finger that occurred after a three-run home run. Adams gave a detailed recitation of the meeting in Sawyer's office, and the ultimatum to "even the playing field." He described his discussions with Bobby Carson, and the demeanor of Sawyer at the team meeting, with emphasis on the directive to keep secret what was said at the meeting. That would help shore up Jaime's assertion of a conspiracy. He also used the articulate pitcher to explain the difference between the 15-day and 60-day disabled lists to bolster his argument that Sawyer may well have been looking for a long-term disability for the Mets' victim, and thereby sought serious bodily injury.

Then Jaime focused on Charles as a rookie and the pressure he got from Herrera, and to a lesser extent some of the other players, to show some leadership in the cause of team honor. Jaime used Adams unwittingly to establish that

Tim was a control pitcher despite his speed, and that he was encouraged by the coaching staff to move batters away from the plate with inside pitches so that they didn't feel comfortable. Adams admitted that Tim never hit a batter before Leyton.

On cross-examination, Cavanaugh did not believe in the necessity of long and drawn-out questioning. All that did was lose the jury's interest. He knew he had friendly witnesses, so the questions were short and to the point.

"Did my client say anything at the team meeting when Sawyer called for retaliation to suggest that he would do what the manager asked?"

"No, he said nothing."

"And isn't it true that Tim threw up before his start on Sunday?" inquired Cavanaugh.

"Yes, that was the only time I saw him so nervous. I think he was feeling the pressure."

"Now, it's true that Charles never hit a batter even though he was told to pitch inside, isn't that right?"

"That is absolutely correct," responded Adams.

"So he didn't always follow his manager's or coaches' instructions"

"Is that a question or a statement by Mr. Cavanaugh?" asked Jaime.

"I'll withdraw the question." Sean knew he made his point by merely making the statement. The jury got his message.

"Now, you advised Tim that Sawyer was likely a short-termer, and that Tim could disregard his manager. You told him to throw some, quote 'chin music,' isn't that so?

"Yes"

"But he never told you, or anyone else for that matter, that he would retaliate, isn't that true?" demanded Cavanaugh.

"Sure."

"But if he had taken your advice and thrown 'chin music,' that would have been perfectly acceptable as a message pitch, wouldn't it?"

"Objection, that calls for speculation and opinion," said Jaime.

"I'll rephrase the question. Are message pitches like balls thrown near the chin commonplace in baseball?"

"Absolutely."

"No further questions of this witness."

"The State calls Bobby Carson, Your Honor."

Carson was an important, although reluctant, witness. Jaime had him corroborate what the jury heard from Adams. Then he led him to the game itself.

"Had Charles walked any batter up until the sixth inning of the Sunday evening game?"

"Not that I can recall."

"How fast was Charles throwing during that game"?

"He had a good heater, and it was reaching 99 at times in the earlier innings. By the sixth, he was down around 95-96 miles per hour."

" What pitch did you call for on the pitch that struck Ken Leyton in the head?"

"I signaled for a slider, down and away."

"And a slider is a breaking pitch, not thrown as fast as a pure fastball, am I correct?" asked Jaime.

"That is generally accurate."

"In your opinion, which one of the Mets' players was the sparkplug of the team - a guy that made the team go?"

"Well, I guess I would have to say that Kenny Leyton was," responded Carson, hesitantly.

"And Leyton was the Mets' player that cleated your teammate Colby Green, correct?

"Yes".

"Was Leyton comparable to Elliot Butterworth on your team?"

" Because he's younger, Butterworth may have the edge, but I wouldn't want to have to choose."

"Unfortunately, that's not a choice that anyone can make now, is it?"

"Judge, that's way out of line, and I ask that it be stricken," said an annoyed Sean Cavanaugh.

"Yes, members of the jury, you are to disregard that statement by Mr. Brooks. Now prosecutor, let's have no more of those editorial statements. Move on."

"So did Charles shake off your signal for a slider away?

"I can't recall prosecutor".

"You can't or you refuse to?"

"I don't think he shook me off, but I can't be positive."

But you would agree that you only gave him that one signal, am I right?"

"Yes."

"That's all, your witness".

On cross-examination, Cavanaugh was precise. "You cannot say that my client brushed off your slider signal, can you?"

"Not really."

"Because, in fact, he made no head movement, nor did he in any other fashion shake off your pitch as the prosecutor indicated in his opening, did he?"

" No, he just took the signal and threw."

"So he could have merely accepted your pitch, and the ball may have gotten away from him, isn't that right?"

" Judge, now I object," came Jaime's retort. "That calls for speculation and asks for a mere possibility. We aren't dealing with what is possible, but what is more probable than not."

"I'll sustain the objection."

"Mr. Carson, did my client have an aversion to pitching deliberately inside to batters?" continued Cavanaugh.

"He certainly did. It was well known around the clubhouse. It was as if he were unable to move a batter back for fear of hitting him, much to the frustration of his manager."

"That's all."

On redirect, Jaime scored a point back. "Mr. Carson, to your knowledge, had any manager ever ordered Tim Charles to deliberately hit a batter before that June night?"

"Not that I'm aware of."

"And was Tim the kind of player that followed his manager's orders"?

"Yes, he was loyal to his manager."

"Nothing further, Judge."

Both sides made their points with Carson, and the time was already 3:55 PM, so Judge Johnson called it a day. Court would reconvene the following morning. Jaime would spend a couple of hours at the office getting his witnesses ready for the next day.

Chapter 44

One juror was late getting to court on Tuesday and the trial was delayed until 9:45 AM, but Jaime was ready to mix up his witnesses a bit for dramatic effect. He put on an expert witness to explain just how little reaction-time Leyton had when Charles threw the fatal pitch. In essence, he wanted the jury to believe that Leyton was a catastrophe waiting to happen when Charles threw a 95 mph fastball at his head.

Jaime called Arnold Golden, a Ph.D. whose specialty at Cooperstown was baseball science. He testified that studies he conducted, as well as literature presented by the Exploratorium Museum in San Diego, found that a ball thrown at 95mph would get to home plate, a distance of sixty feet and six inches, in four-tenths of one second. To hit the ball, the batter must be able to see it within twelve feet of the ball leaving the pitcher's hand. Then, at midway of the path, the batter must mentally measure the speed and decide whether to swing. That swing has to begin when the ball is still 25-30 feet from the plate. At that point, the ball will reach the plate in about 0.0025 seconds, which is at the limit of possible human reaction time.

He went on to say that a ball thrown at 100mph would give the batter only 15 hundredths of a second to react. At 95 mph, he has one-tenth of a second to react, and at 90 mph, he has two-tenths of a second to react to the pitch. Then Jaime asked him a hypothetical question, using the factual setting of this case.

"Dr. Golden, if Tim Charles threw a 95 mph high inside fastball at Ken Leyton, who was in a bunting position at home plate 60.5 feet away, can you offer an opinion as to why Leyton stood there without moving as if, as described by observers, he was 'paralyzed'?"

"Yes, in my opinion that ball would have gotten to him in four-tenths of a second and he would have only had one-tenth of a second to react to the inside pitch. He was in a squared position to bunt, and he was likely unable to move his head because the ball was coming directly at him. He didn't have enough time to get his body to react to his brain's signal to duck. His mind was, in essence, slowed down by the incredible speed of the pitch and the angle of his body toward the pitch."

Cavanaugh chose not to ask any questions. The science was pretty much indisputable, and there was not much he could do to change the hypothetical since the facts were there on video for everyone to see. There was no benefit in trying to attack the expert's qualifications either, because the defense did not have their own expert to contradict the testimony of Dr. Golden. He was stuck with the reality that Leyton did not react in time. He still had his defense to put on, and therefore decided not to challenge the testimony.

Next, Jaime resumed with the ballplayers, including Herrera, who he reluctantly called because of the fact that Julio had initially lied at the grand jury. Jaime wanted to establish that peer pressure from players like Herrera influenced Charles and led him ultimately to deliberately throw at Leyton's head. So Jaime brought Julio again to the statements he made to Tim before the game, and on the pitching mound at the start of the game. This time, Julio admitted his encouragement of the retaliation and the rationale behind it.

On cross-examination, Cavanaugh impeached Julio with his prior sworn statements at the grand jury when he disavowed any plan or encouragement to seek revenge. He once again followed-up with the conclusion that Charles never told him that he intended to follow Julio's request. That was the best he could ask for because Cavanaugh was stuck with the reality that Adams, Carson, and several other players corroborated the substance of Julio's in-court testimony.

After the lunch break, the prosecution put Tim's roommate on the stand. It was a difficult thing for both men to see each other in a court of law, one sitting on the witness stand for the prosecution, the other seated at counsel table as a defendant in a murder trial. Brad nodded towards Tim - gave him a thumbs-up sign, and Tim smiled broadly for the first time at the trial. Jaime used it to his advantage in his direct examination of Schofield. He could later argue that the witness was obviously testifying only because he was subpoenaed , that he was biased in favor of Tim Charles, but that what he said, though given under duress, was truthful.

Jaime needed Bradley to tell the jury just how much angst his friend felt after the team meeting that had several coaches, players, and his manager counting on him to make a statement for the team. Brad reluctantly admitted that he may have contributed to his friend's critical decision by facetiously telling him that he would be called "yellow" by some of his teammates if he passed the buck to a relief pitcher. He related that Tim feared being labeled a prima donna if he failed his teammates. This was critical from the prosecution's standpoint because it helped establish a personal motive that Charles would have for purposely throwing a ball at Leyton.

On cross-examination, Cavanaugh knew he had a friendly witness and he could lead him to some favorable facts.

"It is true, isn't it, that Tim told you that he admired Doug Adams because he chose not to throw at Luther Wynne in a vulnerable part of his body?"

"Yes."

"And he never told you that he intended to do what his manager expected, correct?"

"Yes."

"And the day or evening after Leyton was struck, he told you it was an accident, correct"?

"Objection! judge, that is clearly self-serving and inadmissible."

" Yes he did, Mr. Cavanaugh. He was as upset as I've ever seen anyone in my life."

"Judge, I object again and ask that it be stricken."

"Yes, members of the jury, you are to do your best to ignore that last response from the witness. It shall be stricken from the record. Mr. Schofield, when there is an objection, you are to wait until I rule before you answer."

For Sean, he knew it was virtually impossible for the jury to erase what they just heard, even if he wasn't allowed to make reference to that answer in his final summation to the jury. He would follow-up that point if Tim decided to testify.

He ended his short questioning with the fact that Tim wanted badly to go to the funeral and actually drove with his parents to the viewing.

"Did they go in the funeral parlor to your knowledge"?

"No sir, they were not permitted to go in by the Leyton family, I mean the widow".

That last statement raised a few eyebrows in the jury box.

The session ended for the day, and court would resume after Wednesday's Veterans' Day holiday. Jaime was happy to see Barbara in court. She moved her piano teaching schedule around to permit her to attend the opening statements and to observe all of Tuesday's witnesses. Jaime didn't intend to work that night, so he was delighted to get her take on the trial. They decided to go to the Bonefish Grill for some well-earned draft beer and a fish dinner. She gave him her impression of the case at that juncture.

"I think you were great in the opening, but then again I sleep with you and I think you're great there too. Just don't try doing that with any of the jurors. Seriously, I think you're doing a wonderful job with what you've got, but frankly I'm still not convinced. If you want the truth, I don't think you have much of a chance for a murder conviction. I would never convict, but I could conceivably compromise and find him guilty of reckless manslaughter. I hope you aren't offended by my honesty."

"To be perfectly frank with you, I never felt this was an appropriate murder case, but the grand jury indicted and I have no choice but to advocate. I offered him a deal on manslaughter, but he didn't want it. I guess I can't blame him, but I have to tell you that if I were a juror, I might convict him of reckless manslaughter. He needs to make a very good impression on the jury when he testifies, or he is at great risk to go down."

"Do you think he will definitely testify?"

"I would bet on it. It would be too dangerous not to, but you never know. I 'm never surprised at anything in a trial after all the years I 've been practicing."

"Yes, I do remember you telling me that you were mentored by Clarence Darrow."

At the same time, a similar but more compelling conversation was taking place amongst the partners, their client, and his parents at Ralph's a neighborhood Italian restaurant near the firm. They needed to make a decision very soon about whether Tim would take the stand in his own defense, because it looked like Jaime would soon be nearing the end of his case. Raymond Hunter and his wife, Lynn, were generous in offering Lois and Jeff Charles one of the five bedrooms at his home for the duration of the trial, and they had gratefully accepted. Both parents took a leave of absence from work to support their son. Tim decided to remain in his Center City apartment with Brad Schofield so that he could get away from the trial atmosphere. Sean summed up his beliefs about whether Tim should testify in his own behalf.

"Look, we could still pull this off without putting you on the stand, Tim. We'll have the testimony from umpire Kastle in the record probably Thursday about your state of mind, and we'll be able to argue assumption of the risk by Leyton as a corollary to the reckless manslaughter charge. We'll also try to raise some doubts in the jury's mind about causation. We'll have testimony that the helmets could have prevented the death. We can argue that Leyton and his wife contributed to his death by leaving the hospital too soon, or by not bringing him back when she saw symptoms. But that's one hell of a blarney tale for anyone to swallow. If the jury wants to acquit they can hang their hat on that theory, but I couldn't argue it with much conviction.

"On the other hand, you have no prior record and the jury will expect to hear from you. If you don't testify, they'll wonder why, even if the judge tells them you have a right to remain silent, and they aren't supposed to discuss your silence in their deliberations. The biggest challenge we have to overcome is the testimony from Carson that he gave the signal for a slider down and away from the hitter. If you don't testify, we have no way to explain why you threw a fastball up and in. You're the only one that can answer it, and I can't just argue that you didn't see the signal or that you saw one finger rather than two.

"We also have character witnesses to put on, and if you don't put a live voice to their claims of your honesty, I'm afraid they won't mean a hill of beans. I recognize that you bear the risk of coming close to admitting recklessness if you do testify, but I think on balance you need to."

Kemper and Hunter agreed and urged Tim to follow Sean's advice. Jeff Charles told his son that he felt confident that his son's honest nature would translate well before the jury. Arlene Gantz volunteered to help Jaime through a mock examination, while Kemper played the role of the prosecutor.

By the end of Tuesday evening, the team decided that Tim would testify.

Chapter 45

On Thursday, after careful consideration of the double-edged sword that would come with calling umpire Mike Kastle, Jaime nonetheless believed he had no choice. He needed Kastle to act as an advisor to the jury as an expert witness who could explain the various combative and provocative acts done by both teams during the three-game series. He also needed Kastle's opinion as an expert, and the underlying reasons for it, on whether Charles' pitch was intentionally thrown at the batter.

Cavanaugh made a motion before trial to preclude Kastle from offering an opinion as an expert witness. Judge Johnson ruled against the defense and found that the testimony would aid the jury on the issues in the case, and that Kastle, an umpire in the league for fifteen years, was clearly competent to provide an expert opinion.

Jaime took Kastle through the same testimony that he gave at the grand jury so the jury could use the same circumstantial evidence that Kastle relied upon in ejecting Charles and Sawyer from the game for their own analysis of Charles' intent. Once again, Jaime took him through the video of the game to highlight the foundation for his opinion. Cavanaugh could do nothing but anxiously wait his turn because the video was in evidence and Jaime was entitled to use it again. It was very compelling evidence, and the jurors seemed by their body language to be in sync with the umpire's expertise.

Then it was time for the other edge of the sword that Jaime knew was coming and was now powerless to prevent. Judge Johnson had previously ruled that Cavanaugh could question the umpire about the aftermath of the pitch. Sean began by asking the witness to describe what Charles did after he hit Leyton. Kastle repeated virtually word-for-word his earlier description of Charles' physical reactions.

"What did my client say to you after you ejected him?"

"As he sat on his haunches, he said 'Mike, I didn't mean to hit him.'"

"Could you describe his demeanor when he said that to you?"

"Well, he was white as chalk, and looked to me to be distraught over what happened."

Then, for the first time in the entire history of the investigation, Kastle added "when he was on his knees, he looked at Leyton and asked God to make sure Leyton was alright. He was really shook up at that point."

That statement was like a knife to Jaime's abdomen. How, he thought, was a jury to believe that Charles intended to cause Leyton serious bodily injury if he was asking for divine intervention on Leyton's behalf? If the jury believed Kastle's last statement, murder was out the window. That would lessen the prosecution's leverage for a compromise verdict. The effect on Theresa was equally profound. She stared at Kastle as if he, rather than Charles had thrown the fatal pitch. She realized the import of that piece of evidence for the defense. She didn't buy it one bit, and her anger was reflected in the pallor of her face.

Cavanaugh finished with an acknowledgement from Kastle that his ejection and opinion was not based necessarily on a judgment that Charles intended to hit Leyton, but only that he intentionally threw at the batter.

On redirect, all Jaime could do was to emphasize that Kastle never, in a police interview or at the grand jury, mentioned that Charles invoked God on Leyton's behalf. The problem was that he could not fathom a reasonable motive for why Kastle would be lying to protect Charles. His only solution was to ask one more question.

"Mr. Kastle, did you take into consideration what Charles said at the mound in deciding whether to eject him?"

"No, I did not."

"In other words, you ejected him despite what he said?"

"Yes, I did."

"That's all I have, Judge." Jaime could now argue in summation to the jury that Kastle did not believe that what Charles said was sincere or believable.

As Kastle made his way from the courtroom, Theresa followed him into the hallway. She rushed him and physically turned him around to face her.

"How can you live with yourself? Who got to you? Who paid you off to say that on the stand?"

"Mrs. Leyton, I realize you're upset, but that accusation is just crazy. I had a lot of time to think about those moments over the last few months, and I remembered it not long ago. I have no pony in this race. I'm not trying to protect the kid. I'm only telling what I remember."

"It's a lie, dammit! Tell me who got to you!" As she said those words, she literally grabbed Kastle by his collar and shook him. It took the intervention of a lawyer and sheriff's officer to pull her away from the startled umpire.

Theresa went to the ladies room to control herself, but she was no longer able to be strong. She felt her body and mind deteriorating. She was losing whatever little confidence she had in the justice system. She began to let herself think about the offer in the letter. Could she actually bring herself to seek his help? Could she be that desperate to get what she wanted, regardless of the heinousness of the means?

Chapter 46

Next, Jaime called the record keeper for 911 communications calls in Camden County to authenticate Theresa Leyton's call on that Monday in June. Cavanaugh asked that the jury be excused so that he could make a motion. Judge Johnson felt it appropriate to give the jury their mid-morning break, and asked Cavanaugh to proceed.

"Judge, I move to exclude the 911 call on two grounds. First, it is inflammatory and will be unduly prejudicial to my client, while not adding anything material to the issues in this case. I say that, Your Honor, because Theresa Leyton is on the State's witness list and it is the prosecution's intention to call her to the stand. If that is the case, the 911 call is not only prejudicial, it is also cumulative. The same evidence is available from Mrs. Leyton, and if the call is permitted the jury will hear the same inflammatory evidence twice.

"I would not attempt to keep Mrs. Leyton from testifying. I have agreed to permit her to watch this entire trial, despite the fact that I could have asked for a sequestration order to keep her out until she actually is called to testify. The tape of the call is simply unnecessary, and therefore I ask that it be precluded."

"Mr. Cavanaugh, I can appreciate your thoughtful gesture towards Mrs. Leyton, but to me the 911 tape is clearly relevant and admissible. The only issue in my mind is whether it is unduly prejudicial. Every piece of evidence against your client is prejudicial. If that were the test, no evidence could come in. I have heard the call, and I do not think it will divert the jury's focus from the evidence to their passions. I will permit it."

Once again, a jury heard the chilling sounds of a desperate wife on the verge of shock. The courtroom audience and the jury sat transfixed during the short but compelling tape. Two female jurors could be seen holding their hands to their mouths, and one dabbed tears from her eyes. It had an even more profound impact upon the widow herself.

This was the first time she had heard the tape, and it brought her back to that late Monday afternoon when her life changed completely. She was not prepared to relive it and broke down into a sob. She had to get up and leave the courtroom as the entire jury watched and collectively shook their heads in sympathy. Whatever impact Cavanaugh had made with the points he scored with Kastle, were now greatly diminished by the drama that unfolded from the State's last volley of ammunition.

Judge Johnson called for another short break. Cavanaugh did all he could to refrain himself from a temper tantrum and, as the jury left the room, he moved for a mistrial. He argued again that the judge grievously erred in allowing the 911 call to be heard and that it caused his client irreparable harm. Johnson felt for Cavanaugh on a personal level, but he was not about to terminate the trial and start over. He denied the motion and told the lawyer that he would have an appeal issue if his client were convicted. In the corridor outside the courtroom, Lois sat on a chair praying the rosary while Jeff chatted with Tim and Sean.

Donald and Elizabeth stood nearby with their grandson as Theresa went to the ladies room to compose herself for her testimony. Jimmy watched Lois intently, and then pulled away from his grandparents and went over to her.

"What are you playing with"?

"I'm praying with these beads, Jimmy, for my son and for your father."

"Can I try it"?

But at that moment, Theresa returned and went over to her son, who stood with the beads in his small palms.

"I'm sorry about that Mrs. Leyton, but he just came over to me."

Theresa pulled her son away sharply and exploded at her parents.

"Dammit! Can't you control him? I don't want him anywhere near that family! Stay away from them, Jimmy"!

That exchange startled the Charles family, especially the already angst-filled defendant. He longed to be able to hug the child and console him, but he knew better: that could never be. The emotional outburst further destabilized Theresa, just as she was about to testify.

Jaime took Mrs. Leyton slowly through the preliminary questions of her identity and those of her family so she would relax a bit before the emotional questioning came. Then he went directly to her appearance at the Sunday night game, and she explained how she jumped out of her seat to stand at the edge of the playing field until she saw her husband in the training room. He took her through the hospital exams in Philadelphia, the teasing between she and her husband, and the shared optimism they felt when they left the hospital.

She described how tired he was at her parents' home, and how he forced himself to swim with their son despite his exhaustion. Then she breathed deeply and in a narrative form, described her difficulty in waking him after his afternoon nap, her insistence that he go back to the hospital, and her panicky state when she heard him slurring his words. When Jaime asked if she could make out what he was saying, the emotional toll of the prior fifteen weeks hit her and could not be diverted any longer. She broke down uncontrollably on the stand. Her body shook from her heaves and it looked as though she might fall from her seat when Judge Johnson called a halt to the proceedings. He called for the third break that morning so the witness could compose herself.

This was no act, and Jaime was perhaps even more surprised than Sean Cavanaugh. The tough, determined, and uncompromising persona that he and his staff had seen from the start had dissolved in seconds. In its place was a woman, who perhaps for the first meaningful time, gave herself permission to emote and grieve for a loss that she had believed needed to be repressed until justice was done.

Chapter 47

Sean Cavanaugh knew he would be on a tightrope as he began his cross-examination of Mrs. Leyton. He felt he needed to raise a few doubts in the jurors' minds about the cause of death, or whether other intervening factors may have changed the result. But he had to tread most delicately with the grieving widow, or risk alienating the jury forever. To each question, she was only left to answer "yes."

"Your husband didn't like being in the hospital, so he was not interested in staying, am I right"?

"In fact, he disregarded the recommendation of the physician that he stay overnight for observation, isn't that true"?

"He initially wanted to play in the next game on Tuesday, didn't he"?

"By the way, your husband didn't like the idea of wearing the newer helmets mandated in 2013 isn't that true"?

In fact, he chose to be exempt from the new helmet because he had enough years of service in the majors, correct"?

"And Dr. Howard Sheldon told you on that initial hospital visit that Ken should rest for a couple of weeks, correct"?

"Yet he went swimming in the pool for over an hour the very next day, isn't that true"?

He debated with the idea of placing some of the carelessness at her feet as well, for not being more forceful in demanding that Ken stay overnight at the hospital. He concluded that he made his points respectfully and didn't want to end on a hostile note. He ended his cross and court was adjourned for lunch.

Jaime informed the court that his only witness after lunch would be a medical examiner, and that he would rest his case after that testimony. Judge Johnson urged Sean to be ready with the defense case.

After a light lunch at his desk, Jaime went over the testimony with the pathologist who performed the autopsy, and they walked the two short blocks back to court. Dr. Valerie Cutillo was a regional medical examiner, but she worked on a regular basis with the prosecutors of Camden County by virtue of their joint responsibilities in sudden death investigations. Regardless of her familiarity, she was an independent woman and would provide an unbiased opinion in any case. This one was no exception.

On the stand, Dr. Cutillo summarized her findings for the jury. Leyton was described as a well-nourished male weighing 180 pounds and standing six feet in height. There was no indication of heart disease or any other medical problem that contributed to or caused his death. It was a straightforward presentation that ruled out any other explanation for death other than brain trauma. When asked by Jaime whether the Doctor had an opinion as to the cause of death, she stated flatly that the death was a case of homicide. In other words, the death was a result of human agency and not attributable to natural causes or accident.

The medical examiner testified that her opinion was based upon the medical records supplied from Virtua Hospital as well as the investigative reports from the Prosecutor's Office. Those materials, as well as her own observations, allowed her to opine that, to a reasonable degree of medical certainty, the swelling of the tissue around Leyton's brain and skull were directly linked to the trauma from the pitched ball. That was all Jaime needed to prove a necessary element of the crime of murder or manslaughter. Namely, **but for** the pitched ball striking his skull, Leyton would still be alive.

On cross-examination, Cavanaugh followed-up on the line of questioning he used with Theresa Leyton.

"Doctor, you have relied upon the hospital records, which reflect a refusal by the decedent to remain at the Hospital for observation overnight, and I'm wondering whether you have an opinion about whether that decision may have contributed to his death"?

"I object, Judge. That is purely speculation."

"She says she relied upon the medical records. I'll permit it."

"I would have to say that if he had stayed at the Hospital, the staff may have prevented the extensive swelling that later occurred, and which, by the time he returned to the Hospital, made his chances for survival very unlikely."

"Now, Dr. Cutillo, I'd like you to assume that the decedent, on the very next day, after having been diagnosed with a concussion, went swimming in a pool for one whole hour. What effect, if any, would that have on the individual"?

"In my opinion, any rigorous physical activity would have had a harmful effect upon the patient, and may have contributed to the swelling."

"Thank you, Doctor," concluded Cavanaugh.

On redirect, Jaime got the witness to admit that she was unable to state to a reasonable degree of medical certainty that

Leyton would have survived if he had remained in the hospital. Moreover, Jaime was also able to point out that Leyton's fatigue that caused him to sleep until 10:00 AM could have been a signal that swelling was taking place even before he went swimming.

All in all, he was stuck with the fact that Leyton may have contributed to his death, but Jaime was confident that if the jury listened carefully to the law, they would not be lulled into blaming the victim for his own death. He stood tall and confidently announced **" The State rests Your Honor**."

Chapter 48

The defense began its case by calling its first expert witness, Steve Ries. Sean laid out his credentials for the jury. A former minor league player who later managed for a Dodger's minor league team, he managed the Oakland A's during the 1993 season. He next became manager of the Boston Red Sox for the 1995 and 1996 seasons. Later, he became a broadcast analyst for ESPN, and was a part-time analyst for the San Francisco Giants. He currently co-hosted an MLB Radio show with Bill Levine, a former general manager for the Twins and Orioles.

Having established Ries' bona fides, Sean took him through the baseball culture that recognized an unwritten law amongst managers and players that teammates must be protected. That unwritten code of conduct, said Ries, meant that it often fell upon the team's pitcher to retaliate against an opponent who threw at or actually struck one of his teammates with a pitch, or taken out one of his players with an overly aggressive slide. If a manager or pitcher were to ignore the opponent's offensive behavior, he risked the loss of his own team's respect, and, by his inaction, encouraging future wrongs by opponents.

"Have you ever ordered one of your pitchers to retaliate by hitting an opposing batter"? asked Cavanaugh.

"Absolutely I did, and on more than one occasion."

"In the baseball culture, would that practice actually qualify as a custom of the trade"?

"Yes, it is embedded in the way the game is played."

"If a pitcher lost the team's respect for failing to protect his teammates, do you have an opinion of what the consequence would be"?

"It would be my opinion, based on experience and observation that his teammates may very well shun him socially, and even play with less intensity than they would otherwise when he pitched. It may cause such a schism that the general manager may actually look to trade the pitcher."

"Do you have an opinion of whether the players themselves accept the fact that they will be targeted at some point for retaliation by the other team for some perceived offensive act by their teammate against the opponent"?

"I would say, without question, that they assume there is that risk, either in the same game or in some future game down the road, and that they accept that proposition as an inherent part of the game."

On cross-examination, Jaime made just a few points by leading Ries to answer negatively to every question.

"Did you ever order your pitcher to deliberately hit a batter in the head or stick the ball in his ear"?

"Did you ever direct your pitcher to hit the batter so hard, or in such a vulnerable location of his body, that he would end up on the disabled list"?

"In general, is it the custom, even when retaliating, to throw above the neck"?

"Are you suggesting that players assume they are going to get hit in the head as part of the customary practices of the game"?

Jaime ended his questioning on that note, and felt he had neutralized the expert's impact.

Then Sean Cavanaugh brought a collective sound of shock and awe from the courtroom as he announced that his next witness was the legendary Sandy Kallison. The courtroom doors opened and the still lean and tall figure of the nearly eighty-year-old Hall of Fame pitcher, with the receding white hair, appeared with Hank Kemper by his side. Kemper looked like he was in the presence of a deity. To the press and the public, this was the moment they had anticipated since the commencement of the trial. Despite his reluctance to attend public events, much less a criminal trial, Kallison waived any expert fees other than his expenses. He felt that the indictment was absurd based on what he had seen and known of the facts, and he felt the game needed an acquittal.

Cavanaugh established his twelve-year career, his election as the second youngest man ever to the Hall of Fame at the age of thirty-seven, his .665 winning percentage, and his three Cy Young Awards. Jaime stipulated to his expertise in the game. He, too, was in awe of the man.

Cavanaugh wanted Kallison for his gravitas and to present the jury with a pitcher who stood and toiled on the same mound as Tim Charles. His testimony was brief, but meaningful to the defense.

"Mr. Kallison, please tell the jury, if you could point to one reason for your success in the game of baseball, what would it be"?

"I would have to honestly say, the primary reason was talent. A close second would have to be my intense drive for winning, because that's what the season is all about."

"Did you subscribe to any particular philosophy on the pitching mound"?

"Yes, I believe in the famous quote from the 30's that 'pitching is the art of instilling fear in a batter.'"

"Did you have an opinion whether a pitcher needs to throw inside to be effective"?

"Let me put it bluntly, Mr. Cavanaugh: a guy who won't throw inside is going to be a losing pitcher until he learns to pitch inside. If you don't control the plate and take the corners away from the batter, you aren't going to stay in the Majors."

Cavanaugh had what he needed and sat down.

On cross-examination, Jaime wanted to lighten the mood because Kallison had been so riveting.

"Who was a better pitcher, you or Bob Gibson?" That brought some chuckles from the audience, and even Cavanaugh and Charles got a good laugh. Then Jaime again kept his questioning to a bare minimum, but he had done his homework.

"Pitching inside to intimidate the hitter is not the same as deliberately trying to hit the hitter, am I correct"?

"Yes, of course."

"And in the course of your entire career, how many batters did you actually hit"?

"Gee, I couldn't really tell you off the cuff."

"If I told you that, of all the pitchers in the Hall of Fame, you hit the third fewest number of batters, would that aid your memory"?

"Not really, but I'd accept your statement."

"If I told you the number was only seventeen, would that help you remember"?

"Yes, I think that's about right."

"So, would you agree with me that you can be a great pitcher without hitting a large number of batters"?

"Yes, provided you show them you aren't afraid to pitch inside."

"Thank you, Mr. Kallison. It was an honor to have you with us today."

Once again, Jaime made his point tactfully and respectfully.

Cavanaugh next called Guy Michael, a baseball historian with a long resume of books to his credit. He was qualified as an expert in the field of baseball history and practices. Sean wanted to continue his theme that what his client did was an accepted custom of the game, and a necessary ingredient for a successful pitcher - albeit one that ended unexpectedly. Michael's testimony went one step further than Kallison's theory of intimidation of the batter. He traced the bean ball pitch from as far back as 1910, when John Evers, the great second baseman of "Tinkers to Evers to Chance" fame, called the pitch an *art*, and the term "bean ball wars" came into the vocabulary of the game.

Michael quoted extensively from a book that Sean successfully offered into evidence as a learned treatise, which Michael used in his expert opinion testimony. The book, by Paul Dickson, was called the *Unwritten Rules of Baseball*, and established that there existed an unofficial layer of rules that governed the game.

It was, as Joe Garagiola once suggested, "a game ruled by unwritten laws of survival and self-preservation that had passed those rules down from generation to generation." Among those rules was the law of retaliation, so that if your hitter was hit by an opposing pitcher, we will hit one of yours. Sean was establishing that players lived by the code described in Dickson's book, and that it was a part of the game that was known by and accepted by all who played.

Michael gave other examples where certain managers built their style upon a willingness to intimidate, even if that meant ordering his pitcher to hit an opponent. Michael cited a passage in Dickson's book that referred to the universally feared Sal Maglie, who pitched in the '40s and '50s and was nicknamed "Sal the Barber" because of the close shaves he gave to batters' chins. Maglie, said Michael, actually credited his illustrious .657 winning percentage to the bean ball. Moreover, most players, such as Frank Robinson, who was hit 198 times in his career, accepted it because it was an unwritten rule of baseball.

Next, Michael provided a compelling case on the practice of intimidation through the use of statistics. He cited an article written by Darren Everson of the Wall Street Journal who looked at the career of recent inductee Randy Johnson to the Hall of Fame. Johnson ended his career tied for second place with 190 hit batsmen since the modern era of baseball began. The article suggested that Johnson's 303 lifetime wins were, in large measure, due to the fear factor, especially amongst left-handed batters who were at a disadvantage against the lanky lefthander.

Managers and players alike were so intimidated that, in 1995 his Cy Young Award year, Johnson only faced 92 lefties of his 866 hitters because lefties would sit out the games against him. Michael agreed with Everson that intimidation was a deliberate strategy, and pointed to the fact that in his postseason career Johnson never hit any of the 434 batters he faced. Those games are usually too close to risk putting men on base.

Michael concluded his statistical argument by showing a chart that reflected the hit-by-pitch records for pitchers, starting with Walter Johnson at 205 and downward. Of the top dozen in that list, all but three are Hall of Fame pitchers, and one is Roger Clemens. In Michael's expert opinion, there was a high correlation in terms of success and legacy to the number of hit batsmen in their career.

On cross-examination, Brooks asked "if bean balls, or getting hit by a pitcher, are so accepted as inherent in the game, how would you explain the custom of a batter charging the mound"?

"Well, that isn't all that frequent in terms of all the number of batters who are hit, but in most instances the batter and his team wait for retaliation when it isn't so obvious. It may be in another series or even a season later, nonetheless it is not inconsistent with my opinion. There are occasions when a player loses his cool or feels the necessity to make his own statement to the pitcher."

"Wouldn't you also agree that Paul Dickson makes clear that hitting a batter is accepted, provided it is thrown well below the neck line"?

"I would agree with that."

"And that, although hitting above the neckline is reserved for extreme cases, it is still very controversial because of the grave danger that exists. So it is not a practice widely accepted in today's game, correct"?

"Yes, it is true that in today's financial climate, a case can be made that such message pitches are not as acceptable as they once were."

"Isn't it true that Sandy Koufax only hit eighteen batters?"

"Yes, but the fear factor was still there because he threw inside."

"Isn't it true that there are multiple Hall of Fame pitchers who hit very few in their career? For instance, Lefty Gomez with 19. Lefty Grove, with 42, is tied with Warren Spahn in 586th place in history. Jim Palmer only hit 38 in his long career, and Juan Marichal only had 40, am I correct"?

"Yes, there is no denying the statistics, sir."

"So using intimidation is not the only way to be a successful pitcher, wouldn't you agree"?

"I would agree it isn't the only way, but it sure is an important ingredient."

Jaime had enough. He wanted to end the debate. The real issue in the trial was not whether the custom existed, but whether the defendant's conduct went beyond the norm. He felt the point was made, and Michael had made some concessions. It was the right tone to end the day, and Judge Johnson dismissed the jury for the evening.

Chapter 49

Generally, Friday was set aside for sentences of defendants and various legal motions, but Judge Johnson cleared his calendar to accommodate the trial and the defense witnesses. Cavanaugh called Jonathan Dana, a representative from the Rawlings Company that makes baseball helmets. He testified that they produced a new model helmet in 2009 called the S100, and later modified in 2011, called the S100 Pro, which was vastly superior for safety needs than the helmets worn by Major League players before 2013. Their studies showed that a pitch thrown at just 70 mph could dent the helmet and damage the player, while the new helmet could withstand fastballs up to 100 mph.

In addition, the new model had two earflaps to make sure it stayed on the batter's head if a ball struck it. Dana testified that the helmet was adopted in the Major Leagues beginning in 2013, but met resistance because of its alleged discomfort and bulk. As a result, its use was modified to permit exceptions for players with at least five years of experience. It was his expert opinion that it was likely that Ken Leyton's helmet did not fit his head properly and therefore came off when he was struck. He also offered an opinion that if Leyton had voluntarily chosen to wear the new S100 Pro model, as most others had, his injury may have been considerably reduced.

On cross, Jaime merely pointed out that the League had not mandated its use across the board and suggested by his questions that Dana's testimony was irrelevant. As for the medical opinion, Dana conceded that his degree was a Ph.D., and he was not a physician. Nor did he examine the brain of Leyton, or read the autopsy report.

Cavanaugh was nearing the end of his case, but before he let Tim testify he wanted to precede him with character witnesses. Jurors could, in close cases, be swayed by a series of good character witnesses into acquitting a defendant. They would be instructed at the end of the trial by Judge Johnson that they could acquit Tim based solely on the basis of the good character testimony, if that raised a reasonable doubt in their minds.

Cavanaugh lined up thirty-two such witnesses, but Jaime objected that they were cumulative and would delay the trial. Johnson knew that generally a defendant could present an unlimited number, but nonetheless he restricted Cavanaugh to eighteen. Several of them were ordinary people from his neighborhood.

There was his local priest, a former retired high school baseball coach, a local executive director of a charity that Charles sponsored, but there were also two teammates on the Major League roster, as well as a member of the Phillies' top brass.

.

Sean also had Jeff and Lois testify so the jury could see that Tim was from a strong, intact, middle-class family. He wanted the jury to see the pain and sorrow of those decent parents as they spoke lovingly of their all-American son.

In each case, they were restricted to giving opinions of Tim's character for honesty and non-violence, as well as the reputation in the community that Tim enjoyed for those same two traits. They were unable, because Jaime's objections were sustained, to discuss awards he had received, or good deeds in general that he had performed. For his part, Jaime did not ask the parents a single question. All he asked of the baseball personnel and two of the Sarasota residents was "when was the last time you sat around with your friends and discussed how honest Tim Charles is?" He would follow up with the same question regarding non-violence. No one could recall such a conversation, and Jaime was content that the jury understood his view on the value of character witnesses.

The court recessed for lunch, but Sean and Tim stayed in a conference room and went over his testimony one last time. Sean's secretary, Rosemary Fortuna, brought them both a pasta dish with bread because she wanted to relax them before the testimony. To her, pasta was a panacea for *agita*. Neither of them could eat anything but the bread because of their anxiety. Arlene Molinaro did a good job anticipating Jaime's cross-examination, so it was just a matter of trying to relax Tim.

They talked about the free agent market, and which teams were likely to bid on some of the bigger talents in the National League. It had the desired effect, because Tim let his mind turn to the next season, and he began to hope that his nightmare might soon be over. He longed to find himself back in a baseball uniform once again, but he questioned how he would feel throwing inside again to a hitter.

The hour break flew by, and they sat at counsel table waiting for their turn to tell their side of the tragedy. Tim was bolstered by the presence of his siblings and parents, as well as many of the character witnesses who stayed to support him. He was almost ebullient when he took the stand. Sean eased him into the material facts, just as Jaime had done with Theresa. Tim was relaxed as he told of his youth in Sarasota and his baseball career in high school. It was odd to hear him say in response to the question "what do you do for a living?"

that "I am a professional baseball player for the Philadelphia Phillies." It was evident, but still necessary, as a transition into the Mets' series in June.

Tim acknowledged the veracity of everything in his teammates' testimony earlier in the trial. He described his angst over the team's expectations of him - especially his manager.

"After your talk with Brad Schofield in your apartment, did you come to a decision about whether you would act on Buck Sawyer's order"?

"No, I still hadn't made up my mind. I felt obligated to do what the skipper told us to do, but I just couldn't bring myself to deliberately hurt someone in a game."

"Did you ever come to a decision before that fateful pitch"?

"Yes, Mr. Cavanaugh, it was right after Doug Adams told me there was another choice. If I just threw some chin music at Leyton, it would satisfy my teammates. I decided then that I would throw a high heater at Leyton, and then get tossed from the game. That was the only option I could think of."

"Are you telling this jury that you deliberately threw a high fastball at Leyton's head area"?

"Yes, that's the truth, sir. I felt I had to do it, but I never intended to hit him."

"So is it your testimony that the ball was not accidentally thrown at him"?

"What I mean is that I meant to throw it high and inside, but the ball must have taken off on me because I surely didn't want to hit him. He never seemed to move out of the way. It was almost as if he let himself get hit. I know that sounds crazy, but it's how it looked from the mound."

"What did you do after you saw him get hit"?

"I held my breath-it seemed like forever. All I could think of was to pray to God that nothing serious happened. I don't even remember saying anything to the umpire, because I was in a state of shock. All I could do was watch him lie on the ground until they took him to the clubhouse. Then I went in, iced my arm, and waited for word about Kenny's condition."

Cavanaugh tried to bring out the fact that Tim attempted to go to the funeral, but Jaime objected on the grounds that it wasn't relevant, and he was sustained. Nonetheless, the jury heard it from Brad, and Jaime neglected to strike it from the record. Cavanaugh finished with a simple question.

"Did you throw your last pitch with revenge in your heart and with an intention to avenge your teammates, Tim"?

"As God is my witness sir, I did no such thing."

Cavanaugh took a calculated risk with the crux of the testimony. He knew that Tim would not stray from the truth of the fact that he had thrown at Leyton. The best he could do was to hope that the jury appreciated his honesty, and secondly show that his conduct was not grossly reckless in the context of the sport and the custom of retaliation.

Jaime looked at the jury, as did Kemper, who sat in the second row. If the jury was moved by his testimony it was not clearly evident. They were more contemplative than emotional in their collective appearance. Neither side could safely predict the outcome from their body language.

Jaime's cross-examination was intended to build the framework gradually and then reach a crescendo that would tear down the picture that Cavanaugh painted of Charles. He began by suggesting that Charles and Sawyer had a close relationship because Sawyer was the scout who signed him and gained the trust of Tim and his family. He was his mentor and guided his development from the Minors into the Major Leagues. Tim readily agreed that he owed Sawyer a great deal, and that he would always feel a strong loyalty to him. The next questions were posed so that Tim had no choice but to answer "yes."

"You were a rookie on a veteran team, weren't you"?

"You still had the advantage over other clubs because they still hadn't seen your stuff that much, right"?

"So you were still trying to prove your worth to your teammates, am I right"?

"Weren't you criticized by some on your coaching staff for not pitching inside enough to move batters off of the plate"?

"Would you agree that there were strong feelings amongst your teammates about the need to retaliate against the Mets"?

"You were certainly aware of the team's reaction to Adams' failure to honor the team's needs, weren't you"?

"You saw the fight between Adams and Herrera over that issue, too"?

"You struggled with the pressure that you felt from your teammates - and especially from Sawyer – right"?

"You didn't want to do anything that would disappoint Buck, did you"?

"You would have done almost anything for your manager and benefactor, wouldn't you"?

Then Jaime changed the style of his approach.

"Mr. Charles how many pitches do you think you had thrown in the Majors up to that June 21st evening"?

"Gee, I'd have to guess, but it was probably over a thousand".

"Had you ever hit a batter before"?

"No."

"Isn't it true that you had the fewest walks in the league that season"?

"Yes."

"So you would agree that you have good control of the ball"?

"Yes, I do, but I'm not claiming that..."

"Please, you have answered my question, thank you," interjected Jaime. "Now, you have told the jury that you made a decision to throw some 'chin music' after Adams suggested it, but you never told him that you would be taking his advice, did you"?

"No."

"And when your catcher put down the signal for a slider, you didn't shake off the pitch, did you"?

"No."

"And you were keenly aware that Bobby Carson was on board with some form of retaliation because he said so to Herrera in your presence, and he had caught for Adams the previous day, correct"?

"Yes."

"So my question is, why didn't you shake off the slider until he flashed an inside fastball signal"?

"I didn't want to telegraph it to Bobby or anyone else."

"In other words, you actually thought about it in advance and decided the best way to cover up your plan was to make it look like the pitch got away from you, isn't that a fact"?

"No, that's not what I said."

"You were just following orders weren't you, Tim, just being a good soldier"?

"Well that's not true, either."

"Tell me, Mr. Charles, after you threw the *final pitch* of your career..."

"Objection, that is outrageous,"! Cavanaugh shouted. "Has the prosecutor become an advocate and the jury "?

"I'll rephrase the question, Judge."

"See that you do, Mr. Brooks," instructed Judge Johnson.

Jaime stood closer to the witness and glared at him defiantly.

"Let me ask you this Mr. Charles, and I trust you will answer with a yes or no. Your lawyer will have a chance to let you explain later if necessary. After you threw the last pitch of your *outing,* and you saw the ball moving towards Leyton's skull, did you at any point, yell 'watch out"?

"No."

"Did you rush off the mound and yell 'duck"?

"No."

"Did you say or do anything whatsoever to alert Ken Leyton that the pitch was headed towards his skull"?

"Not that I can remember."

"When umpire Mike Kastle came out to eject you, you said you didn't mean to hit him, correct"?

"Yes."

"And you were still awfully upset, right"?

"Sure I was plenty upset."

"Yet you didn't say, 'Mike the ball just got away from me,' did you"?

" I honestly can't remember that."

"That's because you never said it. Because you wanted to hit him- isn't that a fact"?

"   ."Asked and answered" shot back Cavanaugh.

"No more questions judge", and Jaime sat down.

"Just a question or two on redirect, Your Honor," said Cavanaugh."

"Is there a reason you didn't yell to Leyton"?

"It happened so fast; it was over in a split-second. I didn't have time to react."

"Thank you, that's all."

"One more question on re-cross", said Jaime. "How much time did you give Ken Leyton to react, Mr. Charles? He had only one-tenth of a second to react, didn't he"?

Tim didn't have time to answer because Jaime announced he was finished. The answer was left hanging for the jury. The direct and cross-examinations had taken an hour and a half, so the judge excused the jury to discuss timing issues. Cavanaugh wanted to sum up his case and leave the jury with the lasting impression of his words over the weekend. By that time, some on the panel might decide to bond with his client, and they would be less inclined to alter their opinion after Jaime spoke on Monday. The prosecutor, as one might expect, objected, and asked that both summations be carried until Monday. Judge Johnson agreed and advised the jury that summations and his legal instructions would come promptly Monday morning.

Chapter 50

Jaime and Barbara agreed that it would be best if she came over Sunday morning and stayed the night so she could watch the summations. Jaime spent all day Saturday drafting his argument to the jury. He was not one of those orators who could argue to a jury without notes. He needed the comfort and security of a fully written summation, which he would read over and over again until he could literally see the words in his mind. Then he would keep the notes nearby as a failsafe.

Cavanaugh's view of a summation differed from his adversary. He believed that the case was won or lost well before the final arguments. If you didn't convince the jury that there was reasonable doubt by then, you were unlikely to do so in summation. He would shoot from the hip when his time came. As a result, he spent the weekend catching up on other work, watching football games, and going out to eat with his wife, Carol.

It was during that late Saturday afternoon that Frederick Rosen sent an email to both men. The stroke center at Magee Hospital called to tell him that Buck Sawyer suffered a second stroke in the early morning. The email indicated that he was comatose and had the lowest score on the GCS scale. That scale evaluates the degree of unresponsiveness of the patient to stimuli. Rosen said the staff was very pessimistic that he would recover, let alone be able to stand trial. Not long after the email, a hospital spokesman issued a statement confirming his condition. As a consequence, only one jury would cast its judgment on who was responsible for the death of Ken Leyton. Theresa his widow would have only one chance at justice.

On Sunday, Barbara and Jaime went out for a late lunch and then a movie. When they came home, Jaime was still preoccupied and tense over his upcoming appearance before the jury. He didn't want any alcohol, lest it spill over to the morning and affect his energy level. Barbara offered to help.

"I have an age-old tonic for what ails you. It's been proven for centuries to be effective, and I'll give you a money-back guarantee if it doesn't work."

"Really, what is it, some kind of Chinese herb? I don't like to fool with things like that."

"Let me show you how it works." She unbuckled his jeans and let them fall to the floor.

Twenty minutes later, after they mastered the art of sexual healing, they snuggled in bed and the topic returned to the trial. Barbara wanted to know how Jaime felt the trial went.

"I think it could go either way. This isn't a black-and-white decision. There are nuances, and frankly I'm not sure what to think. I'm going against two hundred years of baseball tradition. It's a game I love, and I would hate to be responsible for changing it. At the same time, that's a decision for the commissioner to consider. We have our own roles to perform. I don't want to sound self-righteous, but I can't let that influence my duty as an advocate.

"How would you feel if they found him not guilty?"

"You know, there's always that competitive side of me that wants to win. You work so hard, and you start to convince yourself that you have a good case; that you will win. It's because you've invested so much of yourself in the process.

"I felt confident at the start. Now I'm not so sure. I still think it's a manslaughter case, but I'm conflicted because I feel for the kid. He's basically a very decent guy, and he was under a great deal of pressure from his peers and Sawyer. I guess what I'm saying is, I wish they would convict for reckless manslaughter, but have the judge depart from the sentencing guidelines and drop the sentence to three years."

"Are you going to advocate for murder at all"?

"I'll make the points, but I'm spending the majority of my argument on the lesser charge. I don't expect the jury to convict on murder, and I would be sick to my stomach if they did. What do you think"?

"I thought he was very impressive and came across truthful. Maybe you're right and it's technically a crime, but I don't think they will convict him. I hope that doesn't deflate you."

"No, the last half hour did that. I feel like I could sleep twelve hours."

"Let's eat some cereal with fruit and hit the sack," offered Barb.

"Sounds great."

In her parents' home in Voorhees, Elizabeth and Donald Cox tried to prepare their daughter for the worst. They shared the belief that the jury would not convict on murder. They tried to no avail to get Theresa to look at the case objectively.

But now she was well beyond the facts of the trial. She was having her own personal debate about the end-game. She too now believed the chance of a conviction for murder was minimal. Could she trust the offer of a stranger? She had been consumed by the thought of the offer for the last several days. Now in desperation, she made up her mind.

She called the phone number in the privacy of her bedroom. She couldn't believe she was doing it, but what choice did she have? The jury was on the verge of reducing the charge, or even worse, and she had not come this far for that outcome.

Meyer was gleeful that the widow took the bait.

"I'll do the job for $7,500, but I want half up front. I'll pull up next to your car in the parking lot across from the courthouse. No checks lady, just bring cash."

"Look I don't know if I can do this, or if I can trust you. You may be a cop for all I know. I'm not thinking straight, but if I do agree, can you be ready in a short time to do it"?

"I'm ready whenever you say, and I'm local so I can meet you within fifteen minutes of your call."

Both were left wondering if the call would ever be made. Just in case, Theresa went to the bank the next morning and withdrew $3,750 from a money market fund.

Chapter 51

The defense always sums up first in New Jersey, and Cavanaugh was true to his philosophy. His summation took just twenty-five minutes. He pounded away at the lack of any definitive evidence that his client actively agreed to accept Sawyer's challenge to put a Mets' player on the disabled list. He argued that there was no testimony which contradicted Tim's statement that he threw high and inside to satisfy his manager, but never intended to hit Leyton.

He asked the jury to recall the crucial testimony of the most important witness to the case, umpire Mike Kastle, as well as the video of the fatal pitch and its aftermath.

"That picture of grief and regret so clearly evident from the body language of my client is worth ten thousand words of argument in summation. With the color drained from his face, without any anticipation that he would face criminal charges, and without any time to fabricate a defense, he fell to the ground in anguish and told the umpire that he didn't mean to hit Leyton. And from the eyewitness' accounts, Tim was really shaken up. All he could do was ask God to make sure Leyton would be okay. Does that sound like the description of a murderous heart? Does it sound like someone intent upon causing serious bodily injury?

"You heard him admit, at his own peril, that he threw the ball deliberately high and inside, but he never wanted to hurt the man. He wanted to get tossed from the game. Then he would be in a position to tell his teammates that he had tried but just missed putting Leyton out of action. That is the *only* reasonable interpretation of the evidence.

"Now, I brought in experts of the game to show you the need of the pitcher to dominate the plate by means of throwing inside to intimidate the batter. You have seen and heard statistics about the greatest pitchers in the game who used 'chin music' or purpose pitches. It is simply a part of the game. You have also learned about the customs in baseball that recognize the need for teammates to protect one another when opposing teams play the game rough. There is a law of survival, and it calls for retaliation when it is necessary for survival.

"I'm not suggesting that the laws and customs of baseball take precedence over the law that governs the rest of society. But I am suggesting that when you play Major League Baseball, Ken Leyton, as well as every other player, knows there are those inherent risks of the game that can, in rare instances, lead to grievous injury. You have heard experts say that that risk is assumed by the players.

"It has only taken two lives in the history of the game, so just how substantial was the risk when Tim threw his inside and high pitch? I want you to listen to the judge's instructions on what constitutes reckless conduct. Then ask yourselves whether what Tim did was a gross departure from the conduct that a reasonable person would have done in the context of the game of baseball. When you ask yourself whether it was a substantial and unjustifiable risk, consider whether Major League Baseball itself should suffer part of the blame when it permitted exemptions to certain players from the newest and safest helmet equipment available.

"Now I am not suggesting that the victim of this tragedy bears the blame for his death. But you will hear from the judge that to find Tim guilty, you must find that, *but for* Tim's conduct, Ken would not have died. And you must also find that it was not too dependent upon another's voluntary act. In other words, I am suggesting to you that we have raised more than a reasonable doubt from the testimony that Ken Leyton may have been the actual cause of his death. It was he who refused to remain hospitalized. Medical experts warned him to stay overnight and to refrain from physical exercise. He did neither of them. Perhaps if he had worn the best helmet available to him, and perhaps if he had heeded the advice of the experts, he would have survived.

"Ladies and gentleman of the jury, you have heard from multiple sources that Tim Charles has been blessed and taught by his family to maintain the highest regard for honesty and non-violent behavior. Eighteen people came in here to vouch for his character. That testimony in and of itself should give you pause when you are considering whether the prosecution has proven its case beyond a reasonable doubt.

"Tim Charles, at his young age, has lived 86,400 seconds a day for twenty years. He has been a model citizen for 1,728,000 seconds in his life. It took just one second to stain his conscience forever, and to put his life in jeopardy of being labeled a criminal with all the consequences that follow. I ask you to absolve his conscience and not to judge him for that one second. I ask you humbly and respectfully to reunite him with his family in Sarasota and with his family on the Phillies' squad. Thank you so very much for your attention."

Rather than give the jury a break, Judge Johnson asked Jaime to address the jury.

Jaime came out swinging. He began with the argument that had brought an objection in his opening statement.

"It may be a kid's game, but it's played by adults who are armed with a potentially deadly weapon. I ask you to listen to the judge's description of the definition of a deadly weapon because you have the right to draw a conclusion that by using a deadly weapon, the defendant Charles' purpose was to cause serious bodily injury resulting in death. Pass the ball around again and imagine the impact that would cause at 95mph at just 60 feet away, and you will have no question in your minds that it qualifies as a deadly weapon.

"The defendant tells you that he never intended to hit Ken Leyton, yet we have the expert testimony of the umpire who evaluated all of the circumstances leading up to the beaning. And what did Kastle do? He ejected Charles and Sawyer because he looked at the circumstantial evidence and was convinced that the pitch was deliberately thrown at the batter to strike him, in violation of baseball's rule 8.02(d). We have Charles telling you he never wanted to hit Leyton, and he is praying to God on Leyton's behalf. Yet what does Kastle do? He disregards those self-serving words, which occurred once Charles knew he was in trouble, and he throws him out of the game because he doesn't believe him.

"Kastle, and you as jurors, should look at the circumstantial evidence. I won't bore you with a recap of all that went on in the two prior games, but they are pieces of the puzzle. Remember Charles' uncanny control, the fact that he never hit a batter before this series, and most of all recall that he disregarded his catcher's signal for a slider away from the batter. And if his intent was merely a brush-back pitch, why couldn't he confide in Doug Adams in advance and tell him that's what he was going to do? He didn't because he had made up his mind that the next pitch would be the payback pitch that made things even for his manager and his team.

"Members of the jury, life for all of us is about making the right choices. Do we follow orders that we feel are morally or legally wrong because our superior tells us to do so? Do we go against our own moral compass because we succumb to peer pressure? If you have a choice and you choose poorly, you must accept the consequences. And yes, you should judge Charles on the one second of his life that was a poor choice, because it cost the life of a thirty-one year-old man. His widow, Theresa, will have no more seconds with Ken Leyton.

"As to the cause of his death, I won't even dignify their argument over causation because it is an insult to his family and to your intelligence.

"Now, even if you find that his conduct does not rise to the level of murder, can there really be any doubt that what he did was so reckless that any reasonable man would not have done it? He threw a hardball at a man who had only one-tenth of a second to react to the ball thrown at his head. Isn't that an unjustifiable risk that can cause serious bodily injury? What is there about a game for kids, but played by adults, that would justify such serious injury or risk of death from such a short distance?

"That is a value judgment you now have it in your hands to make. Can that substantial risk be justified because of some macho code of honor that exists in the world of baseball? Is it justifiable because baseball players understand the pitcher's need to dominate the corners of the plate? Or will you, by your verdict, announce that the laws of society will prevail over any so-called 'assumptions of risk' that may exist in the sporting circles?

"Members of the jury, the evidence is plentiful. It all adds up to an unlawful killing. I leave it in your hands to label it. Thank you for your hard work and your willingness to serve."

Chapter 52

After a fifteen-minute break, Judge Johnson addressed the jurors with his legal instructions. He explained that their verdict had to be unanimous, and they had to be satisfied on either murder or manslaughter beyond a reasonable doubt. If they had a reasonable doubt, they should acquit the defendant. He explained the role of character evidence and the fact that it alone could warrant an acquittal.

He then gave the jury a fuller explanation of the law on homicide, and the jurors seemed to nod recognition when he explained the concept of a deadly weapon, the inference that they could draw if they found one was used, as well as the definition of serious bodily injury. When he got to the definition of reckless manslaughter, he explained that it differed from murder in that it didn't require that the defendant's purpose was to cause serious bodily injury or that he was practically certain such injury would result from his conduct. The crux of the statute, he said, was:

"A person who causes another's death does so recklessly when he is aware of, and consciously disregards, a substantial and unjustifiable risk that death will result from his conduct. The risk must be of such a nature and degree that, considering the nature and purpose of defendant Charles' conduct, and the circumstances known to him, a disregard of that risk is a gross deviation from the standard of conduct that a reasonable person would follow in that same situation.

"Now, the State has another burden of proof, and that is to prove two things with respect to death. The first is that **but for** the conduct of the defendant Charles, Ken Leyton would not have died.

"The second is **that death must have been within the risk of which defendant was aware**, and it must have not been too remote, too accidental in its occurrence, or too dependent on another's volitional act to have a just bearing on the defendant's responsibility. In other words, the death was not so unexpected or unusual that it would be unjust to find the defendant guilty. That concludes my instructions."

The judge asked the clerk to draw two names from the wooden jury box, and those two would become alternates if a juror were removed for any reason. Jaime was gratified to see that both alternates were men. That made the jury's gender even at six. The judge excused the jury, with the physical evidence, to begin their deliberations at 11:30 AM.

Jaime decided to go back to the office while the jury deliberated, but Sean was asked to stay close to the courtroom by Judge Johnson so the jury would not be inconvenienced by any delay. The two families paced outside the courtroom after they lunched, despite the prediction by the lawyers that no verdict was likely that day.

The first word from the jury was a note from the foreperson that requested a read-back of umpire Kastle's testimony. Both sides debated the meaning of that request, but the jury certainly gave no indication of which way they were leaning. The read-back took twenty minutes.

The next communication at 4:15 PM brought dismay to all, including the judge. The foreperson reported in a note that one of the jurors was asking to be excused.

Judge Johnson brought the juror, Jaime, and Sean into his private chambers. She was seventy-nine year-old Evelyn Sobel. With the court reporter present, Sobel told the jury she was distraught over the deliberations, and she didn't think her health would be able to handle the strain if she were forced to continue.

"I have a grandson the same age as Mr. Charles, and I just can't handle the thought that this young man will go to prison for a long time. At the same time I feel terrible for such a young widow and her poor child. I am sick to my stomach, dizzy, and I already have a splitting headache. I think my blood pressure must be way out of control. I just can't sit there and listen to some of those people who are trying to pressure me. I thought I could do it, but I find I just can't."

"Well," said Judge Johnson, "is it the pressure from the other jurors that is making you sick? Or are you telling me it is your feelings for the defendant and the Leyton family that has upset you?"

"It's both. I just can't bring myself to find him guilty even though he is responsible for a death. I just won't go along with a verdict if they want to find him guilty of murder. But I do think somehow he should be held responsible."

"Are you saying you won't follow the law even if you agree with the other jurors on the facts?"

"I don't think I can handle the emotional stress. I would be sick with grief, and I won't ever get over it."

"Mrs. Sobel, I will excuse you for tonight, but ask you to return tomorrow. I want to give the lawyers and myself enough time to make the right decision, because we all have a lot invested in this trial."

After she left, Judge Johnson asked Sean if he would agree to remove the juror and allow just eleven jurors to make the decision. He refused to do so, and Judge Johnson quite understood the soundness of his judgment. The more jurors there are on a panel, the higher the odds that one will have a reasonable doubt.

Back in the courtroom, Judge Johnson told the jury and the public that he would rule on the juror's request to be excused in the morning. He didn't elaborate on the jury's deliberations. He told the panel to return at 10:00 AM the next morning to allow for legal arguments by the lawyers. Most observers, as did Tim, wondered why the judge just didn't replace the woman with an alternate. Cavanaugh explained that it wasn't that easy. A jury could only be excused for illness, death or an inability to continue. If the juror is replaced merely because she is feeling pressure from the other jurors and is at odds with their positions, she can't be excused.

"It wouldn't be fair to you, Tim, if the judge just excused any juror who was sympathetic to you, but felt so pressured by the other jurors that she just wanted off the jury. You would lose jurors favorable to your cause. What bothers me is that he may rule that she isn't capable of following her oath as a juror to base her verdict on the law and the facts, and not on sympathy."

"What happens then?"

"He would have to remove her from the case, but what is worse is that he might have to declare a mistrial and we would be back to square one."

"Sean, I hope you're joking with me because I could end up like Buck - in a coma. I don't have the money for legal fees, and I don't have the stamina for another one of these trials. I'd have to take the prosecutor's deal and just do the time for what I did. I can't put any further strain on my family. We all need to move on, even if it means the end of my career."

"The jury has been out for only four hours" said Sean. "The longer the deliberations continue, the greater the likelihood that, if a juror is replaced, there would be a mistrial. The reason is that when a new juror comes aboard, the entire group has already hardened their positions, and the new juror's influence is made meaningless."

"But I doubt that Judge Johnson would declare a mistrial this soon. Keep your chin up, Tim, and don't worry about what Sobel said. She didn't tell us the breakdown in numbers of the jurors for guilt or innocence. She only said some were pressuring her. For all I know, they may have been pressuring her to get involved in the deliberations."

Chapter 53

Theresa waited in a corner of the empty courtroom. She listened, unobserved, as the bailiff discussed with a sheriff's officer what he learned from the notes left in the jury deliberation room. One juror, likely the foreperson, wrote "one juror is holding us up."

"You know what that means. They're going to acquit him, they haven't been out long enough to convict", said the bailiff.

"Yeah, we'll have a verdict in the morning," replied the officer.

This was all it took to cement the decision for Theresa. She was on the verge of a full blown panic attack. She bolted from the courthouse and made the call from her SUV in the lot. True to his word, Meyer pulled up next to her a short time later. It was dark, and the lot was almost empty. Meyer placed a stolen tag on his car to complicate any police observance of his car. He slid over to his passenger seat and Theresa rolled down her window. She handed him a Wells Fargo envelope that contained half of the payoff money.

"You must do this tomorrow. You can do it as he walks to the courthouse, or after the verdict, but he'll be mobbed by media after the verdict. Anyway, that's your problem. I want to know how I can be sure I can trust you."

"You can trust me. I want the rest of the cash, Mrs. Leyton."

It was after only a few seconds that she realized she knew this young man. She had seen him at the grand jury on numerous occasions when she waited in the hallway during the proceedings.

"You were a grand juror weren't you? I'm positive. You're still wearing the Phillies' hat!"

That startled Meyer and chilled him to the bones. He never meant to kill anyone. He was merely trying to defraud a wealthy widow to save his own ass. Now he was screwed because she could identify him. He made up his mind quickly. He needed the cash as much as she needed Tim Charles to be killed.

"Yeah, that's right, so now we both got something on each other. Give me a number to reach you so I can collect the rest of the money when the heat cools down."

Although hesitant, Theresa capitulated. She wrote her number on a piece of the envelope and gave it to Meyer. Meyer knew where he could get a gun, but he didn't know if he could kill someone. He was now the one under pressure to execute a plan and still evade the police.

With the decision behind her, she felt exhilarated because she was one step nearer to closure.

Chapter 54

The following morning, the legal issue was quickly resolved by Judge Johnson. He had the sheriff's officer escort Mrs. Sobel into the courtroom and explained that he would grant her request to be excused because of emotional distress. She broke down in tears and thanked the judge for his kindness and understanding. She even shook hands with Jaime and Sean before she left. Next, Johnson denied a motion for a mistrial by Sean, who argued that he would be denied the jury that was chosen by Mr. Charles by replacing Sobel at this juncture. The court, however, reasoned that Sobel was unable to continue due to her personal health conditions, rather than from any pressure exerted upon her by jurors to reach a particular verdict. Therefore, the court found there would be no violation of the defendant's constitutional rights if an alternate were substituted. He further found that the jury had only deliberated for 4 hours. That, in the court's mind, was not so long a period as to conclude that the jurors had formulated their opinions- staked out their positions- so that their minds were forever closed to new ideas.

Accordingly, the clerk randomly selected a retired female elementary school teacher as the twelfth juror.

Judge Johnson stressed to the jury that they all had to begin their deliberations anew. In other words, they were to start all over again - as if they had just heard his legal instructions. That was met by sighs of frustration from the packed audience and media representatives. This process was not going smoothly or quickly. They were excused at 10:15. Just one hour later the tension in the courtroom was revived when the judge announced to the parties that the jury had three questions. Johnson read them to the spellbound observers.

'Was anyone else charged in connection with the death of Ken Leyton? If so, what is their status?'

'Can we find the defendant not guilty of murder but guilty of conspiracy to commit murder?'

'Can we find the defendant guilty of the possession of a deadly weapon?'

"Now counsel, said Johnson, "I propose to tell them that they are not to consider whether anyone else was charged, and they are not to allow that to enter into their deliberations. It seems to me we have a jury that is apparently free from the publicity about Buck Sawyer's indictment and medical condition. That is a good thing."

"The second question is also easily answered. I will tell the jury that they **can** find the defendant not guilty of murder but guilty of conspiracy."

"Now, unless there is disagreement, I will hear you on the last question."

Jaime responded that the jury was likely thinking in terms of the baseball as a deadly weapon. Nonetheless, he argued that the grand jury had not included that charge in the indictment and that such a charge was not a lesser-included crime of murder or conspiracy. He therefore urged the court to answer in the negative to the last question. To do otherwise, he went on, could perhaps taint the verdict. Jaime feared such a charge would give the jury an easy option and allow them to acquit on the murder/manslaughter.

Sean was conflicted in his emotions. If the jury was permitted to find Tim guilty of the relatively minor offense, there would likely be no jail time as a consequence, and little chance of jeopardy to his baseball career. If the jury was not given the choice on such a charge, the result could be a conviction on the serious homicide count. Cavanaugh knew that Jaime's position was legally correct, but he had to take the risk.

"Judge, the prosecutor argued in his opening that a baseball was a deadly weapon that was used in a murder. Therefore we were on notice that this was the state's theory and we are not claiming unfair surprise if that charge is considered by the jury. If the jury believes the baseball at the moment it was thrown was a deadly weapon, we consent to that option for the jury. Under the totality of all of the facts, it should be considered a lesser-included offense."

"While I appreciate your strategy, Mr. Cavanaugh, I agree with the prosecutor's analysis of the law. Accordingly, I will not permit the jury to consider that charge."

The jury was then brought back to court to listen as Johnson replied to their questions. There was no discernible reaction from the individual jurors to assist the lawyers in their assessment of where the jury stood. They looked only at the judge or themselves and not the parties.

Both counsel shook their heads and shrugged their shoulders as the jury left the courtroom. What were they to make of those questions? Law clerks and other visiting lawyers buzzed in speculation about the meaning of the trifecta. Tim Charles looked to his legal protector for guidance, but Sean could not bring himself to tell the young man what he thought. He didn't like any of the questions, especially when they were read together. They could all mean that the jury was ready and willing to convict for something. The first question certainly seemed to suggest that someone was going to pay for the death.

The second question could be interpreted to mean they were leaning towards a compromise of conspiracy rather than murder, but Sean knew that decision would bring a long prison term for his client. The last question could be good news or bad. Maybe the jury was looking for a minor offense to compromise upon, or maybe it was just looking to pile on. In any event that was no longer an option. Sean merely put his hand on Tim's shoulder and told him he stopped trying to read anything into jury questions long ago. Something about the tone of his answer did not sit well with Tim, and his anguish only mounted.

Theresa, on the other hand, was more convinced than ever that Charles was about to beat the murder case. She had virtually stopped talking to Jaime, but she calculated that it was time to act. She went into the corridor and phoned her accomplice. She urged him to come to the Hall of Justice and watch for Charles to leave for lunch. She assured him that she would make another withdrawal during the interim.

The jury was, of course, sequestered since they were now in deliberations, and word leaked out that they intended to work through the lunch break. Judge Johnson would not return unless the jury had a verdict or question. At 1:45, all of the principals were back in court save the defendant. For Theresa Leyton, his absence only brought titillation. She imagined the scene in the streets of Camden with the prone body of Charles riddled with bullets. She could almost imagine hearing the sounds of an ambulance outside.

But as court was adjourned for lunch, Tim had told his legal team that he needed some space and fresh air; he was not interested in food. He announced that he would walk to the Victor Café on Camden's waterfront and be back by the afternoon session of court. As he walked out into the breezy November afternoon, an anxious Chris Meyer stood outside his car in the lot across the street and watched intently as Tim turned right onto Mickle Boulevard. Meyer decided he needed to follow in his car because it was too risky on foot. He had his revolver in his waist covered by a navy pea coat.

He waited until Tim was well beyond the courthouse until he approached an area that was largely made up of barren employee parking lots. It was the perfect spot for Meyer to pull off a quick drive-by shooting. Meyer lowered his window and pulled his gun out. Tim was a clear shot. He was oblivious to his assassin's presence. Meyer slowed his car to a crawl. Now he would earn his pay by overriding the jury's pending verdict.

But others were equally engrossed in the scene outside. As part of the prosecution team, Lt. Falconetti and Investigator Arroyo attended every session of the trial. As they left for lunch from the same lot where Meyer had just stood, they immediately recognized the former grand juror they had once arrested and who was now a fugitive.

With Meyer's attention directed towards Charles, the two law enforcement partners tailed him closely in an unmarked car. When Arroyo saw Meyer display a gun she jumped out of the car and drew her weapon. She screamed for Charles' attention as she gained on Meyer's car. Meyer made a split second decision that it was now or never and fired two quick rounds towards his prey. Charles screamed and Arroyo saw him fall motionless on the ground. Simultaneously Arroyo fired three rapid shots at Meyer which blasted out the windshield. The crashing glass forced Meyer to pause long enough for both officers to surround him at gun point. Meyer let the unfamiliar gun drop from his hand and Arroyo retrieved it. Falconetti rushed to check on Charles who sat up holding his chest. Falconnetti feared it was a fatal shot and began to radio for paramedics but Charles, with a mortified look, assured the Lt. that it was just a case of skipping heart beats. The plot had failed and Charles was unhurt. He had dodged one bullet but there was yet another one that faced him in court.

Falconetti left Charles to assist his partner. "Hey scumbag! It's so nice to have you back where you belong!" said Falconetti, as he held Meyer while Arroyo cuffed him.

"You're under arrest dirtball. Looks like you just elevated your game to attempted murder."

"Thank you again for being such an asshole. This will guarantee you ten to twenty years on top of the shitload of time you'll be doing for the corruption charges. You're going to be a ward of the State for a very long time."

"But I got some shit to cooperate with man. You'll want to hear about it."

"That ship sailed a long time ago, brother," said Arroyo.

As they read him his *Miranda* warnings, they drove the few blocks back to the Prosecutor's Office to process him on the new charges. Meyer wouldn't stop talking. He kept chirping about a plot to kill Tim Charles by Theresa Leyton. That didn't get their attention until they fully searched him and found the $3,750 in cash in the bank envelope. Then they found a torn piece of paper with a phone number on it that Meyer insisted belonged to Leyton. They quickly called the victim/witness coordinators and were stunned to find that the numbers matched their records for the widow. What followed next was a call to Jaime for advice.

While Tim Charles had avoided an assassin's bullet, Theresa had gone to Wells Fargo and withdrawn the remaining $3,750 that she hoped would bring her peace of mind.

Chapter 55

Lawyers and trial watchers spoke quietly in small groups. At 2:00 PM, Tim strode into the courtroom bolstered by his faith and his lawyers. Sean had given him permission to relax and be on-call for court within ten minutes. Theresa, on the other hand, looked like she was struck with the judge's gavel. Her face was distorted with rage as she scowled at Charles. She could not contain herself. How, she asked herself, had that two-bit low life bungled the job? All she could do now was hope that the hit could be accomplished after the jury freed her tormenter.

Stunningly, she would not have long to wait. At 2:45 PM, the jury foreperson handed the court attendant a note. The jury had reached a verdict. Judge Johnson gave the media and the parties a half-hour to return to court. It was a short period of deliberation. Tim asked Sean if that was a good sign, but again Sean could only say that the verdict must have been consistent with the jurors' collective beliefs, which made it easier to agree. No one knew for sure what it meant.

For virtually everyone in court, those thirty minutes were excruciatingly painful. Even those who had no interest in the outcome of the case felt their blood pressure rise. For lawyers, there exists no more anxiety-driven moments than those awaiting the return of a jury's verdict. Sean sat at counsel table looking down and at times reassuring Tim that the jury would do the right thing. Jaime could not sit and paced around the courtroom seeking distractions from members of the media or colleagues. Theresa used her time trying in vain to reach Chris Meyer.

The families of the parties, Brad Schofield, Colby Green, Nolan Albright, Barbara Jay, and the assistant GM of the Phillies, all assembled for the final reckoning. Two minutes before the jury entered, Falconetti and Arroyo sat down on the front row behind Jaime. They nodded, and Jaime gave them the thumbs up. Sitting between them was Chris Meyer. This did not go unnoticed by Theresa Leyton, whose shoulders noticeably slumped.

As the twelve jurors took their seats in the jury box, everyone's eyes were locked on the jury for signs of which way the verdict would go. It is usually believed that if jurors look at a victim before the verdict, it will be a guilty verdict. If, on the other hand, they look at the defendant without rancor, that is a good omen for the defense. In the matter of Timothy Charles, the jury was split. They looked at both Theresa and Tim.

As the bile rose in the esophagus of Jaime Brooks, the clerk stood and asked the jury if they had a verdict. The response was in the affirmative. **"Is your verdict unanimous**?" she asked.

"It is," replied the foreperson.

"What is your verdict on the charge of murder"?

At that moment, the hushed court watchers were startled when five members of the jury stood in unison and announced that they wanted to protest the verdict. One juror spoke for the group of five. "We want to make a statement about the verdict your honor". Unabashed bedlam broke out in the packed courtroom. "Silence in my courtroom!" cried Johnson as he pounded his gavel "I'll hold everyone in contempt if I hear another outbreak." Tim braced himself for yet another legal calamity and the potential of a mistrial.

"Those jurors standing shall sit down immediately" Johnson said sternly." Do you disagree with the verdict in your foreperson's hand?" When they attempted to explain, the judge confined them to answering only whether they agreed with the verdict to be announced. Reluctantly, one by one each juror gave an affirmative response. Until the last juror responded, the tension in the court did not dissipate. Yes it was unanimous. Soon the whole country would learn the fate of Tim Charles and possibly the game of baseball as we knew it.The clerk asked the critical question once more. Johnson then addressed the audience and warned of harsh consequences for any outbreaks from either side after the verdict.

"We the jury, find the defendant, Tim Charles, **not guilty** of murder or conspiracy to commit murder."

"What is your verdict as to manslaughter?" Again, the defense braced for the verdict.

"We the jury find the **defendant not guilty of manslaughter or aggravated manslaughter** as well."

Jeff almost broke Lois Charles' rib as he squeezed her. She sobbed uncontrollably with relief. Her son turned to his family and friends with tears flowing from his eyes while Sean Cavanaugh did all he could to hold back his own flow.

Theresa cried as well, but it was through shrieks of anger directed at Tim.

"I will not rest until I have avenged my husband's murder!" she screamed in agony, and then crumbled to the floor.

Judge Johnson, in an effort to shield the jury from the frightening reaction of Leyton, excused them with his thanks. Several smiled at Tim and waved. A few even tried to go over to counsel table but were interrupted by court staff. When the jury left, Jaime nodded to his investigators who approached

Theresa Leyton and cuffed her in full view of the media. When reporters shouted in unison at her seeking an explanation, for the first time since her husband's death, she had nothing to say to the press.

Jaime leaned over and told Sean he would explain later and congratulated the defense team that also assembled for the verdict.

"Do you have any interest in joining our firm when you retire?" asked Sean.

"Thanks for the offer, but I'd rather go out having played on the same team for my entire career. No offense, Sean, but it's just not in my DNA to defend. You take care, and for the record, you did a hell of a job."

"You do the same too, Jaime. You had me sweating bullets."

"Let's get the celebration going," encouraged Raymond Hunter. He invited the Charles contingent to have dinner on the firm at the Capitol Grill in Cherry Hill. It didn't take much arm-twisting to get them on their way to their first night of freedom from fear since the indictment shattered their lives.

Barbara Jay led Jaime from the courtroom and suggested that she had a great idea for a consolation prize if Jaime was up to it. There was no arm-twisting needed for that idea either.

POSTSCRIPT

As a sports columnist, and as one who watched the entire trial, I still needed closure. What had the jurors meant by their protest? They declared Tim Charles *not guilty*, but was that the same as declaring him *innocent*?

My editor and I actually went the distance. We got a court order to interview the jurors in the case. It turned out that the gang of five wanted desperately to make a statement that Tim Charles bore some criminality for his actions. They wanted to find him guilty of **the possession of a deadly weapon**. Can you believe that? They wanted the game to know that they considered the baseball a deadly weapon in the death of Ken Leyton but were denied the opportunity by the judge.

I can tell you one other thing that reeks of irony. I spoke with personnel in Judge Johnson's courtroom and learned about the note written by a juror. I figured it would give me a take on the verdict. Sure enough, it was written by the foreperson. The phrase was "one juror is holding us up." But here's the kicker.

A juror was late getting to the jury assembly room one morning. The foreperson wrote the words on the pad and was about to ask the bailiff to take it to the judge. At that moment, the juror appeared and the note was never delivered. Apparently, the clerk found the note later in the afternoon and believed that the jury was close to a verdict, but they got it all wrong. Apparently so did Theresa Leyton.

During the lunch break and after Meyer was questioned, investigators prepared search warrants for Theresa's person to find evidence of a conspiracy to murder Charles. They found a Wells Fargo bank envelope with $3,750 that matched the money and envelope found on Meyers during his arrest. They also corroborated Meyer's story by examining her cell phone and locating phone calls to and from Meyer. Finally, an examination of her bank records reflected two separate withdrawals of $3,750 within a day of one another. Theresa Leyton and Chris Meyer were indicted for various serious offenses which if found guilty could lead to upwards of twenty years in prison for both.

What do I think about the effect of the trial on baseball? The bottom line is that those guys who were willing to use the bean ball in their arsenal will continue to risk suspension, just like some will risk the penalty for steroid use. But in my opinion, the dust-off pitch above the neck has diminished a great deal ever since that protest group of jurors warned the sport that they were not afraid to brand that behavior a crime if serious injury or death occurred.

As for Tim Charles, he returned to the Phillies the following season and pitched magnificently. He did so without the necessity of throwing chin music. He was fourth in the balloting for the Cy Young Award for the new World Series Champion Phillies. Tim visited the gravesite of Kenny Leyton each season whenever his team played in New York. No one tried to keep him out.

I still follow the career of Jaime Brooks. At the urging of his fiancé Barbara Jay, he stayed on at the Prosecutor's Office rather than retire. The political gossip has it that he will succeed Grace Moore as Prosecutor when the latter's nomination for a judgeship is confirmed. He is currently engaged in pre-trial motions in the long delayed trial of Theresa Leyton. The primary state's witness is Chris Meyer, who is cooperating with the prosecution. Mrs. Leyton posted bail and remains at her parents' home with her son James.

By John Cowan

EPILOGUE

It was December, and Commissioner Wilson's special committee filed its report regarding their recommendations for remedial steps in the aftermath of Leyton's death. They recommended three items be implemented. The first was to mandate, once again, the use of the S100 Pro Rawlings batting helmet. Next, they urged a mandatory period of suspension for pitchers who threw a bean ball. Lastly, and the most controversial of all, was to raise the pitching mound from ten-and-a-half inches to fifteen inches above home plate.

They argued that this would greatly benefit pitchers by increasing their dominance and power over the batter, and accordingly, reduce the necessity of using brush-back pitches above the neck area. Thus batters would still be able to dig in at the plate because they would know that mandatory suspensions would flow if they were hit in the head zone, but pitchers would gain an advantage with the higher mound.

Commissioner Wilson held a press conference at which he announced a 50 game suspension for anyone who struck a batter in the head if, in the opinion of his office, the pitch was intentionally or recklessly thrown. He also issued an order implementing the use of the newer helmets for the next season. On the last suggestion of the committee, Wilson said:

"The one historical instance in baseball where the mound was substantially raised provides us with ample evidence that the game will be fundamentally altered for the worse. I do not want the game to sacrifice the joy of the home run as well as large run- scoring rallies because of an overreaction to an isolated, albeit tragic, episode in our history. I will not step back in time to 1968 to achieve a result that has already proven to lessen the game's vitality."

There were noticeable, verifiable signs that the game changed to a degree as a result of the Charles case. In the next season, the total number of home runs increased to 5001, up from 4552 a year earlier- almost a 1% increase. The average home runs hit per game increased from 1.76 to 1.87. There were 16 batters in the National League that batted over .300, versus 11 the prior year. The National League composite batting average jumped from .253 to .256. A comparable increase was evident in the American League. The National League ERA also increased from 3.81 to 3.89, and the DH league increased from 4.08 to 4.17.

Moreover, the number of batters hit by a pitch increased dramatically, from 816 to 889 in the National League. The statistics are always open for debate, but it did appear that the diminished risk of the bean ball did lead batters to be more aggressive at the plate. While pitchers hit more batters, they were below the neck, and did not seem to deter hitters as did the threat of a bean ball. In fact, only 3 bean ball incidents occurred in, but just 2 were found to have been intentional.

One such incident occurred after a batter stood at the plate and marveled at his 464-foot-long home run. He was plunked in the helmet at his next at bat. He suffered a serious concussion and was out for two months. The matter is under investigation by Philadelphia DA Nancy Artis, who will determine whether to file aggravated assault charges against the Giants' pitcher, Rueben Velez. If indicted and convicted, he could face up to 10 years in prison.

FROM THE AUTHOR

Obviously this is a work of fiction. The characters are entirely fictitious, although some of the names of people in the book bear resemblance to friends or acquaintances of the author. Naturally, some of the Phillies' players, as well as some other former baseball players named in the book, are real but were named only for historical perspective.

I chose the Phillies because they have been my beloved team since I began attending games in 1951 with my dad. The history of the rivalry between them and the Mets since 2006 led my legalistic mind to imagine what could hopefully only conceivably happen.

Thank you for reading my book. If you enjoyed it, I would appreciate it if you would take a few moments to write a review on amazon's website and like my Facebook page. The gratification I get from a good review is enormous, and it helps other potential readers decide if the book is worth the time and money. And I'd love to hear from you as well. My email is thehman999@yahoo.com

http://amzn.com/B007AIQO0A

https://www.facebook.com/APitchForJustice

Made in the USA
Middletown, DE
24 July 2018